PAULA DANZIGER

The Cat Ate My Gymsuit
There's a Bat in Bunk Five
Can You Sue Your Parents for Malpractice?

DEAN

Dean in association with
Heinemann Young Books

The Cat Ate My Gymsuit first published in Great Britain in 1986
There's a Bat in Bunk Five first published in Great Britain in 1987
Can You Sue Your Parents for Malpractice? first published in Great Britain in 1986
This edition published in 1992 by Dean
an imprint of Reed Consumer Books Limited
Michelin House, 81 Fulham Road, London SW3 6RB
and Auckland, Melbourne, Singapore and Toronto
Reprinted 1992 and 1993
Text copyright © Paula Danziger 1979, 1980, 1982
All rights reserved

ISBN 0 603 55028 2
Printed in Great Britain by The Bath Press

CONTENTS

The Cat Ate My Gymsuit

To John Ciardi
because he dedicated a book to me,
because he is my good friend and teacher,
and because he never collects gin-rummy debts.

INTRODUCTION

In *The Cat Ate My Gymsuit*, a teacher's refusal to say the Pledge of Allegiance becomes an issue, causing people to take sides.

I've been asked to explain the Pledge to my non-American readers. So here goes.

In most American schools, at the beginning of the day, students go first to homeroom. Here, attendance is taken and useful and useless information is given out. Then either the teacher or a voice over the intercom says something like, "Please stand now for the Pledge of Allegiance." Most of the kids stand up. Some don't, for either religious or political reasons. Those who do, put their right hands over their hearts, turn to the American flag, which is hanging somewhere in the room and recite, "I pledge allegiance to the flag of the United States of America, and to the republic for which it stands, one nation under God, indivisible with liberty and justice for all."

Then everyone sits down. That's basically the explanation.

The reason that Ms Finney's action caused such an uproar was that for many people, saying the Pledge to the flag is symbolic of patriotic pride and commitment to country. For others, not reciting the Pledge is also symbolic.

I hope that all of my readers respond and relate to *The Cat Ate My Gymsuit*, to the feelings, to the humour, to the sense of perspective.

Please know that my books are very important to me and so are my readers.

Paula Danziger

Chapter 1

I hate my father. I hate school. I hate being fat. I hate the principal because he wanted to fire Ms Finney, my English teacher.

My name is Marcy Lewis. I'm thirteen years old and in the ninth grade at Dwight D. Eisenhower Junior High.

All my life I've thought that I looked like a baby blimp with wire-frame glasses and mousy brown hair. Everyone always said I'd become an adolescent blimp with wire-frame glasses, mousy brown hair, and acne.

My life is not easy. I know I'm not poor. Nobody beats me. I have clothes to wear, my own room, a stereo, a TV, and a push-button phone. Sometimes I feel guilty being so miserable, but middle-class kids have problems too.

Mom always made me go to tap and ballet lessons. She said that they'd make me more graceful. When it came time for the recital, I accidentally sat on the record that I was supposed to dance to, and broke it. I had to hum along with the tap dancing. I sing as badly as I dance. It was a disaster.

Father says that girl children should be born at the age of eighteen and married off immediately.

Stuart, my four-year-old brother, wants to be my best

friend so that I can help him put orange pits in a hole in his teddy bear's head.

I'm flat-chested. I used to buy training bras and put tucks in them.

I never had any friends, except Nancy Sheridan. She's very popular, but her mother and mine are PTA officers and old friends, so I always figured that Mrs Sheridan made her talk to me—Beauty and the Blimp.

School is a bummer. The only creative writing I could do was anonymous letters to the Student Council suggestion box. Lunches are lousy. We never get past the First World War in history class. We never learned anything good, at least not till Ms Finney came along.

So my life is not easy.

The thing with Ms Finney is what I want to talk about. She took over for Mr Edwards, our first English teacher. He left after the first month. One rumour is that he had a nervous breakdown in the faculty lounge while correcting a test on noun clauses. Another is that he had to go to a home for unwed fathers in Secaucus, New Jersey. I personally think that he realized that he was a horrible teacher, so he took a job somewhere as a principal or a guidance counsellor.

When Mr Edwards left, we got a whole bunch of substitutes. None of them lasted more than two days. That'll teach the school to group all the smart kids in one class. We were indestructible.

The entire class dropped books, pencils, and pens at an assigned time. Someone put bubble gum in the pencil sharpener. Nancy pulled her fainting act. We made up names and wrote them on the attendance list. All the desks got turned around. Mr Stone, the principal, kept coming in and yelling.

And then Ms Finney came.

Chapter 2

Celeste Sanders was the first to spread the news.

"Hey, we got a new English teacher. A real one, not a sub. First-period class says she looks like a kid."

"A new one. Let's walk in backwards."

"Everyone give a wrong name."

"Let's show her who's boss."

Everybody rushed down the halls and into class. Some of the guys started to make and throw paper air-planes. Alan Smith played 'Clementine' on his harmonica. He'd learned it from the instructions on a Good and Plenty box. Jim Heston played the Good and Plenty box, and Ted Martin played a comb. There was applause and cheering after the performance. At 1:15 the coughing started. A few kids didn't do anything, but I did. I really didn't like what was happening, but if you're a blimp with fears of impending acne, you go along with the crowd.

Ms Finney just sat there. She was young and wore a long denim skirt, a turtleneck jersey and had on weird jewellery—giant earrings that hung down to her shoulders, and a macramé necklace. She didn't smile or yell or cry or read a paper or do any of the things that teachers normally do when a class gets out of hand. She just sat there and looked at everybody.

Finally it got quiet. Everyone started to squirm. It was really creepy after a while.

"OK. Give her a chance," someone muttered.

We all looked around to see who was talking. It was Joel Anderson, the smartest kid in the class. When almost everybody else would be fooling around, he would sit there reading a book. Some of the kids thought he was a little weird, but everybody usually listened to him.

He put his book down, looked at Ms Finney, and said, "Are you going to teach us anything?"

Somebody giggled.

The class got very quiet.

I looked at Joel and thought how brave and smart and cute he was. We'd been in the same classes since kindergarten, but I hadn't said more to him than "Hi" and "What's the homework assignment?" I didn't like to embarrass anyone by having them be seen talking to me.

Ms Finney stood up, looked at the class, smiled, turned to the blackboard, picked up a piece of chalk, and wrote:

"Ms Barbara Finney."

Turning around again, she smiled and said, "That's my name. I'm your new English teacher, and I hope this year is going to be a good one for all of us."

I thought about that. First of all, she'd written 'Ms'. Was she just trying to be sharp, or was she really into it? And she'd written her first name. Teachers never do that. They never admit to having first names. They're always Miss or Mr or Mrs, hardly ever Ms, and never with first names. It's supposed to be a big mystery, like do teachers really have to go to the bathroom or do anything but teach and go to meetings?

She spoke again.

"I decided to be an English teacher because I care about people communicating with people. That's why I'm here. I want to do it and help you all to do it too, as effectively as possible. A poet named Theodore Roethke once said, 'Those who are willing to be vulnerable move among mysteries.' Please, let's try to move among mysteries together."

The class looked at her and at one another.

Alan Smith laughed and said, "What is this gonna be, a class of detectives?"

Ms Finney looked at him without smiling. But she didn't yell, either.

"I know that this may all seem a little strange to you now. Maybe it won't work, but let's try. Take out a piece of paper, and for the rest of the period think about communication and write about what it means to you."

We all took out paper. I stared at mine and then snuck looks at Ms Finney. She was young and pretty and seemed nice. She sounded smart. She was different, but I wasn't sure how, and I didn't know if I could trust her. I mean, she was a teacher, and an adult.

During one of my looks, she stared right at me and smiled. I lowered my head and pretended to be writing. Dumb teacher. Who did she think she was? What does a blimp know about communication? How could she know what it feels like to be so fat and ugly that you're ashamed to get into a gymsuit or talk to skinny people? Who wants to say. "This is my friend, the Blimp"?

Class was almost over, and I still hadn't written anything. I stared at my paper again and began:

COMMUNICATION
is
NOITACINUMMOC
spelled backwards

For the rest of the year, I want to improve my handwriting so that I can write legible letters to the Student Council Suggestion box.

Marcy Lewis

The bell rang. Grabbing my books, I rushed up to the front and put my paper face down on the desk. No one else was going to see what I wrote.

Going to gym class, I overheard some of the kids talking about Ms Finney.

"She seems OK."

"Weird."

"I like her."

"She's a creep, like the rest of 'em."

In the locker room all the girls rushed to get dressed, except for me. I sat on a bench.

Nancy came over and said, "Marcy, not again! You'll flunk."

I just sat there. Trying to change into a gymsuit while

hiding my mini bra and fat body would have been a gymnastic feat in itself.

Once the class started, I walked up to the gym teacher, Schmidt.

"All right, Lewis. What is it this time?"

"The cat ate my gymsuit."

She shook her head, frowned, and wrote another zero in her marking book.

I sat down to watch my eighty-millionth volleyball game.

Chapter 3

Things got better at school after that, at least for me. For a while, some of the kids were mad at Joel for spoiling their fun. But a lot of the kids were glad that everything had settled down. And we started doing some really neat things in class. There was a lot of writing, but I like to do that. Sometimes it is easier to write things down than it is to say them out loud. Ms Finney said that to communicate is to begin to understand ourselves and others. She wanted us to be honest in our thinking, and to write well. That's really hard, to be honest and remember things like commas and paragraph structure and stuff like that.

The really nice part is that she never asked us to discuss anything that she wouldn't discuss herself. One day we had to write about the things that bothered us. Ms Finney stood in front of the class and said, "I remember that when I was a kid, I used to be so embarrassed because I wore braces on my teeth and everyone used to call me 'Tinsel Tooth'."

That may not sound important, her telling us that, but it made it easier for us to write about and discuss things that bothered us. You know, like mothers who insist on being Girl Scout leaders when you don't even want to be a

Girl Scout; falling down steps when you are trying to make an entrance; bad breath; having to take your younger brother to the movies; aunts and uncles who keep asking if many people 'shoot up' marijuana; dumb stuff like that. It surprised me how many people had problems. I'm sure that lots of people had more trouble than we talked about, but Ms Finney was careful not to let it get too personal.

One time, she talked about some guy named Marshall McLuhan, who wrote about people getting turned on by music and films and stuff. Then Ms Finney turned off all the lights, put on a whole lot of light boxes that blinked on and off, turned on an album real loud, and told us to experience it. She said she wanted us to decide for ourselves whether this type of thing was an escape or a way to get really involved. It was really neat, but then the vice-principal, Mr Goldman, walked in and called Ms Finney out of the room. When she came back in, she looked very upset and put the lights back on and stopped the lesson.

We also put on a play. Ms Finney asked me to be assistant director. That was very hard for me. I had to get up and walk around the room and get stuff ready. I always feel safer sitting behind the desk, where nobody can see my body. But Ms Finney asked, and it would have been hard for me to explain to her why I didn't want to do it, so I did it. It ended up being OK.

Don't get me wrong. Ms Finney wasn't perfect. She never got reports back on time, she gave hard tests, and once in a while she got mad. She also did weird things like holding on to a piece of chalk, forgetting what it was, and trying to smoke it. Sometimes she let kids get away with too much. But she really tried.

And we really dug her. In the beginning, some of the kids were worried because they were afraid they wouldn't learn what they had to know to pass the college entrance exams. Other kids thought that Ms Finney was just plain weird. But eventually we all said that we did learn. We wrote more for her than we had ever written before. She never gave true-false or multiple-guess tests. I think most teachers like them because they're easier to correct. Instead, she made us write our own interpretation of what we'd read.

She brought in all kinds of books to read. And a lot of us bought paperbacks from the book club. It was like a celebration the day the books came in the mail and Ms Finney sorted them out and gave them to us. I spent most of my allowance on books. We shared and swapped them. I feel like I'm addicted to the printed word. Like I need a book fix when I get upset.

We talked about poetry and current events and plays and movies. Ms Finney knew an awful lot, and she made us feel that we knew a lot too and were important. She really listened. It was amazing.

And she didn't talk to us just in English class. During her free periods she'd walk around the school and drop in on some classes, like home economics and shop and art, classes where there were times that she wouldn't be interrupting other teachers. She'd taste the food that the kids made, admire the sewing, and look at all the projects in shop. It made everybody feel good, like she knew that there was more to us than just the time we spent in her class.

One day she came to my gym class. I had just told Schmidt that my little brother had misplaced his security blanket and was now using my gymsuit instead. Ms Finney looked at everybody playing volleyball and then came over and sat down next to me.

"Hi, Marcy."

"Hi, Ms Finney."

"Who's winning?"

"The blue team."

"Don't you feel well?"

"I'm OK. Why?"

"Just wondered."

We sat and watched the game for a few minutes. I didn't know what else to say.

She turned and said, "I'm going to ask Ms Schmidt if I can play. I'm a real clod at volleyball, but it's fun. Do you want to play too?"

I shook my head. Looking at me as if she wanted to say something else, she just smiled and walked over to the game. Schmidt obviously said that she could play, because she took off her shoes and joined the red team.

She really was bad. When someone hit the ball to her, she ducked. When she served, she didn't always get it over the net. But she looked as if she were having fun, making up her own rules as she went along.

"It's a do-over. I forgot to call out the score."

"English teachers get an extra serve."

"People named Barbara get two extra serves."

Someone yelled across the net, "Hey, Ms Finney. Just pretend that the ball is a direct object and our team is the indirect object."

Ms Finney smiled and volleyed. The ball just missed hitting Nancy on the head. Nancy turned around, laughed, and yelled, "She said a direct object, not a dangling participle."

Schmidt blew her whistle and said, "Everyone hurry up. Into the showers and then get dressed."

Ms Finney yelled, "Thanks, everyone, for letting me play." Then she came over and said, "That was fun."

I just smiled at her and followed the rest of the kids into the locker room.

One day in class, Nancy raised her hand and asked Ms Finney if we could do more about how we felt inside. Ms Finney thought about it and said that we had to use the class time to do what was in the syllabus, the guide that schools give teachers. She said that she felt a responsibility to go over the assigned material. After thinking awhile, she smiled and said, "Why don't we start a club after school? That'll work. I'll tell my other classes and you all tell other friends. We'll start Monday after school."

That's how Smedley got started.

Chapter 4

Smedley wasn't a person. It was the club. What happened was that twenty-five kids came, which was really good because a lot of the kids had to take buses to school and staying after meant a long walk or having someone pick you up. We figured that the club should have a name. Nancy suggested 'The Self Club', Joel wanted it to be called 'Interpersonal Persons'. Alan Smith said that we should be named 'The Sherlock Holmes Crew', because we all would be searching to find ourselves. That kid is probably going to be a detective some day, or a peeping tom. A kid from another class said, "Why don't we just call ourselves Smedley, after that dopey guy in our grammar book who is always looking for the right way to say things?" Everyone liked that.

Ms Finney said that we should begin by examining what had just happened, that each of us should look at how we acted in the group and how we all finally agreed. This, she said, was group dynamics in action. She said that she had taken college courses involving that sort of thing, and that she had had a minor in something called Human Organizational something or other. I don't remember exactly, but it sounded good.

So we talked about it and saw that some people have different roles in a group. Some are leaders. Some are reactors. (Alan thought that meant that he was like an atomic reactor.) Joel said that Alan and Robert Alexander always acted like clowns when they wanted attention or were afraid of something. They both got mad at him and called him a brainy creep. He called them cretins, and finally Ms Finney had to tell them to stop.

"OK. That's enough. If you want me to be adviser to this club, you all have to try to work things out. Let's begin with an exercise to get acquainted."

Nancy raised her hand and said, "Ms Finney. That's silly. We've known each other since kindergarten."

Ms Finney looked around the room. "You may have known each other since kindergarten, but do you really know each other? I bet you don't. I've noticed that some of you don't even talk to people who aren't in your classes."

She split us up into pairs and told us to spend fifteen minutes getting to know the other person. I thought I was going to die. She had put Joel and me together.

Joel pulled his desk near mine and said, "Hi, I'm Joel Anderson."

I just nodded my head.

"You should tell me your name now."

How could I tell him? I was so nervous, I couldn't remember anything. Finally, it came to me.

"Hi, I'm Marcy Lewis."

Joel asked, "Have you always lived here?"

Again I nodded my head. I couldn't stand it. I felt like

such a blob, a real idiot.

Joel tried again. "What would you like to tell me about yourself?"

I didn't know. Was I supposed to tell him I was a blimp trying to disguise myself as a real person; or that I probably had a horrible case of contagious impending pimples; or that I had this weird brother with a teddy bear filled with orange pits; or that I thought that he was cute and brave and probably thinking about how suicide would be better than talking to me?

I finally looked down at my desk and said, "I'm Marcy Lewis . . . thirteen . . . I hate dancing lessons . . . grammar tests . . . and questions."

He said, "Don't you like anything?"

I thought for a while and said, "Yeah. I like Ms Finney, reading books . . . and felt-tip markers."

Then I sat there, trying to think of something, anything to ask him.

"Joel, do you like Ms Finney?"

"Yes I do."

"Were you scared when you got mad at the class and told them to give her a chance?"

"Why should I be scared saying what I believe?"

"Aren't you afraid that people won't like you?"

Joel just looked at me. I decided that I'd better change the subject.

"Do you have any brothers or sisters?" I asked.

"No."

"What do you want to be when you grow up?"

"Joel Anderson."

28

Ms Finney told the class to pull the desks into a circle, and that each of us had to introduce our partners to the group. Everybody seemed to know new things about the others. When my turn came, I said, "This is Joel Anderson. He doesn't have any brothers, sisters, or pets, and I think he's smart." Then I sat back and waited for Joel to introduce me.

"This is Marcy Lewis. She says that she doesn't like lots of things, but I bet she really does . . . and she has a nice smile."

I couldn't believe it. I'd been sure he was going to say something like "This is Marcy Lewis. She's a real creep and doesn't know how to talk." Or "This is Marcy. She might even look human if she didn't look like a Mack truck." I wasn't used to anyone saying anything nice, except Nancy and my mother, because they had to.

Once we had finished with all the introductions, Ms Finney told us all to reach out to the people at the desks on either side of us, hold hands, close our eyes, and think about the group. Joel was on one side of me, Ms Finney on the other. All I could think about was how scared I was that my hands were sweaty. I was also afraid that they would notice that my finger-nails were all bitten down.

The group sat like that for a long time. Then everybody sort of let go, and Ms Finney said that we should all go home and write a self-description to bring in for the next week, one that only she would read.

I was afraid to look at Joel. All of a sudden, I heard him say, " 'Bye, Marcy. See you in class tomorrow." He had talked to me in front of all those people! I was so excited, but I just smiled and said, "Yeah. See ya, Joel."

Nancy and I walked home, Beauty and the Blimp, Wonderwoman and the Blob Who Ate Brooklyn. Nancy was really excited about Smedley. She kept saying how much fun it would be, how she liked to get to know people, and how she thought it would be good for me. I asked her why.

"Oh, Marcy. You know. You're so hung up about your weight . . . you and your family don't talk to each other . . . and you're so afraid of things . . . and you shouldn't be."

I just clumped along, biting my nails and thinking about what she had said.

Chapter 5

School went on as usual. I kept getting good grades in everything but gym. My anonymous letters to the Student Council suggestion box were ignored. Lunches continued to be lousy. We were only up to the Civil War in history class.

It was different in some ways, though. I didn't sit alone at lunch any more. I sat with some of the kids from Smedley. Ms Finney's classes were still great, but the rest of the classes seemed even more boring than they were before she came. We kept asking the teachers to be more like her, but they made faces and told us to keep quiet. We talked out in classes more and asked more questions, but they didn't like that. We even asked some of them to join Smedley, but they said things like "What are you doing? Getting your heads shrunk?" and "My contract doesn't say I have to stay after school past last period."

What changed a lot was my home. It got even worse. My father has a horrible temper. He doesn't hit, but he yells. Even worse, he says awful things to me, like "I don't care if you get good grades. You do stupid things. Why do I have to have a daughter who is stupid and so fat? I'll never get you married off."

My mother would try to tell him to stop, but he wouldn't listen. They'd get into a fight and she'd start to cry and then go get a tranquillizer.

Then my little brother, Stuart, would cry and run for his teddy bear. While all this was happening, my father would scream at me. "Look at what you've done. We'd never fight if it weren't for you. Apologize." By that time, I'm crying. It usually ended with me running upstairs, slamming my door, throwing myself on my bed, and rocking back and forth. My mother would come in and hug me and tell me everything would be OK, but that I really should lose some weight and look like everyone else.

I hated it. That's what usually went on in my house but, as I said, things got much worse.

In a way, it was because of Smedley. We did lots of neat stuff in there, and I wanted to try some of it at home.

One day in Smedley we broke up into small groups and told each other how we saw each other and felt about each other. I was really excited. Nobody said that they hated me. They said I was smart and nice, but too quiet and shy. No one made fun of me. They didn't say I was skinny and beautiful, but they didn't tell me I was ugly and fat either. So I thought that maybe it would be good to try it at home.

My mother was all for it. I had told her about what we were doing in Smedley, and she really dug it, because she said it was making me different. I didn't tell her how scared I still was, though. I wanted her to be proud of me.

So one night at dinner, she explained that she wanted us

all to sit around and talk like a family.

My father said, "I've worked hard all day for this family, Lily. Isn't that enough? I don't have to talk to all of you too, do I?"

Mom very quietly said, "Martin, I think it's important. Please."

So he said, "OK . . . for a little while."

Mom and I cleared off the dishes, and then we went into the living room, where my father was watching television. Stuart was sitting on the floor, stuffing pits into the hole in Wolf, his teddy bear. Stuart watches a lot of commercials, and he once saw that oranges are supposed to keep you healthy. He used to try to put whole oranges in Wolf, but things got pretty sticky, so we convinced him that pits are best for bears.

My father frowned and said, "No, let the kid stay here. He's part of the family too. And anyway, I want to talk to him about his stupid thumbsucking and that idiot teddy bear."

Stuart held Wolf in his arms and started to suck his thumb. "I love Wolf. He's my friend. He never yells at me."

"Look, kid. You're four years old . . . What are you going to be? Forty, hugging that bear and sucking your thumb? You'll never get a job that way."

Stuart started to cry.

I was scared, but I said, "Daddy. Please don't yell at him. He's just a little kid."

He started to yell. "Don't you start. First I have problems at work. And then I have to come home to all this. All I want is a little peace and quiet. I was an only child. I'm not used to all the noise in the house. Your mother is always busy with you two. She never has enough time for me."

My mother said, "Martin. Please calm down." He kept it up. Stuart started to cough really hard. I started to shake. I didn't want to show him that I was upset, but then I yelled. "You don't want to talk because you think I'll say that I hate you."

"I don't care if you hate me. Don't you ever talk to me that way, young lady. Go up to your room."

"Martin. Give her a chance to talk. You don't give anyone a chance to say anything."

"You just keep quiet. What do you mean, I don't give anyone a chance to talk?"

"That's exactly what I mean."

My father stood up and yelled, "Marcy! This is all your fault. You and that stupid group-dynamics crap. Why can't you leave well enough alone."

I screamed, "I hate you! Just leave me alone," and ran up to my room. I could still hear them fighting. Crying, I heard the door open. It was Stuart, with Wolf.

"Can I come in?"

"OK." I tried to stop crying.

He sat on the bed. "Marcy. I love you. Wolf loves you. Don't cry. Please."

"Stuart. I love you too."

"Why is everybody always yelling? Why can't we be happy?"

"Don't worry. It'll be all right."

"I don't like yelling."

We just held on to each other. My mother came in and said, "Daddy doesn't mean anything when he yells. That's just his way. Don't be frightened. He loves you very much. He just doesn't know how to show it."

I could see that she had been crying. I felt so bad. Nothing that I ever did turned out right.

"Your father says that he's sorry and that we should go shopping Saturday and buy you some new clothes. He thought you'd like that."

"I don't want his dumb money for clothes."

"Please, Marcy. Be reasonable. He's sorry."

"I hate him."

"Please don't say that. You're upsetting me."

So we stopped talking about it. Stuart and I went downstairs, and Mom gave us large bowls of ice cream. My father walked into the kitchen. Stuart started sucking his thumb. I finished up my ice cream and asked for more.

"Marcy. Did your mother tell you that you are both going shopping?"

"Yes."

"Buy anything you want." Then he walked out of the room.

When I went to bed that night, I thought about how bad it was in my house, how much I loved Stuart, and how glad I was that Smedley and Ms Finney were at school.

Chapter 6

English class was really good. We worked hard, but it was fun.

Certain things were always the same. Every Monday we had to hand in compositions. Wednesday we took our spelling tests, and then there were 'The Finney Friday Flicks'. We could bring in popcorn while we watched the movies. After seeing the films, we discussed them.

Book-report times were great. Once we had to come to school as a character in the book that we'd read. It was like the thing in Smedley, only we were the characters, not ourselves. Getting into small groups, we talked about who we were and what happened in our lives. Then we joined with the other groups and introduced one another. It seemed as if the characters from the books were real people.

Another time, after studying what propaganda is all about, we made up one-minute television commericals to 'sell' our book. We videotaped each one with the school's equipment, and after watching all of them we talked about how they worked or didn't work.

Writing a children's book was another assignment. First we talked about what kinds of things were important, like plot, theme, time, place, and stuff like that. Then we each wrote a story and gave it to Ms Finney to be typed up. After that we illustrated them. She taught us how to bind them into books. When we finished, she tried to get school time off to use our books in a special project. But Stone wouldn't give it to us, so we met on a Saturday at our town hospital. We visited little kids who were sick, read our stories to them, and then left the books there so that the hospital would always have books for the kids to read. Some of the class even asked for and got permission to visit every Saturday.

Another time, we talked about humour, satire, and parody. We decided to write our own television show, and called it *Dr Sickbee at Your Service*. It was the story of an orthodontist who moonlights in a rock band, lives next door to a weird family, has a younger sister who ran away to join the roller derby, and solves mysteries in his spare time. We put it on video-tape and picked out the best of the book commercials to use with it, and some of the other English teachers let their classes see it.

Once we had to learn a list of literary terms, vocabulary and spelling words, and parts of speech. I spent a whole weekend studying because I figured that the test was going to be a killer. Getting to class, we saw that Ms Finney had made up a large game board that read 'This Way to Tenth Grade.' Each row was a team. We rolled a die and landed on one of the categories. If we answered correctly, we got to stay there. If not, we had to go back. There were all sorts of penalty cards, like 'Misses the bus', 'Wait one turn', 'Your locker is messy. Lose two turns cleaning it', 'Talking during assembly. Go back three steps'. The first team to make it to the end graduated to tenth grade.

Another time, we walked in and there was a weird-looking guy standing with Ms Finney. He wore a trench-coat and a cap, and had a pipe.

"Class. I'd like to introduce you to my friend, Sherlock Houses, the defective detective."

"Hi, kids. I have a problem, and Ms Finney says that you're pretty smart and can help me. You see, I'm working on The Case of the Missing Drummer."

"I'd rather work on The Case of the Missing Beer."

"Cool it, Robert," said Ms Finney with a smile.

Sherlock continued. "The kidnappers left a ransom note. But I accidentally spilled coffee on it, and some of the words are blurred. Could you help me figure it out?"

We groaned but agreed to play their game, and Sherlock and Ms Finney handed out copies of the note with certain words messed up. We spent the rest of the period trying to figure out the missing words.

At the end of the period, Ms Finney told us that Sherlock was really a friend of hers from graduate school and that what we had done was an exercise in understanding words in context.

It was fun.

Chapter 7

We should have guessed that Smedley and Ms Finney were too good to last. There were all sorts of clues. We noticed that the principal came in to observe quite often. But they sometimes do that with new teachers. We were extra good when he was there. After all, it was Ms Finney's first year as a teacher, and we saw that she got kind of nervous when someone came in to check her out. So we tried to remember to raise our hands and wait to be called on. Ms Finney always said hand raising wasn't necessary if we all respected one another.

One day Mr Stone walked in, sat down in the back, and put his clipboard down on the desk.

We had been working when he came in, but everyone stopped.

Ms Finney said, "Let's continue. Who knows what images are used in this story?"

Seven hands were raised. Robert Alexander waved his.

"All right. Give one example, Robert."

"He's stubborn as a mule. That's a metaphor."

Thomas Shaw yelled, "No, that's a simile."

Ms Finney said, "Who's right? Joel, do you know?"

"It's a simile," Joel answered. "A comparison of two

dissimilar things using *like* or *as*."

"Very good. Now, Robert. Try to find a metaphor."

"OK . . . How about 'The room is a pigsty'?"

"Very good," said Ms Finney.

We were real careful to do our best. We didn't answer more questions than we would have, but we didn't laugh as much, and it just wasn't as much fun. But we all knew that things like that are important to principals. I think that at Principals' School they are taught to look for things like raising hands, checking hall passes, making sure that the window shades are at a certain level, and making announcements over the loudspeaker that begin "This is your principal speaking. I must have your attention please." Anyway, Mr Stone must have gotten A's in all these areas.

So we tried hard that day. When Ms Finney asked Robert Alexander to use 'philosophy' in a sentence, he said, "The derivation of that philosophy obviously was influenced by a group of loquacious siblings." It made no sense, but it sounded erudite (another word that Ms Finney had us look up).

When Mr Stone left, Ms Finney laughed and said, "Look, don't try so hard. Just be yourself."

Robert said, "I thought Mr Stone would be impressed. That's how he sounds at school assemblies."

"But your sentence didn't make much sense."

"That's why he'd like it."

Then Ms Finney picked up a piece of chalk and wrote a quote from Shakespeare, something about sound and fury signifying nothing. Sometimes she got into stuff

40

that's hard to understand, but maybe someday I'll put it all together.

Two weeks later, we came into class and found a substitute.

Chapter 8

We figured that Ms Finney must be sick or taking a mental-health day to recuperate from teaching us.

The substitute made us diagram sentences on the blackboard. Halfway through the period, Mr Stone walked into the class, stood in front of us, cleared his throat, and said, "Miss Finney will probably not be returning to this school. Mrs Richards will be here until we find a new full-time English teacher. Now get back to work."

Get back to work, he said. How could we do that?

Alice Carson raised her hand and asked "Mr Stone. Is Ms Finney all right? Is she sick . . . or in an accident . . . what happened?"

Mr Stone looked at us. "Miss Finney will no longer be a teacher in my school. I want all of you to forget everything she taught you.

The room was still for a minute. Then Joel stood up and said, "Ms Finney taught me the proper methods of punctuation. Should I forget that?"

Mr Stone got even madder. Turning to Joel and glaring, he said, "Joel Anderson, you're a trouble-maker. Detention for the rest of the month."

Before I even realized what I was doing, I stood up and

said, "Ms Finney is the best teacher in the whole dumb school, and I want her back again."

Mr Stone looked shocked. "Marcy Lewis! This isn't at all like you. Now sit down and keep quiet."

I was sick of hearing that. First my father and now Mr Stone. So I kept standing there, and said, "You have not converted a man because you have silenced him." That was a quotation that Ms Finney had had us write about.

The whole class applauded.

Mr Stone said, "You all have detention, and Marcy, this is not like you. Your mother is president of the PTA. She will be very upset when she hears about this."

The bell rang. He told us to go to our next class. We didn't move.

"I said, go to your next class. You will be very sorry. I will put this on your school records."

He stormed out of the room, and we heard him screaming at some kid who was at his locker at an unassigned time.

We still hadn't moved. Some of the kids started to cry. I did. My whole world seemed upside down.

Joel finally spoke. "Come on. Let's go. We're not helping ourselves or Ms Finney. Let's find out what's happening."

Everyone got up to leave. Joel came over to me and said, "Marcy. You were great. You really told that fool off. I'll see you in detention, and we'll figure out what we're going to do." Then he left.

I didn't believe it. Joel spoke to me and said that he liked what I did!

Nancy stood there and said, "You really did it. I'm glad."

We had to run to the gym. Nancy didn't want to be late. I didn't care. When we got to gym, I went up to the gym teacher and told her that I had been mugged on the way to school by a syndicate specializing in stolen gymsuits. Then I sat down and watched another thrilling volleyball game.

The day went quickly. I called up my mother and told her that I was staying after to do something extra with my English class. I didn't mention that the something extra was detention. That would have been tranquilizer territory. She was pleased, and said, "Marcy, I'm so glad that you are getting involved in school activities."

After the last class, Nancy and I rushed to the bathroom. She combed her hair and I checked for pimples. Then we headed for detention.

Joel was standing by the door. He smiled when he saw us, and said, "We'd better hurry up. They give added time if we're late."

So the three of us sat down in the back.

Nancy whispered, "What do you think is happening?"

Joel said, "I don't know, but my Dad is on the Board of Education. I'll try to find out."

I whispered, "It must be something awful. They usually let teachers at least finish out the year."

"Maybe she starred in an X-rated film and Mr Stone saw it." That was Nancy's idea.

The detention teacher kept looking at us. Joel told us that we had to quiet down or else we would have to stay

44

later. He and Nancy had had detention before, but this was all new to me.

I sat there and pretended to read. Usually it's easy for me to read, but this time I was so upset that I couldn't do anything.

The teacher finally told us that time was up and we could go. Everyone rushed out of the room.

"Marcy, I'm going to ask my father what's happening. I'll let you know as soon as I find out. Then you can call Nancy and she can let some other kids know."

"OK. Please find out. Joel, do you think it's really bad? I'm scared."

Joel shrugged and shook his head. "I don't know," and then he walked away.

Nancy and I headed home.

"Hey, Marcy, what are we going to do if she can't come back? What happens to English class and to Smedley? They won't let us have Smedley without a teacher."

I could feel the tears coming down my face. I couldn't say anything.

Nancy stopped and grabbed my hand. "Don't cry. It'll be all right." She thought for a minute. "I take that back. Ms Finney says it's good to show emotions. Marcy, go ahead. Cry if it makes you feel better."

That's why it was all so important to me. The kids from Smedley and Ms Finney still cared about me even if I showed my feelings. I felt as if someone had taken a vacuum cleaner and cleaned all my insides out and left me with only my blimp outside.

"Marcy, I think Joel likes you. He said he was going to

45

call you tonight, not me, and he's been talking to you a lot lately."

I guess Nancy told me that because she thought it would make me feel better. But it didn't.

Chapter 9

When I got home, my mother was waiting for me at the door.

"Honey, what happened at school today? Mr Stone called and was very upset."

"Did you have to take a tranquillizer?"

"Oh, Marcy, don't be mean. I can't help it. You know things aren't easy for me."

I knew that. I mean, her husband is related to me too. And she also worried about me and Stuart.

"Mom, I get scared that you use them too much. In school they say that prescriptions shouldn't be abused."

"I'm careful. Look, Marcy, what happened?"

So I told her about what had happened. I started to cry when I got to the part about Ms Finney and Smedley. She held me.

"Honey, do you love Miss Finney more than me?"

"No . . . It's different. She's not afraid, and she's helping me not to be afraid. And she teaches good stuff in class. It's not fair. Mr Stone is an idiot."

"Oh, honey, don't talk like that."

"It's true. He's an idiot, a dope. He's just rotten."

"Marcy, he's a human being. Remember that."

"Nothing you say can make me believe that. Stone's not human. There's not one nice thing about him."

"You know, Marcy, life's not like that. No one is all bad or all good—not Mr Stone, not your father, not me, no one. You've got to learn that."

I just shook my head. "Stone's a fool."

Just then, Stuart came running into the house. He'd been riding his bike, and had fallen. We ran over to him.

"Stuart, where does it hurt?"

He just kept crying.

My mother looked for broken bones and blood. Finding none, she said, "I think you'll live. Did you break the sidewalk?"

Stuart shook his head.

"Would you two like some ice cream?"

We said yes and headed for the kitchen.

"Wolf wants some orange pits."

"We're out of oranges. We'll get some later."

I decided to say something. "Stuart, I love you."

He smiled, and I smiled back. It's so easy to love him sometimes. He's a little weird, but he's a good person, for a four-year-old. Ms Finney says that age doesn't matter, but sometimes it's hard to talk to a little kid. But the thing with Stuart is that we say a lot without talking.

We heard a car door slam, a scary sound when you know that it means your father is home. My mother went to the front door to meet him.

"What a rotten day," he said. That's what he always says. It's always the same. My mother then kisses him and hands him a Scotch and soda. It's one of our few family traditions.

"Martin, I want to talk to you about something. Please, stay calm."

My mother has a fantastic sense of timing. It got quieter, and then I heard my father scream, "Marcy Lewis, get in here!"

I ran into the living room and tripped on the rug.

"You're such a klutz. I thought sending you to dancing school was supposed to make you more graceful."

"I wanted drum lessons, not dancing."

"You'd probably give yourself a concussion with the drumsticks," my father said. "What's this I hear about school?"

"Mr Stone's wrong. Ms Finney's a good teacher."

"How many times must I tell you to respect your elders?"

"But he's wrong."

"I doubt that, but even if he were, you must learn to respect those in authority. How do you expect to get ahead?"

"I don't care about that. All I care about is Ms Finney."

"I never did like her, young lady. She's been feeding you a lot of garbage, with that sensitivity-training crap and calling herself Ms. What's wrong with Miss? Just be good and play by the rules and you'll be a much happier person. Your mother and I know that."

"Martin, I think Miss Finney has helped Marcy."

"Don't you start. Look. I know what's best for this family. Don't I support you and take care of you?"

49

Stuart came over, hugged me, and smiled.

"Why is the kid so dirty?" my father asked.

"I fell off my bike," Stuart remembered.

"Just what we need. Another clumsy kid in this family."

My mother said, "Let's all wash up for dinner. Marcy and Stuart, let's go set the table."

We went into the kitchen while my father sat down to read the paper in the living room.

Once the table was set and dinner ready, we all sat down. My father talked about how hard his job was. Stuart kept sucking his thumb. I stared at my plate, and my mother suggested how nice it would be for all of us to go on a weekend trip.

"I work hard all week," my father said. "I want to relax on the weekends."

Everything got so quiet, you could hear the milk going down Stuart's throat. The phone rang. My mother got up to answer it. I figured it was Mr Stone again. I got really scared.

"Marcy, it's for you. A young gentleman."

I had forgotten. Joel had said he'd call me if he found out any new developments. I got up from the table and went to the phone as if I were used to getting calls every day from boys.

"Hi, Marcy. I just found out. It's serious."

"What happened. Did she lose her marking book?"

"Very funny. She's been suspended because she won't say the Pledge of Allegiance in homeroom."

I thought about that for a while.

"But lots of kids don't say it."

"She's not a kid, she's a teacher. And anyway, my father thinks it's more than that. He says a lot of people don't like her—Mr Stone, some of the teachers, Mr Goldman, and some of the parents."

"How can't they like her?"

"Look, Marcy, she's different. Not everybody likes you when you act and dress differently."

"Joel, I really care about her. What can we do?"

"I'm not sure. Listen, meet you in front of school tomorrow half an hour before classes start OK?"

"Yeah. Well, I'll see you."

I called Nancy right away, told her what was happening, and had her spread the word. My father was yelling that I'd better get back to the table, so I hung up and went back to the dinner table. As I sat down, my mother started gushing. "Our daughter is growing up . . . her first call from a boy."

My father grumbled, "Can't you tell your little friends not to call during dinnertime?"

"Oh, Martin. It's her first call from a boy. Did he ask you out?"

I couldn't stand it anymore. "Look. I'm sorry he called during dinner. He wanted to know if he can borrow Wolf to cut it up in science class."

Stuart started to cry. Sometimes I feel really sorry for the kid, but it was the only way that I could get my parents to stop bothering me about the call.

"That's it, young lady. Go to your room!" my father screamed.

"Martin. She hasn't finished eating," my mother said softly.

"That's all right. That girl won't waste away to nothing."

I ran upstairs to my room and cried.

A while later, my mother knocked at the door and immediately came in. She didn't even give me time to say whether I wanted company.

"Honey, I'm sorry it's like this. You've got to learn to live with it. I'm sorry. I love you very much."

We hugged each other, and then she left and I cried myself to sleep.

Chapter 10

My alarm went off in the morning. I got up, dressed, and went downstairs. Both my parents were eating breakfast. The morning paper was lying on the table. Ms Finney's picture was on the front page. The headline read 'Junior High Teacher Dismissed; Refuses to Pledge Allegiance.'

Miss Barbara Finney, teacher of English at Dwight David Eisenhower Junior High School, has been suspended from her duties until further notice for her refusal to say the Pledge of Allegiance.

Mr Frank Stone, Principal, stated, "As a good American, I am chagrined to think that this type of individual is allowed to influence impressionable young people."

Miss Finney was not available for comment at publication time.

A hearing will be held on Tuesday, 15 October at 8:00 PM, in the auditorium of J. Edgar Hoover High School. The public is invited to attend.

Finishing the article, I put the paper back down on the table.

My father started. "I suppose you are impressed by this woman's actions."

"I've learned a lot in her class."

He slammed down his coffee cup. "I want you to stay out of this, Marcy. You are not going to turn into a revolutionary. Learn to play by the rules."

I concentrated on pouring the milk on my cornflakes.

My mother put her hand on mine. "I'm sorry. I was very impressed by her when I met her at the PTA meeting."

I asked, "Can I go to the hearing?"

"Martin. Why don't we go together—you and me and Marcy. I know it's important to her."

"All right. I suppose so. It'll be interesting to see Miss Know-It-All's teacher get fired. But I'm warning you, young lady. I want you to stay out of trouble."

"Can I be excused? I have to meet someone at school to go over homework."

"All right, but remember what I said."

I ran up to my room, grabbed my books and jacket, and ran out the door before anyone else had a chance to say anything to me.

When I got there, Joel was waiting. A bunch of other kids were also standing around. They were from the different classes that Ms Finney taught. Also from Smedley. All of them were pretty upset.

Joel said, "What we have to do is get all of the kids together and make plans. Each of you go around now and get lists of kids who are willing to help support her."

The group broke up, and Joel turned to me.

54

"Marcy, we have only four school days and a week-end before the hearing. We've got to organize fast. And listen, Nancy's decided to have a party Saturday night. Would you go with me?"

Just like that, I got asked out for my very first time.

"Yeah, if you want to take me, I guess I can go. But I have to ask my parents first."

The bell rang for homeroom, and we got up and went into the school. I was in a daze. Joel and I went to our separate lockers. I ran into Nancy.

"Hey, Marcy, you had to hang up last night before I had a chance to tell you. I'm having a party Saturday. Can you come?"

"Yeah. Joel just invited me . . . I think."

"What do you mean, 'I think'?"

"Yeah. He asked me."

"Don't be so surprised. I said he liked you. See?"

Mr Stone walked up to us. "Good morning, girls. Marcy, I want to see you in my office after homeroom. Be there promptly." Then he walked on.

"Marcy. Are you going to get it because of what happened in class yesterday?"

"Probably. What's it like to go to the principal's office?"

"I don't know. I only get detention a lot."

Just what I needed to think about. Maybe we'd have an earthquake during homeroom and I wouldn't have to go. Or maybe I'd be lucky enough to trip and break my leg so that the ambulance would carry me away before I got to the office. Probably if that happened Mr Stone would yell and tell me to go to the nurse, who would tell me to take a nap and then go back to class.

Going into homeroom, I tripped over someone's feet, but I didn't break anything.

When it came time to say the Pledge, I looked around to see what everyone was doing. Some kids said it. Others passed chewing-gum sticks and notes. A couple of kids talked. Not too many seemed aware of the words. What did it all mean? It seemed to say everything that Ms Finney believed in, liberty and justice for all, one nation. Maybe it was the under-God part. She never talked about religion, but maybe that was it. I didn't know.

The bell rang, and I headed for the office. Lots of kids were there. Some had come to school late, and now they were waiting around until the secretary had time to make out late passes. A couple of kids were there because they had been caught sneaking cigarettes in the bathroom. They should have gone to the faculty room. The smoke there is so thick, no one would have seen them. I sat down, chewed on my nails, and waited to see Mr Stone.

About forty-five minutes later I was called into his office. He had a picture of his family on his desk. It was the kind that you get on a Christmas card with a dittoed letter about how the family was doing and how they had grown. Mr Stone frowned at me.

"Marcy, you were very rude to me yesterday. I don't understand it. You've always been such a good student. I don't want you or any other student to get involved in this situation. It's a matter for grown-ups to handle."

I was scared, like when you go to the doctor to get a flu

shot. But I couldn't let him bully me.

"Mr Stone, it involves us. Ms Finney was our teacher, and she's a good teacher."

He kept frowning. "Don't you understand? I'm very concerned. Miss Finney has a great many philosophies and teaching techniques that are not good."

"No, I don't understand."

"Marcy, the younger generation just doesn't understand they've got to play by the rules. Let me tell you about my oldest daughter. She was a good student, just like you, and she was accepted to a fine college. When she got there, she met some people with very radical ideas. Now she's dropped out of school and is living in a commune and spending all her time making quilts and gardening. Can't you see now why I am so concerned about Miss Finney and her strange ways?"

"But, Mr Stone, she's not strange. She does teach us regular English. And I don't think your daughter is doing anything wrong."

Mr Stone exploded. "That's it! I've had it! Now you listen, young lady. You'll be very sorry some day. I've spent my whole life trying to keep America's ideals in mind, and this school a good place to educate young people. And then along comes a teacher who talks about feelings and being in touch with yourself and she doesn't believe in grades and argues at teachers' meetings and doesn't dress like a teacher and won't salute the flag. And I also have to deal with community pressure. Well, I just won't have it."

I got really scared. It's horrible to be yelled at. Then his phone rang. He picked it up, listened for a minute, and looked up and said, "Marcy, I hope that you understand that I only want the best for all of you. You may now return to class."

I left the office. I was very confused. I had gotten a late pass to go to gym. As long as Mr Stone kept me out of class, he should have let me miss that class. But since he didn't, I went up to the teacher, told her that I gave my gymsuit to a poor starving orphan who needed it to trade for a bowl of rice, and sat down to watch another volleyball game.

Afterwards, in the locker room, everybody came over to ask me what had happened. Nancy really knows how to spread news quickly. I just said that Mr Stone was mad at Ms Finney and didn't want students to interfere.

It was strange. In Ms Finney's class we had read *To Kill a Mockingbird* and talked about the part where Atticus tells Jem that you can't understand someone until you've walked around in his or her shoes. So now I tried, in my head, to put myself in Ms Finney's place, and in Mr Stone's, and in my father's and mother's. It was horribly confusing. It sure gets tough when you get older. It's much easier to be a little kid whose big problem is learning to tie shoelaces.

Next period, while I was still trying to think, Nancy passed me a note, trying not to let the teacher see it.

> Marcy,
> Some of the kids are coming
> over to my house after school

to make plans about how to
help Ms Finney. Can you come
over? Joel will be there.

Nanci

That's just like Nancy to change the spelling of her name and to dot the i with a big dumb circle. I guess it's a stage people go through, but I'm never going to do it. The dot looks too much like a blimp. When I looked up, I smiled at Nancy, who was pretending to solve an algebra equation.

Finally the bell rang, announcements were made, and I headed for my locker. Joel was standing there.

"How did it go with Mr Stone?"

I just shook my head.

"He called me in too."

"Did he tell you about his daughter?"

"No. He said that I was a troublemaker and that I was a bad influence on you."

That was amazing. Why did everybody keep trying to team Joel and me up? I mean, we'd just started talking to each other.

I just stood there and blushed. I blush a lot. That's really embarrassing. So, rather than just standing there, I opened my locker. When I did, some of the books fell out. My locker cleanliness would never get *Good Housekeeping's* Seal of Approval. Joel just laughed and helped me pick up the books.

Then he said, "We'd better hurry up. Nancy's expecting us."

59

We walked over to Nancy's house and talked. It was getting easier to talk to him. But I still felt like a blimp. I mean, I was fat. That hadn't changed. Although I had stopped eating a lot of junk, I still hadn't lost much weight.

When we got to Nancy's house, I offered to help her get the food ready. Joel went downstairs, and Nancy and I worked in the kitchen.

"Marcy, how come you never take gym?"

"I don't like volleyball."

"But you never play when we do anything else."

"I'm not coordinated."

"A lot of kids aren't."

"Nancy, I don't want to talk about it."

"But, Marcy, you should. Ms Finney always said it's better to talk about things that bother you instead of keeping them inside."

I thought about that. Maybe I should tell her. But I was afraid that she would laugh or tell someone.

"Promise not to tell."

"Yeah."

"I hate getting into a gymsuit. I'm too fat and ugly and I hate dressing and undressing and showering in front of everybody."

Then I started to cry.

"Marcy. Come on. You're not ugly. You *are* too fat, but you have good points too. It's just that kids think you're stuck-up because you won't play and because you're smart."

"Do they care?"

"Sure. You can be fun to be with, and you say good things when you're not scared."

"Nancy, are you friends with me just because your mother makes you do that?"

Nancy thought about that and said, "It sort of started out that way, but then I really got to like you."

I didn't know what to say about that, so I said, "I guess we should bring the food downstairs now."

We brought the stuff downstairs. There were a lot of kids there. I sat down next to Joel because he asked me to.

"Marcy, what took you so long?"

"Do you think I'm stuck-up?"

"No. Who told you that? Nancy?"

"Yeah. She said some other kids thought I was."

"People always say that about other people who are quiet, because they are harder to know and more mysterious. But look at you lately. You've been talking a lot."

"That's because you're a bad influence on me. That's what Mr Stone says, so it must be true."

We both laughed at that. I was proud of myself for that line. For a minute, I almost forgot that I was a blimp.

Nancy passed around cookies, but I refused to have any. She smiled at me when I did that, but didn't make a big deal about it. Then she said that we should all get down to business.

Everyone started making suggestions. The meeting got pretty wild, so rather than trying to explain it, here are the secretary's notes of the meeting:

PROBLEM:

What to do to show everyone how we feel about Ms Finney and her being fired.

PROBLEM SOLUTIONS:

1. Clog up the faculty room toilets with *The New York Times* school supplements.
2. Sit in at the Board of Education offices, the front office, and the cafeteria.
3. Demand aspirin from the school nurse.
4. Steal all the chalk in the entire school.
5. Put out an underground newspaper.
6. Put out a contract on Mr Stone.
7. Short-sheet the beds in the nurse's clinic.
8. Go to the Guidance Counsellors and ask for guidance.
9. Boycott the school cafeteria.
10. Capture the intercom system and announce that school has been dismissed.
11. Picket.
12. Steal the faculty-room coffee pot.
13. Put a padlock on the faculty smoking lounge.
14. Circulate petitions showing support of Ms Finney.
15. Have every kid in the school light up a cigarette at an assigned time, so that the entire student body would get suspended at once.
16. Burn all the copies of the intelligence tests, or make Mr Stone take one and announce the results at the next PTA meeting.

17. Plant grass on Mr Stone, call the cops, and have him busted.
18. Deflate all the volleyballs.
19. Call all the major TV networks and have them cover the story.
20. Try to get our parents to support Ms Finney.
21. Turn in all our assignments written in crayon.
22. Refuse to leave homeroom until we get a promise that Mr Stone will listen to us.
23. Cut school and then forge notes saying that we were absent because of cases of acute acne.

Needless to say, we decided not to do most of those things. What we planned to do was get petitions signed, try to get our parents to help, and refuse to leave home-room until we could talk to Mr Stone. We thought that if we could organize and get at least ten kids from each homeroom to refuse to leave, we would mess everything up, and then Mr Stone would have to listen to our representatives. They voted and elected four of us, Joel, Nancy, Robert Alexander, and me. They said that we were the logical choices because Joel and I had nerve enough to talk up in class, and Nancy did some nutty things but had sense, and Robert knew how to speak Mr Stone's language. Another first for Marcy, the kid who was afraid of being chosen last for gym teams.

Mrs Sheridan came down to the recreation room and told us that it was time to be heading home for dinner. I said goodbye to Nancy, and she said she'd call me later.

Joel walked me home. We talked about what would

happen when our families found out that we were leading what was happening. I said that my father would probably yell and threaten to cut off my allowance and tell me how stupid I was, and then my mother would try to calm him down. After that, I wasn't sure what would happen. Joel said that he thought his father would approve, but even if he didn't he'd still allow Joel to go ahead with it. I asked what his mother would say and he said, "That's a long story. We'll talk about it at Nancy's party, if you can go."

I said, "OK, I'll ask my parents tonight." Then we were at my door, and I said goodbye and went inside.

Chapter 11

My mother immediately came up and said, "Marcy, did you have a nice day? Who was that young man? Is he the same one who called? Where did you go? What did you do?"

I waited to make sure that she was all done asking questions. Then I answered.

"Yes, I had a nice day. His name is Joel Anderson, and he called last night. I went over to Nancy Sheridan's to talk about school. And Joel asked me to go to a party at Nancy's on Saturday night. Can I go?"

My mother just stood there and beamed.

"Oh, yes, of course, dear. What are you going to wear. Do you know anything about his family? Is his mother in the PTA?"

"I don't know. All I know is that his father is on the Board of Education. And I'll probably wear blue-jeans and a sweatshirt."

"Oh, Marcy, you can't. We'll have to go out Saturday afternoon and buy a nice new dress. What will everyone be wearing?"

I was so happy that she said yes that I didn't say I didn't care what everyone would be wearing.

"Look, Mom, I have to go do homework," I said, and headed up to my room.

While I was sitting at my desk, trying to study and thinking about Joel, Stuart walked in.

"Marcy, play with me."

"What do you want to play?"

"Play teacher."

I took out paper and a felt-tip marker and printed the alphabet in large and small letters.

"Here, Stuart, practise your letters." Stuart sat on the floor and went to work. He was really getting good at it. I continued to do my homework.

Mother called us down for dinner. My father had a late business meeting, so it was just Mom, Stuart, and me. We laughed a lot. It was really fun.

After dinner, Stuart and I went upstairs and I read to him. In the middle of a story, Stuart asked, "Who's Finney?"

"Do you mean Ms Finney?"

"Yeah. Mommy and Daddy fight about her."

"Oh, Stuart, she's this really great teacher. She talks about good things, like feelings and people and good books and lots of stuff you should like."

"Will she be my teacher when I grow up?"

I thought about that and sighed. "I don't know. I really hope so. I don't know anything anymore."

Then I kissed him good night and watched him shuffle out with Wolf, leaving a trail of orange pits.

Once in bed, I immediately fell asleep and had very strange dreams about my being caught in a bowl of jello.

When I got up in the morning, I dressed quickly and ran down to breakfast. The rest of the family was already there.

My father said, "I hear that you are going to a little party Saturday night with a young man. I'm not sure that I like the fact that my little girl is growing up, but I suppose that I've got to get used to it."

Then he smiled. I smiled back. He continued, stirring his coffee very slowly.

"His father is a radical on the school board. Goes for busing and progressive education. I don't want my daughter involved. You understand, don't you?"

My cornflakes got caught in my throat.

"You know, Marcy, I really don't understand you any more. You used to be such a good child. Now I just don't know you."

My mother interrupted, "Martin, please don't start. Marcy is a good child. She's just going out. All the girls do at her age. Why, lots of them have been going out for much longer. And I'm sure that Joel is a nice boy."

I just sat there.

Stuart smiled at me across ths table. I really loved the weird little kid at that moment. I smiled back and said, "Stuart, tonight I'll read you and Wolf another story."

My father just grunted and said, "That kid and his teddy bear! Stuart, you'd better start growing up."

First he complains that I'm growing up too fast and then he complains that Stuart isn't growing up fast enough.

I asked to be excused, and got my books and went to

school. Joel met me outside the building. It felt really good seeing him. A bunch of kids, the same ones who had been at Nancy's, gathered and we made plans. All of us were supposed to spend the day rounding up anyone who would be willing to remain in homeroom after the bell rang. The plan was to organize and be prepared to do it the next day. We settled things pretty quickly, and the day went on.

It was a strange day. Everyone was walking around very quietly. Even while passing between classes, it was almost too silent. People walked around whispering, trying to figure out who was in on it and who wasn't. Nancy, Robert, Joel, and I knew, because we were given the lists, but no one else was positive.

Then it happened. We were sitting in English class, still diagramming sentences, when the room phone buzzed. The sub went to it, and stared around the room while she was listening. She kept shaking her head, and then said, "All right. I'll send them right down."

Then she put down the phone, paused, and said, "Robert Alexander, Joel Anderson, Marcy Lewis, and Nancy Sheridan are wanted in the principal's office immediately. Take your books with you. I don't think you'll be coming back here today."

Everyone turned and looked around. Then all of a sudden someone said, "Uh oh, you guys are gonna get it." The four of us got up, grabbed our books, and left the room. The sub closed the door after us.

We all stood outside the door to the classroom. "What now?" Nancy asked.

"Maybe Stone wants us to audition for the talent show," was Robert's answer. "Perhaps my fame as a harmonica player has spread."

Nancy laughed and said, "I can always do my imitation of an electric toothbrush."

Joel said that he could play his guitar, and I started to tap dance. All the money my parents had put into my lessons finally paid off. We all stood there laughing.

Then I said, "Listen, I'm really scared."

Nancy looked down and said, "Me too."

Joel said, "We're all scared, but we've got to go . . . unless we all plan to run off to Alaska, and that doesn't seem too sensible. We knew what we were getting into, so let's go through with it. At least we'll get our chance to talk to Stone."

We got to the office and went to the front desk. The secretary had the look on her face that she always had whenever a kid was going to get it. I bet when she was a kid she always told on others.

We filed into Mr Stone's office. It was filled. My mother was there. So was Nancy's. And there was another woman and a man that I didn't know. I glanced to my right and saw Stuart sitting there, clutching Wolf and sucking his thumb.

Mr Stone said, "I have called your parents here to discuss your plot to undermine my school."

We all stood there. Then Joel said. "There has been no plot to undermine your school. We just want to make ourselves heard in *our* school."

Then the man who was with the women said, "See here,

Mr Stone. I'm not sure what you're trying to accomplish. I've already told you that I trust my son and approve of him."

I looked at Joel, and he nodded his head. "Dad, I would like to introduce Marcy Lewis, Nancy Sheridan, and Robert Alexander—"

Mr Stone interrupted, "Look, there is a time and a place for everything. I have called all of you together to discuss the student rebellion of which you four are the leaders. What I want from you are the names of all of the students who are involved in this plot, or you four will be in serious trouble."

I said, "Oh, no. That's not fair. No way."

Mr Stone turned to my mother. "I told you, Mrs Lewis. See what she has turned into."

My mother looked at him and said, "My daughter has turned into someone I'm very proud of, and I'm not sure that she is doing anything wrong. I don't appreciate your threatening her."

All of the parents started talking at once. So did we. Everything got noisy and very confused.

The phone rang. Everyone shut up. Mr Stone picked up the receiver. He listened for a while and then said, "Thank you. That solves a lot of my problems."

Then he got up and started walking around. That was sort of hard. There were so many people in such a small place. But I guess Mr Stone thought he would win the 'Principal of the Year Award' for his performance.

Anyway, he turned and said, "Your plan has no way of working. The Superintendent's Office has ordered school

70

to be closed until the Tuesday hearing."

Then he walked back to his desk. On his way he accidentally knocked over Wolf. Orange pits fell all over the rug, and Stuart started to cry. My mother ran over to Stuart, and so did I. All of a sudden, everybody in the room started to laugh, except for Stuart and Mr Stone, who turned around and said, "For everyone's information, these four student ringleaders are suspended for ten days. It will go on their permanent records, and they will not be allowed to make up work missed. You might as well take them home. I don't want them on school grounds for the entire time that they are suspended."

We all walked out of the office and into the hall. I heard my mother inviting everyone over to our house to discuss the situation. Then she, Stuart, and I went to my locker to get my coat and books.

I said, "Thanks, Mom. I'm sorry to get you involved in this."

"Marcy, do you believe in what you're doing?"

"Yes, I do."

"Then I'm very proud of you. I wish I had nerve enough to do it. But I'm scared. What is your father going to say?"

"Mom, I've spent thirteen years worrying about that, and I've never been happy. So now I've got to do things that I think are right."

Then I closed my locker and we walked out to the car.

"Honey, don't think I'm mad at you, but shouldn't you clean out your locker? People will think that I never taught you to be neat."

I just looked at her and laughed. That's just like my mother—in the middle of everything, she worries about my locker. But she certainly had surprised me. She was on my side.

On the way home, I asked, "Mom, how come all of you came to school?"

My mother explained. "I got a call from Mr Stone's office. Naturally, I had to bring Stuart with me. When I got to school, I ran into Nancy's mother and the other parents. Mr Stone called us into the office, told us how bad you all were, and how we should support him, especially me, because of the PTA. Mr Anderson told him that he was proud of Joel and would personally congratulate his son, not punish him. The only one who went along with Mr Stone was Mrs Alexander, who cried the whole time. Then he called you in, and you know the rest of the story. Oh, Marcy, what are we going to tell your father?"

"Mom, I don't know. He's gonna yell a lot, but I don't know what to do."

Stuart sat in the middle and kept pretending to drive. Poor kid. He's in the middle most of the time.

Getting to our house, we rushed inside to get ready for everybody else.

"Mom, how do you think Mr Stone found out who the leaders are?"

"He said that a student told him."

"What a rat."

"Marcy, you shouldn't talk about Mr Stone that way."

"I meant the kid, but Stone's a rat, too."

"Marcy!" But then she laughed.

"Mom, Stone stays Ms Finney never taught us anything, but I know that 'Stone's a rat' is a metaphor. I bet he doesn't know that."

"Marcy, stop fooling around. We have company coming."

The bell rang. Everybody came in. We all sat around for a few minutes, getting food and staring at one another.

Mr Anderson started. "I'm very proud of our children. Although I think their scheme was drastic, I feel that Mr Stone has treated them as mindless children, and they've proved him wrong. They know what they want and are willing to accept the consequences. I think they've learned a very important lesson."

Mrs Alexander just kept crying.

My mother said, "This won't keep our children out of college, will it? We do want Marcy to get a good education."

Mr Anderson put down his coffee cup and lit up a cigarette. "Listen, don't let Mr Stone intimidate you. We have bright children, and many schools will respect their minds and their initiative."

Robert, Nancy, Joel, and I sat on the floor watching the whole scene. Finally Nancy said, "Look. We made the decision to support Ms Finney, and I'm glad. I'll use the suspension time to study."

"Yeah," I said. "We can get the assignments and do them anyway."

"But, we won't get credit for it. Why bother?" Robert asked.

Joel said, "We can use the time to learn something, instead of diagramming sentences."

We all laughed.

"I think you should go to the library and get some books out concerning legal rights and privileges," Joel's father suggested. "You can learn some interesting things. This situation can turn into a real learning experience."

Finally Mrs Alexander spoke up. "I don't know about the rest of you, but my Robert will be punished. I don't agree with the stand he is taking or your attitude about it. Come, Robert, we're going home." She got out of her chair and turned to leave. "Robert, I told you that we are leaving. Now, let's go."

Robert got up. He looked upset and mad. I didn't blame him. I knew what he was going through.

They left. The rest of us talked about the upcoming hearing. No one was sure that Ms Finney would win. Mr Anderson said that he was in a funny position, being a school-board member and everything. He had a feeling that Mr Stone would try to get him disqualified.

My mother offered to contact those members of the PTA who might help.

Mrs Sheridan offered to work with her.

Mr Anderson said that he would help, but it would have to be during evenings.

My mother said, "Perhaps Joel's mother would like to help during the day."

Joel looked uncomfortable. His father smiled and said, "My wife and I are divorced. She doesn't live around here."

I jumped up. "Does anyone want Coke or coffee or anything?"

They all said no and that it was time to go home for dinner. I said goodbye to Mrs Sheridan, Nancy, Mr Anderson, and Joel.

After they left, I turned to my mother. "Why did you have to do that?"

"Do what?"

"Ask them about the mother. If they wanted to say anything, they would have."

My mother looked surprised. "Oh, I'm sorry. I didn't realize. Do you think they think I'm horrible?"

"I don't know. I doubt it. But please don't do it again, Mom. I'm happy that you're helping me with this school thing." I hugged her.

"I did a lot of thinking," she said. "I'm very proud of you. I never could have done that when I was your age. So now, at my age, I'm learning and you're my teacher. The world is changing . . . and I'm glad."

I hugged her again. Sometimes it's very hard to say anything.

"Joel is very nice, Marcy. Do you like him? Does he like you?"

"I don't know, Mom. Yeah, I like him. But it's no big romance. Don't bug me about it. I think he just thinks I'm a good friend. We like some of the same things."

Stuart walked in and asked for an orange. We both ate one and spent the rest of the afternoon stuffing orange pits in Wolf's head. Actually, we turned it into a game, putting Wolf in a corner and trying to pitch the pits into the hole. I won, 84 to 39. It took almost all afternoon to get that score.

I heard the car door slam and the front door open. The ritual had begun. Only this time it was a little different. This time he called me downstairs before he was even handed his drink.

I walked in and said, "Hi. How was your day?"

"Apparently not as exciting as yours, young lady. I warned you about getting involved. Maybe it's about time that you got punished for your actions. I had to hear all about this from a business associate. I understand that both of my girls are involved in this? Is that true?"

My mother said, "Let's all sit down and discuss this quietly."

So we all sat down. I looked from one to the other. Then I said, "I'm doing the right thing. I'm not always wrong."

"Martin, Marcy's right. You should've heard Mr Stone."

He just sat there, chewing on his smelly cigar. My mother continued, "She's got to make her own decisions. And I've made my own decision too. I'm going to support and help her. She's helped me to realize some things."

My father turned on me. "Are you satisfied now? Your mother and I never disagree."

"Don't blame her," Mom said. "I've made up my own mind."

"Can I please be excused?"

"Oh, no you don't, young lady. You cause all the

trouble and then you try to slip away."

"Martin!"

"Oh, all right. Marcy, I want you to go to bed without your dinner. You may leave."

I went up to my room, closed the door, and looked in the mirror and searched for emerging acne. There was none. So I sat down at my desk. Then I realized that I didn't have anything to do. I'd been suspended. Me, of all people. So I spent the next hour thinking of Joel.

Joel was a special person, I decided. He was smart. He was brave. He was cute. And he liked me. Amazing.

I stayed in my room all evening and watched television. TV comes in handy when people can't talk to each other. Then I went to bed and dreamed about going to Nancy's party and falling down a flight of stairs.

Chapter 12

The next morning my mother came into my room and woke me up.

"Marcy. I let you sleep late today, but it's time to get up. We're going shopping for your dress. And I want to talk to you."

I hate waking up out of a sound sleep. She expects me to talk and make sense immediately. So I rolled over on my stomach and put the pillow over my head. She started to tickle me. I hate that too.

It was easier to get out of bed than to be tickled. My mother thinks she's being cute when she does that. I think she's being a pain.

"Mom, what do you want?"

"I'm getting nervous about what's going on. I don't like to fight with your father. I'm not used to it."

I flopped down on the bed and put the pillow back on my head. I could feel her sit down on the edge of the bed. I tightened up, expecting to be tickled again. When that didn't happen, I peeked out from under the pillow. I could see her crying.

Sitting up, I reached over, and touched her hair. "Aw, Mom, please don't cry. It'll be OK. I'm sorry."

78

"Marcy, it's not your fault. It's not anybody's fault. It just happened. I never really thought much about women's liberation. Now I'm beginning to."

"Look, Mom, let's go shopping. Don't worry."

So we went shopping, taking Stuart and Wolf with us.

I hate to go shopping. I love clothes, but they always look awful on me. All those skinny tops, and the clothes that expect you to have a waist. And when you find something you like, they never have it in your size. It's horrible. One of the worst things is that I have to go into the store, go past the junior boutique, and step into the 'Chubbies' section. They should give out paper bags to wear over your head while you shop there.

So there we were at the 'Chubbies' section. Stuart was swinging on one of the coat racks. My mother was looking at ugly dresses. I was trying to avoid the saleslady.

She waddled up to my mother. She was what the store people would call a 'stylish stout'. She was what I would call a 'senior blimp'.

"Can I help you, dearie?" she asked.

"We are looking for a party dress for my daughter."

"Oh, isn't she sweet. What do you want, honey?" she asked me.

"I want a pair of size five bluejeans."

"Marcy," my mother began.

"Mom, she asked what I wanted, not what I was going to get."

"You'll have to excuse my daughter. She gets upset when she shops."

The lady smiled and said, "I can understand. I used to be that way myself."

I felt like throwing up when she said that.

My mother must have understood, because she said, "Perhaps it would be best if we browsed by ourselves. We'll be sure to call you if we need help. Thank you." My mother's OK sometimes, even if she is skinny.

We took lots of stuff into the dressing room. Finally, I found a purple pants suit that I liked. My mother liked it, even if it wasn't a dress. I guess she gave in because she was getting tired of pulling Stuart out from under racks, and of searching for the perfect outfit that was going to turn me into an all-American princess.

Then we went to the jewellery department. That's fun. It doesn't matter what size you are when you buy a necklace. I bought a pair of hoop earrings, a necklace, and a ring. I felt really good. And it was nice to see my mother happy. Even Stuart was happy. My mother bought him a pair of sneakers, and the salesman gave him a balloon.

In the afternoon I went over to Nancy's house. She's going out with a tenth-grader at Hoover High School. Nancy's been going out since seventh grade, and she knows lots more about guys than I do.

"Nancy, do you think Joel likes me?"

"He asked you out, didn't he?"

"Yeah. But I don't know why."

"Oh, Marcy, come on. You're not so bad."

"Yeah. But he's so nice."

"So are you. Listen, Marcy, Joel's a great guy, a little too serious sometimes, but nice. I don't think he goes out much, though. So if he asked you out, he must like you."

"Really think so?"

"Yeah. I don't think he's the kind to fall madly in love, but I think you and he can be friends."

"You don't think he can fall in love?"

"Marcy, you're weird. First you're afraid that he doesn't like you and then you wonder whether he can fall in love."

I blushed. Can I help it if I get confused easily?

I told Nancy that I was nervous because everyone was going to be dancing and all I knew was tap and ballet, and that wasn't 'in' at parties. So Nancy and I practised all afternoon.

When I got home, I practised all the dance steps in front of the mirror. My mother walked in and tried to do them too. Sometimes I wish she'd act her age.

Dinner went pretty well. My father seemed happy because we had bought clothes.

"See," he said, hugging my mother. "My family can get nice things because I work so hard."

The phone rang. My father answered it and called out, "Marcy, it's your Romeo." I was so embarrassed that I didn't want to go to the phone. But I had to.

"Hi."

"Hi, Juliet."

"Oh, Joel, I'm sorry. My father thinks he's funny."

"I'll live. So will you. What did you do today?"

"Some shopping . . . and then I saw Nancy."

"I talked to some of the kids today. It's hard to get everything together now that school's cancelled. Listen.

Tomorrow, I'll pick you up at 8. OK?"

"Sure."

"Good. Well, listen, I'll see you later."

"OK. Bye."

As I put down the receiver, I looked up and saw my father.

"Hi, Dad."

"Marcy, we never talk any more. Let's talk now."

"Daddy. I have to practise my dancing."

"This will only take a few minutes."

So we sat down in the living room and he started. I could tell that he was going to try to stay calm. And he did try. He hardly raised his voice. It sounded as if he'd rehearsed it.

He said, "I realize you're growing up and have to start making your own decisions. But I don't approve of you not saying the Pledge. And I don't think you should support Miss Finney."

"*Ms* Finney," I said.

"All right, *Ms* Finney, if you insist."

I stopped chewing my nails long enough to explain to him that while I did support Ms Finney, I still said the Pledge.

He said that he hadn't realized that. Still, he disagreed with my support of Ms Finney.

"You've got to learn to stick with the majority, to play the game. And Marcy, now that you are going out, I want you to remember to be a good girl. You must protect your good name."

I laughed. He sat there, looking uncomfortable and

chewing on his cigar.

"Dad, I promise not to elope before I'm sixteen, bring home another mouth to feed, join a motorcycle gang, or mug little old ladies."

He raised his voice a little. "Stop acting like a smart aleck. Can't you understand? I just want my family to be happy."

I said, "OK, but don't worry about me."

Then he said, "I'm glad we've talked." Then he shook my hand. He shook my hand. A hug would have been nicer, but that was better than nothing, and he hadn't yelled too loud.

My mother walked in. "How would you both like some ice cream?"

"No thanks, Mom. I'm going to go upstairs."

I spent the rest of the evening washing my face with special anti-acne soap, brushing my hair, and looking in the mirror to see if giving up the bowl of ice cream had made me skinny.

Chapter 13

The next day, I had to babysit. My parents were going shopping and I had to take care of Stuart and his bear. Sometimes I feel that my parents should claim Wolf on their income tax.

I took him over to the playground, swung him for a while, and then ran him around on the merry-go-round until we both got dizzy. Wolf, of course, never gets dizzy. According to Stuart, that's because he's so healthy from the orange pits.

We sat down on a bench.

"Stuart, are you happy?"

"What?"

"Are you happy?"

He nodded his head up and down.

"Why?"

"I love you."

I hugged him. "Are you always happy?"

He just looked at me.

"Stuart, do you think you're happy because you're just a little kid and don't know any better?"

No answer yet.

I could see that my question wasn't going to get

answered. What can you expect from a four-year-old, the wisdom of Moses?

"Stuart, do you love Wolf?"

"Yes."

"Mommy?"

"Yes."

"Daddy?"

"Yes."

"What makes you cry?"

"When I fall down."

"What else?"

"When you cry."

"Anything else?"

"When Daddy yells."

"Do you love Daddy?"

"Yes."

Sometimes I wish I were four years old.

"Marcy."

"Yes."

"I'm hungry."

So I took him home and made him a peanut butter and ham sandwich. That's what he wanted, and I figured that since it was so easy to make him happy, I should do it. He'll learn soon enough what sad is. He'd just finished it when we heard the car drive up.

"It's Mommy and Daddy," he yelled.

Rushing outside, he grabbed hold of my mother's leg and said, "I miss you."

Nice. The kid doesn't cry or anything all day and then he acts like it wasn't any good.

"What did you get me?"

Great. He sometimes thinks the whole word is like a quiz show.

My mother laughed and said, "Come inside. I'll show you."

Everyone came in. Stuart. My mother. And my father.

"Hi, honey. How did it go?"

"Fine, Mom. We went to the playground."

She picked out two bags. "One for Stuart and one for you."

We ripped open the bags. Stuart got a pair of mittens, and I got a floppy hat.

"Oh, Mom, I love it."

"The saleslady said all the girls are wearing them, and it'll draw attention to your face."

All of a sudden I felt horrible. Why did she always worry about what everybody else is wearing, and why'd she have to remind me that I have to do stuff to draw attention from the neck up because the rest of me is so glunky?

My father looked at me and said, "Don't you start getting oversensitive, young lady. Your mother wanted to make you happy. Now be happy."

I had to laugh.

We all started to laugh. Stuart had taken the hat and put it on Wolf.

Then we put the packages away, and Mom and I started making dinner. Stuart, Wolf, and Dad headed for the TV.

"Marcy, I bought the hat for you because I liked it and thought you would like it. Do I always talk about how everybody else dresses?"

"Yeah, you do. Ms Finney says that clothes can be an artistic expression of the individual, Mom, I don't want to look like everybody else, even if I could."

"I'm sorry. It's just that it's safer being like everyone else."

"Mom, are you happy?"

"What do you mean?"

"Are you happy?"

"I don't think about that much. I'm happy when you are happy. You are very important to me."

"Do you love Daddy?"

"Yes, Marcy, I do. I don't always agree with him, but he's very good to me."

"He's not very good to me."

"Please. Don't say that. Daddy loves you very much. He just doesn't know how to show it."

"Are you sorry that I'm your kid?"

"No, of course not. What a silly question. Marcy, he's your father and I'm your mother. We both love you."

I finished setting the table, and we all sat down to eat. All of a sudden it dawned on me that it really was the night of Nancy's party. It was my very first date. I was kind of calm and frightened to death at the same time.

Once dinner was over, I rushed upstairs to get ready. I spent fifteen minutes brushing my teeth and another ten searching for pimples. I thought that I found one and then realized that it was a blot from my felt-tip pen. An orange pimple would have been a little strange, even for me. So I washed my face.

Getting dressed was a real trip. I got nervous about the colour of the outfit. Purple was a pretty colour, but what if I looked like a large grape in it? I was sure that everyone at the party was going to say "Joel, who is that grape you're dragging around?" Or "Marcy, Hallowe'en is over." When I put on the earrings, necklace, and ring, I felt better. I mean, grapes don't wear jewellery. People would know it was me.

My mother came into the room. She started gushing about how nice I looked, how I was growing up, and how my clothes did express my personality.

The doorbell rang. My mother wanted me to wait a while to make an entrance. I rushed down the steps, trying to get to the front door before my father got there.

I didn't make it. My father and Joel were standing there looking at each other. I walked over and said, "Hi. I'll get my coat and we can leave."

But it wasn't that easy. My mother came down the steps, making the entrance that I didn't make, and said, "Well, hello Joel. Why don't we all go sit in the living room and talk for a while?"

I thought I would die right there. But I didn't, so we all went into the living room. It was horrible. My father kept chomping on his smelly cigar and asking Joel what his plans for the future were. My mother kept gushing about how nice I looked. Stuart wandered in and asked Joel if he was going to marry me. Joel just sat there, smiling and trying to say nice things.

I couldn't say anything. I just sat there, trying not to have a nervous breakdown and wishing that a tornado would strike or that some machine would come out of the sky to rescue us. I was positive that I was developing an ulcer.

Finally I stood up and said, "We'd better go. Nancy's expecting me to help her out."

So everybody stood up and walked over to the door. I felt as if we were leaving for a trip to Mars. All we needed were reporters around, asking questions like "Ms Lewis, how does it feel to be going out on your first date?" and "Mr Anderson, has it been a life-long ambition of yours to go out with a grape?" My father told us to get home early, and my mother kept picking imaginary lint off my coat.

We finally got out of the door and started down the street. Then I looked at Joel to tell him how sorry I was about the scene at the house. Instead, we both laughed.

Chapter 14

By the time we got to Nancy's house, my stomach had calmed down. Ringing the bell, we heard someone running up to the door. It was Nancy, looking absolutely beautiful in a long skirt and a short top. On me it would have looked like a lot of rubber bands above a tent placed on a volleyball.

Standing behind Nancy was this fantastic-looking guy, the kind you always see in ads for aftershave lotion. I had never been that near to anyone who looked like him. Nancy introduced us. It was her boyfriend, Phil. I'd seen him around but had never talked to him. He smiled and said, "Nancy's been telling me what's happening. Wish we had as much excitement at that stupid high school. Maybe it'll get more interesting next year, when you get there."

Joel said, "Why don't all of you at the high school get involved? It's something that could happen there too."

Phil and Joel got really involved in the discussion, and so did Nancy and I. We finally headed down to the rec room, all of us carrying plates of food. The place was mobbed.

Some of the kids were dancing. I kept trying to remember all the things Nancy had taught me. Then Joel turned to me, saying, "Listen, Marcy. I'm a lousy dancer. So let's go talk."

We went over to a couch and sat down. Everyone was either dancing or standing around eating food. I didn't know how to begin talking. I'd talked to him before, but somehow this was different. And he wasn't saying anything either. So I sat there, looking at the dancers and smiling as if I were having a fantastic time.

All of a sudden, a pretzel flew across the room and hit the wall right behind us. We looked around the room.

It was Andy Moore. He's always getting sent to the principal's office because he shoots straw wrappers at everyone in the cafeteria. He waved at us, and we waved back.

Joel began, "That Andy is really dumb. He'll do anything for attention."

I said, "Ms Finney says that we've got to try to understand people, maybe not like them, but try to understand."

He thought for a minute. "Yeah. I guess so, but sometimes it's hard. I wish Ms Finney was still around."

"So do I. Nancy's mother ran into her at the grocery store. She said Ms Finney's going to fight."

He stared ahead, and then looked down at his hands. "I'm glad. She's one of the few people I can talk to. It's kind of hard. My father's a neat guy and I can talk to him. But my grandmother doesn't understand much, and she lives with us."

"Where's your mother?"

"My parents are divorced. She lives in Denver. She's remarried. I don't like her."

It seemed hard for Joel to talk about it, so I didn't ask any questions.

But he continued, "My dad's a lawyer. Gets involved in a lot of controversial cases. He gave up corporate law to start his own practice. My mother got upset and said that he should stay where the money was and not always be defending weirdos. But they're not all weirdos. Some are poor and need help. He's really a good guy."

"So she moved?"

"Yeah. She likes things to be easy. And she didn't like a lot of my father's friends . . . too radical, she said. So one day she decided to divorce my father. She wanted to take me with her, but I didn't want to go. She cried a lot and said she'd go to court to get me, but I told her that I hated her and refused to go."

"What did she say?"

"She said that she'd let me stay with Dad until she got resettled and then send for me."

"Oh, Joel, when's that going to happen," I said, feeling panic. What if Joel had to move away? Joel and Ms Finney gone. I couldn't stand it.

"It won't. One day we got a letter saying that she was getting married to a school principal. I had to go out to Denver to visit her. That's where she's teaching and where she met him. He's just like Mr Stone. I can't believe there are two of them. Anyway, I went out there and was so bad that the principal didn't want me, and she went along with him. I hate her. I really do. I'm glad she gave

92

up after a while."

"Does it bother you?"

"No . . . yeah, I guess it does. Maybe that's why I don't trust that many people."

"You can trust me."

"I know that you're OK, but I just want you to know that I'm not the type to go out much or get hung up on anybody."

"OK."

"Marcy, let's be friends."

"OK."

I felt strange. There was a lot to think about . . . Joel being bad . . . his mother leaving . . . a step-father like Mr Stone . . . Joel not wanting to get serious but still wanting a friend . . . my own feelings about Joel.

Nancy and Phil picked that moment to come over and talk.

"Hey, having fun? Why aren't you dancing?" Nancy asked.

"I don't," Joel answered.

"But Marcy spent all week learning."

I could have killed her.

Joel turned to me and said, "Sorry about that," and we both laughed.

"That's OK. The lessons might come in handy some day," I said.

Robert Alexander came over.

"Hi. Thought your mother wouldn't let you come," Joel said.

"That dope. She's driving me crazy. I snuck out."

"What'll happen if she finds out?"

"She won't . . . Even if she does, I don't care. She said I have to go to boarding school. I hate her."

Phil held up a six-pack and said, "Anybody want a beer?"

Joel, Robert, and Nancy took cans, so I did. I opened my can and took a sip. I'd tasted beer before and thought it was horrible. It still was.

I asked Nancy where her parents were. I was kind of nervous about the beer.

"They went to a movie. I told them I was old enough not to have chaperones. So they gave in. They're cool."

I just nodded my head, then pretended to sip my beer. A cream soda would have been better. We all sat around talking.

At one end of the room there was a lot of noise. Andy Moore was putting beer cans on their sides and karate-chopping them. I asked Nancy if her parents were going to be mad because of the beer.

"Listen," she said. "They're so glad I don't smoke dope that they think beer's OK."

So I just stood there, watching and pretending to drink. Everybody else was dancing or chug-a-lugging. Joel turned to me and said, "Listen, Marcy. Let's go. This party is going to get out of hand. I'd rather just talk."

Waving to Nancy, we left. Joel and I walked back to my house.

"Joel, do you like beer?"

"Yeah. Why?"

"Just wondered."

"Don't you?"

"No."

"Then why did you drink it?"

"Everyone was."

"Marcy, you don't have to drink just because everyone does. Look, you're different. That's cool."

I thought, Yeah, really cool. I don't look like everyone else. I don't take gym like everyone else. And sometimes I don't feel like everyone else.

Instead I said, "I don't want to be different."

Joel stopped and looked at me. "Ms Finney's different. Do you think she wants to be like everyone else?"

That was hard. Ms Finney was special, very special. Some people can be different and still be happy. I personally think that while blimps are different, they are not special and not happy.

We continued walking. I didn't know what to say. I guess Joel must have realized how down I was.

"Remember the time Robert told Ms Finney how he cried while watching *Gone With the Wind* and she said she hadn't realized how sentimental he was and he said, 'Yeah, someone stole my popcorn'?"

We laughed.

Then I said, "What about the time she invited her friend in and they both played guitars and talked about poetry and music?"

"And all the old movies she brought in."

"And the word games."

"And how she let us videotape our play."

"And the time she had us do the Blind Walk and

blindfolded one person and had one lead the other around."

"That was neat. It was a good beginning to *The Miracle Worker*."

"I miss her."

"Me, too."

By that time we'd reached the front door to my house. I was really happy thinking about all the good times with Ms Finney.

We stood at the door. All of a sudden, I got scared. What if Joel wanted to kiss me good night? I'd never kissed anyone before, except relatives, and they didn't count. I mean, kissing Stuart on the forehead to 'make it all better' isn't exactly thrilling. And practising and pretending with a pillow isn't the same as the real thing, either. What if I turned out to be a lousy kisser? Even worse, what if Joel didn't even want to kiss me? Either way, it was going to be pretty hard to deal with.

I opened my purse and started to look for my keys. My purse always has so much junk in it that it takes forever to find anything. I dropped half the stuff on the ground, and then we had to search for everything. I found my keys and just stood there.

"I guess I should go inside now. Thanks for a nice time." It was dumb, but I couldn't think of anything else to say.

Joel leaned over. He was actually going to kiss me. I closed my eyes like they always do in the movies and on TV. I felt a quick kiss on my forehead. It was the type of kiss I get when my mother tucks me in. So much for my career as a sex fiend.

A light went on in the living room, so I said, "I'd better go in now."

We said good night. When I got inside, my mother was waiting.

"Did you have a nice time, dear?"

"Yeah."

"Did everyone like your new clothes–oh, I'm sorry. I forgot. Do you think Joel will ask you out again?"

I shrugged my shoulders.

"Why don't you know? Did something go wrong?"

"Mom, please don't start. I had a good time."

She looked at me and said, "I only want you to be happy, Marcy. I don't want you to be miserable the way I was when I was little."

I didn't know what to say to her. So I hugged her and went to bed. Then I lay awake, trying to figure everything out and wondering whether I'd wake up with pimples all over my face.

Chapter 15

My phone rang and woke me up the next morning. It was Nancy, in a bad mood. The kids had helped her clean up after the party, but when her parents came home they found a couple of the guys in the back yard, throwing up. In the future, they said, they would stay home when she had parties.

I thought she got off easy. If it had been my family, my mother would be in hysterics and my father would be screaming for blood.

Nancy asked if I wanted to come over and listen to some records. I really wanted to but had to go see my grandmother, so I told her that I'd call when we got back.

When I got downstairs, I saw that the Sunday paper had been delivered. I picked up the funny sheets, and my father took them away. He said that since he paid for the paper, he had the right to read it first. Then he put them beside his chair and read the sports section.

I got mad. I screamed, "I hate you! You're a real creep," and ran up to my room and slammed the door and locked it.

It all happened before I realized that I was going to do it. I was scared. I didn't know what was going to happen next.

I could hear him yelling. He was telling my mother and Stuart how bad and ungrateful I was, how hard he worked and all he wanted was peace and quiet and how I never let him have any. Finally he shut up, and then I heard my mother coming up the steps.

She came to my room and tried to open the door. Then she knocked. I sat on my bed and screamed, "Leave me alone! Can't everyone in this dumb family just leave me alone?"

She knocked again and said, "Marcy, please let me in, or else I'll have to tell your father." So I let her in.

"Marcy, don't be mad at me. It's not my fault."

I threw myself back on the bed and put the pillow over my head.

She started to cry. This time I didn't even care. Then I heard my father's voice.

"See what you've done, young lady. You've made your mother cry. Apologize or you won't be able to go out on any more dates."

My head was still under the pillow. I wanted to stay there and smother, but I sat up and said, "Leave me alone. Just leave me alone. I hate you."

My father raised his hand. He had never hit me before, but this time it looked as if I was going to get clobbered.

My mother grabbed his arm and screamed, "Martin! Please don't. Nobody made me cry. I did it myself. Don't hit her."

He looked at both of us. She was trying to stop crying. I was staring at him. He glared at me and said, "Get that snarl off your face. You look like an animal." Then he turned and left, slamming the door.

My mother was still standing there. I wanted to be alone, so I went back under the pillow. I heard her leave. My head ached. It was hard to breathe. I just wanted to be dead.

Someone tapped me on the back. I peeked out. It was Stuart.

"What do you want?"

He patted me on the head and said, "I love you. Give me a kiss."

So I kissed and held him. Poor little kid. It's scary when something like this happens.

My mother came back in and said, "We'd all better get ready. Your father wants to leave in half an hour."

So we went. The visit to my grandmother was horrible. Everyone was in a rotten mood. My father kept telling her what a monster I was.

Sometimes I feel guilty hating him, but he deserves it.

Chapter 16

Joel called the next day. His grandmother was making him buy a birthday present to send to his mother. He didn't want to get one, but figured that it was easier than fighting.

I rushed downstairs to tell my mother that I'd be going out. She got upset because I was wearing bluejeans and a sweatshirt. She said that even though I was 'plump' I didn't have to look like a slob.

I told her that I wasn't going to change, that until I saw her I had been happy with the way I looked, and that if her advice meant that I was going to end up with a guy like my father, I didn't want to bother.

She got really mad then, and told me that I was becoming an unmanageable brat.

I walked out of the house and sat on the front steps, waiting for Joel. My mother came out and said that she couldn't take any more fighting.

"Mom, I don't want to fight with you either. But you can't tell me what to do all the time. I'm not a baby."

"I know, but a child is always her mother's baby."

That seemed silly. Did that mean that my father was still my grandmother's baby, or that Mr Stone was someone's baby? I doubted that Joel was his mother's baby. I bet Ms Finney's mother didn't think she was a baby.

"Marcy, you're so important to me. I don't have anyone else to talk to."

"Mom, what about Mrs Sheridan? Talk to her."

"Oh, I can't. There are certain things that you keep in the family."

"Well, tell Stuart. I can't stand it. You tell me things, and then when I tell you I hate my father, you get upset. What do you want from me?"

"Try to understand. I'm trying to change and grow. Marcy, it's not easy for me. I know it's not easy for you either. Let's try to help each other."

"Why'd you marry him?"

"If I hadn't, you and Stuart wouldn't be here."

"Yeah, I know . . . but that's not why you married him . . . is it? Uh . . . Mom, did you have to get married?"

"Marcy! Your father and I were married for two years before you were born. You know that. I married your father because I loved him. I still do. We need each other. Don't you understand?"

I shrugged my shoulders. Why couldn't she understand? I mean, I'm just a kid. Why couldn't she talk to Mrs Sheridan or someone? Why me?

Joel was coming down the block. He waved, and I waved back. My mother looked and then said, "I guess that's it. You want to be with Joel, not me. Have a nice time," she said, walking into the house.

Joel walked up to the steps.

"Hi."

"Hi. Ready?"

"Yeah."

"Did you and your mother just have a fight?"

"Well, not really a fight. A discussion."

"Was it OK?"

"Oh, Joel, who knows? Let's go."

So we took off, and ended up going to a shopping plaza, one of those places that has every kind of store. All the kids hang out there, so we ran into a lot of people. But we had to go look for a dumb present for Joel's mother.

He was in a weird mood, laughing a lot but also a little angry. At first I thought I'd done something wrong, but Joel said, "No, I'm just mad 'cause I have to get something for my mother."

It was funny. He kept looking in all of the stores, trying to decide what to get. He looked at an anthill farm, a plaque that said 'God Bless Our Happy Home', a rock record, a Monopoly game, a green shade of nail polish, and a button that said 'Kiss me. I'm neurotic'. Finally he picked out a really ugly heart-shaped pin with red, green, and orange rhine-stones. It was atrocious.

We found it in one of those horrible stores that sell lots of junk: striped purple and yellow toilet seats, rock posters, candles, stationery, doorknobs, mink-covered can openers, and other stuff. The pin was on a clearance table with a lot of other disasters that no one else had bought.

Joel immediately picked it up and said, "This is it. It's

fantastic, really perfect. I love it."

I didn't know how to tell him that it was awful. "Listen, Joel. Are you sure your mother will like it?"

Looking at me, he smiled and said, "She'll hate it. Don't you see? She'll just hate it. It's perfect. She'll never figure out if I know how ugly it is or if I think it's beautiful. When she comes to see me or if I have to go there, she'll have to wear it. It'll look awful. And when I show it to my grandmother before I send it, she'll never know either. Those two don't realize a guy can have good taste."

"Is that your mother's mother?"

"No. My father's. But my mother and she are a lot alike. They think everyone has to be a certain way and that's it. I'm glad my father's not like that. He's cool. He listens to me when I talk, and he doesn't make me think the way he does. And I like the things he says and does. He's OK."

"Wish mine was."

"Just don't let them get to you. In three and a half more years you'll be in college . . . or at least out on your own. Just try to survive until then."

"Joel, do you have trouble surviving?"

"Yeah, sometimes. But I'll make it. You too."

"It's easier for you."

"Why?"

"Well, your father's cool and you look OK."

"What's that have to do with it?"

"It's easier if you look OK."

"Marcy, looks don't matter."

Sure, that's what he always says. Maybe he's right, but

it's sure hard to believe that when the rest of the world is skinny.

The salesperson came over to ask if we needed any help. He probably thought that since we had been standing there for a while talking we were casing the place for a giant robbery, or at least planning to shoplift an ugly toilet seat.

I smiled at him and said, "My friend here has just decided to purchase one of the lovely items. We were just wondering if it is a one-of-a-kind piece. It's for his mother, and he wants it to be something that's unusual, that everyone else won't be wearing."

The salesperson looked down at the pin in Joel's hand, tried not to smile, and said, "I'm quite positive that you're not going to see that on too many people. That's an unusual pin."

Joel nodded. "Yeah. It's a special pin for a special person. I try to pick presents that are like the people they're for. This pin is just right for my mother."

"She must be an unusual person."

Joel nodded his head again, and we headed for the cash register. Neither of us said anything else until we got out of the store. Once we did, Joel turned to me and said, "Very unusual," and we both started laughing so hard that we couldn't stop.

Finally I wiped the tears out of my eyes and said, "Joel, let's go back to my house and get some lunch. My mother will have the police out for us if we don't get back, and if we stay here the cops'll get us for disorderly conduct."

Wiping his eyes, Joel said, "You're right. There probably is a law against laughing. And if there isn't, they'll make one. Don't worry, if we get arrested for being happy, my father will defend us. I can see it all now." And he jumped up on an empty chair. "Ladies and gentlemen of the jury. You were young once. Surely the crime of these poor misguided children, laughing in a public place and having fun, is something that you once did. They will learn as they grow up. Young Mr Anderson has already begun reforming. He now dreams of becoming a school principal, and is currently taking mean pills in preparation thereof. Ms Lewis, on the other hand, will not easily reform. She has pledged to follow the example of that awful Ms Finney and become a fantastic English teacher, who teaches kids no prepositional phrases. But, dear ladies and gentlemen of the jury, Ms Lewis will atone in time. Just yesterday, in her jail cell, she asked for a grammar book to read while eating her bread and water."

I jumped on the chair next to Joel's. "We throw the fate of these two misguided innocents on you. Remember, justice must be tempered with mercy."

At that point, one of the shopping centre rent-a-cops came over and said, "Listen, you two. Very funny. Now get down and move on."

So Joel and I hopped down and headed off.

When we got to my house, my mother was sitting on the steps playing with Stuart. When he saw us coming, he ran over yelling, "Marcy, Joel. What did you buy me?" My mother looked over at us. She looked very lonely all of a sudden.

I walked over, hugged her, and said, "What's for

lunch? We're starving."

She smiled. "Is Joel staying?"

I nodded.

Stuart kept saying, "What did you get me?"

I looked down at him. "Nothing."

He started to cry.

Another family scene.

Joel kneeled down, put his hand on Stuart's shoulder, and said, "Stuart, come on, be good. You don't get a present every time you want one. It's not like that."

Stuart held Wolf up. "Kiss Wolf."

Joel laughed. "Don't be silly, Stuart. I hardly know Wolf."

Mother, Joel, and I started to laugh, too. Stuart didn't understand, but he began to smile. We all went inside and had lunch. Stuart and Joel had peanut butter and banana sandwiches and Mother and I had tuna fish, Weight Watchers style.

After lunch, Joel, Stuart, and I went out to the park and played with a Frisbee. Afterwards both of us sat on a bench and watched Stuart swing.

"He's a good kid. Sometimes I wish I had brothers and sisters."

"I think it would be nice to be an only child."

"Don't you like Stuart?"

"Yeah. But I always get blamed when he does something wrong. And lots of times they're nicer to him than me."

"I think you should be nice to him. He's a good kid, and he's fun. The thing with Wolf is funny. I bet he gets lonely sometimes. That's why Wolf is his friend. Doesn't he know any kids his own age?"

I thought about all that for a few minutes and said, "He knows some kids at nursery school and some of the neighbourhood kids, but he's alone a lot. They make fun of him because of Wolf. That dumb teddy bear."

"I like him. He likes you a lot. You should give him a chance."

"It's hard in my family to be just friends with any of them. They always ask me to do things."

Stuart came running. He wanted to play Frisbee again.

Joel, Stuart, and I played until dinnertime. Then Joel left to go home, and Stuart and I headed back to our house.

Chapter 17

I woke up the next morning with a stomachache and a horrible headache. At first I thought that I was doomed to some horrible sickness that teenagers always catch on television shows.

Then I remembered. Today was the date of Ms Finney's hearing. By night I would know if she was going to be back or not.

I got out of bed and dressed. My stomach and head still ached, but I figured I'd survive, and anyway, if I told my mother, she might not let me go to the hearing.

So I went downstairs. My father had already left for work. My mother was sitting down at the table, reading the paper.

"Marcy, look, there's a lot about Ms Finney in here."

She handed me the paper, and I sat down to read it. There was interesting stuff in it, all about how Ms Finney had gone to a progressive college and how she was currently going for a master's degree. The paper said that during college she had been active in drama productions, had been on the literary and humour magazines, the yearbook and newspaper staffs, and had helped organize group-dynamics activities. She had also been involved in college demonstrations. And she'd been elected to a national honour society.

"She's a bright, interesting woman. I hope that she comes back as your teacher."

"Me too."

"Turn to the 'Letters to the Editor' page. It's all about Ms Finney."

I turned to the page. There were lots of letters, about fifty-fifty for and against. The people supporting her tended to use 'Ms' in their letters, and the ones against her would call her 'Miss Finney'. One of them was from Mrs Alexander, Robert's mother. She wrote that Miss Finney was warping young minds and was unpatriotic and should be fired. There was also a letter from Joel and his father, standing behind Ms Finney, saying that she was a great innovative teacher.

"Mom, did you see Joel and his father's letter?"

"Yes, Marcy. Keep reading."

I skimmed the rest of the page; Ms Finney had shown us how to read quickly for important facts. Glancing at the bottom of the page, I saw a letter signed by my mother. It said that as the president of the PTA and as the mother of two children, she was profoundly interested in the state of education and that she felt that Ms Finney had helped the students to learn English and to learn to like themselves.

"Oh, Mom. Why didn't you tell me? It's such a nice letter. Oh, what's Dad going to say when he sees this?"

"He saw it this morning. I showed it to him."

"Did he yell?"

"No. He said that he didn't approve but that I had to do what I thought was right. Then he said that my place was in the home, not being political, and that he hoped I would come to my senses."

"Then what happened?"

"I told him that my place was wherever I wanted to be, and he left and slammed the door."

"Oh, Mom."

"You know, Marcy, I feel very good about this. I feel much stronger. And guess what else?"

"What?"

"I've decided that I'm going to get out and look for a job or maybe go back to school. What do you think?"

I smiled. "I'm happy."

"Me too."

The phone rang. I ran to answer it. Joel was on the other end. He'd seen my mother's letter and called to ask if he could come over and visit. I said, "Sure," then hung up and went back to talk.

"Joel's coming over."

"Good, I'm glad. He's nice, Marcy. I'm pleased that the two of you are going out."

"Listen, we're just friends. Don't send out wedding invitations yet."

My mother laughed.

The phone rang again. This time it was Nancy. She wanted to know if I could come over. I told her that Joel was on his way and we might be over later.

Standing near the phone, my mother said, "I'm so glad that you've made some new friends."

I nodded. "And they don't tell me all the time that I have to look like everybody else."

"They don't care about you the way I do. I'm your mother. I don't mean to hurt you. It would be so nice to see you thin."

"Please don't start. Come on."

We looked at each other carefully. Then I started to walk away.

"Marcy, I love you. Let me help you be all that you can. Please. I want you to help me, too."

I ran back to her, and we hugged each other.

When the doorbell rang, I ran to the door, opened it, and smiled. It was so good to see Joel.

He came in and talked to my mother and me, and then the two of us went over to Nancy's house and spent the day watching quiz shows and talking.

Joel walked me back to the house and told me that he'd see me at the hearing. I was getting nervous again just thinking about it.

Dinner at my house was another scene. My father refused to say anything through most of the meal. As he drank his coffee, he just stared at my mother and me. Finally, he started to talk.

"You know, it'll be great when that Miss Finney gets fired. It'll teach both of you not to get involved in bleeding-heart causes. Watch out for yourself, that's my motto. Don't always be on the side of radicals. It'll get you nowhere."

I bit my lower lip to keep from saying anything. He wasn't going to bother me. I didn't want to let him.

He continued, "Lily, you've managed to get involved. I don't understand you any more. You've always been such a good wife."

My mother frowned and started to clear the table. "Martin, I'm still a good wife, probably better now that I say what I think. Please, let's not fight. I've made up my mind."

Grumbling, he picked up his coffee.

Beginning to help clear the table, I said, "What time are we leaving for the hearing?"

He said, "I've decided. We're not going."

Turning around, my mother said, "Don't worry, Marcy, I still have a set of keys to the car. We're leaving in half an hour."

My stomach started to hurt, and I started to shake.

"So now you're upset. Well, it serves you right, young lady. You've managed to disrupt the whole household."

Dropping the dishes on the floor, I ran upstairs. I couldn't stop shaking. My mother followed.

"Come on, honey, please stop. Please. It's going to be all right."

She held me and rocked me back and forth. "Marcy, please. Honey. Do you want to talk about it? What can I do? Please. I promise I'll get you help. We'll both go to someone for counselling. Even if your father doesn't like it, I'll go to work to pay for it. Please. I'm sorry."

The phone rang. My mother picked it up. It was Nancy. She handed me the phone, but I shook my head. She took it back.

"Nancy, Marcy can't talk to you right now. Could I

113

please speak to your mother?"

She smiled at me and waited for Mrs Sheridan to get on the phone.

"Hello, Sara? Listen, we're having a little problem here. Are you going to the hearing? Good. Could you possibly pick Marcy and me up? . . . No, there's nothing wrong with the car . . . Yes . . . Martin's being impossible . . . OK. We'll see you in about ten minutes." She hung up.

I had calmed down a little. Seeing how calm my mother was helped me. I couldn't believe it. Smiling at me, she said, "Go wash your face. Let's get going."

Once I got my face washed, we headed downstairs.

My father was standing in the living room, holding on to a small piece of the car engine. He held it out to us. "If you're planning to use the car, you'll have to figure out where this goes."

My mother glared at him. "Martin, you know what you can do with that." Turning to me, she said, "Come on, Marcy, let's wait outside."

We waited on the steps. In a few minutes Nancy and her parents drove up. We got into the car. No one said much. It was obvious that things were tense.

Finally, Mr Sheridan said, "I want you girls to remember that Ms Finney may not win. If that happens, she'll probably have to take it to court. This is just a school hearing, you know. Be prepared for anything that happens."

Mrs Sheridan said, "I've heard that she's gotten the backing of the American Civil Liberties Union."

My mother nodded. "I just hope she wins. It's very important."

No one said anything else.

As we got close to the school, we saw that the place was jammed. People were picketing. Others were just standing around. There were even television cameras.

Mr Sheridan let us out and went to look for a parking space. I'd never seen the high school so crowded. An interviewer came up to my mother. "I understand you are president of the PTA. We'd like you to make a statement."

My mother smiled at the man and said, "I feel that Ms Finney is a fine teacher and should be where she belongs, in front of a classroom." Someone booed. Another person cheered. I could see that my mother was a little shaky. The interviewer left.

"Good work, Ms Lewis. You did that well." We turned around and saw Joel, who was smiling. Phil was standing with him.

My mother laughed and said, "Thank you, Joel. I'm happy to have a chance to do my part."

Phil said, "We'd better head in if we're going to find a place to sit."

"Why don't you go in and save seats for the rest of us?" my mother suggested. "We're still waiting for Mr Sheridan."

So Nancy, Phil, Joel, and I went inside.

Finding seats, we looked around. Joel asked me how everything was going.

"Not so good. The scene at my house tonight was

horrible. You wouldn't believe it."

Joel looked at me. "I thought it might have been bad when I didn't see him here tonight."

The Sheridans and my mother joined us, so we stopped talking about it.

All of a sudden everyone in the auditorium started to turn around. Ms Finney was arriving. With her were three people, two men and another woman. One was the man who had played guitar with her in class. The other two carried briefcases and looked official.

I was so nervous, I felt that I couldn't breathe. But it was great to see Ms Finney. She looked very tired, though.

They sat down in the front row in a special section. Then the Board of Education members came out and sat down at long tables in the front of the room. The school board president, Mr Winston, pounded his gavel and said, "There will be no disruptions, nor will there be any cameras used. If these rules are not followed, this hearing will be closed."

Then they began. First they had to talk about old business. The budget was discussed. Bus routes were argued about. Teachers' salary negotiations were mentioned. Finally, after what seemed like hours, Mr Winston said that it was time for the new business.

Everyone was absolutely quiet. Mr Winston said that there were several items on his agenda to cover. I couldn't believe it. They still weren't going to get to Ms Finney. My stomach was beginning to kill me.

They named teachers who were resigning, approved

teachers who were replacing them; decided on when we would make up the days missed; and then Mr Winston said, "We are now ready to begin discussing Miss Barbara Finney. I would like to remind everyone that this room must remain orderly."

Mr Stone got up to speak first. He said that Barbara Finney had been a problem since she got to the school; that she dressed strangely; that her teaching was not traditional, and that he never would have hired her if Mr Edwards had not left suddenly. Miss Finney's students, he continued, were rude to him and were getting wild. Moreover, as a veteran he found her not saying the Pledge of Allegiance an unpatriotic and misguided stand. He finished up by saying that he did not want her in his school any more.

Several people cheered. Mr Winston pounded his gavel and warned everyone to remain quiet. Then he called Ms Finney up. He asked her to reply to Mr Stone's charges.

She stared straight ahead and began. "I don't think it's a crime to dress differently. I never dress immodestly at school, nor do I tell the students how to dress.

"As for teaching differently, that's very true. I'm not at all ashamed of that. I'm hopefully teaching human beings to communicate with one another and to love and respect the English language. I try to do it in ways that will interest and excite students. Everyone complains that children can't and don't read. Well, my students are reading, and their writing has improved. Just check their records. The results are there. Isn't that what's important?"

She paused to catch her breath. Her voice got softer. "As for the Pledge of Allegiance, I choose not to say it. I salute the flag each morning as a symbol of what this country is supposed to be, but I can't say the Pledge. I am sorry to have to say that I don't believe this country offers liberty and justice for all. I will continue to work toward that end, but until I see it happening, I will not say the Pledge. I am a good American. I care about the country and the people in it."

Then she sat down.

We began to applaud. Mr Winston pounded his gavel. "This is your last warning. One more outburst and I'll clear this auditorium."

He continued. "The Board has at its disposal independent evaluation reports on Miss Finney. They are satisfactory. Therefore, our decision will be based on Miss Finney's refusal to say the Pledge. At this time, the Board will adjourn, and will return with its decision as soon as possible."

The Board members got up and went into some meeting room.

Everybody else got up to stretch or go out for a smoke. Joel grabbed my hand and said, "Come on, Marcy. Let's try to see Ms Finney."

We pushed through the crowd. Joel was good at getting by all those people. Finally we made it through the lobby, and outside Ms Finney and her friends were standing near a kerb, smoking cigarettes and talking to reporters. I was scared to go up to them, but Joel moved right in.

"Hi, Ms Finney."

118

She smiled. "Oh, hi, Joel, Marcy, how are you?"

I just nodded my head and started to cry.

She leaned over and put her hands on my shoulders.

"Marcy, it's not easy, I know. But everything will work out all right."

"Hey, Ms Finney. Did you hear? We got suspended."

She nodded her head. "So I heard. Your plans were very supportive. I appreciate that. But you know it's necessary that you take responsibility for your actions. Are you sorry now that you're suspended?"

I said, "It's worth it."

She smiled. "I'm glad. Hey, have you read any good books lately?"

Joel and I told her about the books that we were reading.

She looked at us and said, "I miss all of you very much."

"We miss you too," I said.

"I want all of you to understand that no matter what happens, I care about all of you and want you to do your best to learn."

"Aw, Ms Finney. Don't worry. You'll be back." That was Joel.

Tears started to roll down her face. "Please. I want you to remember all the things I've taught you."

I touched her arm. "I'll remember. Don't worry."

She tried to smile. "Marcy. You've grown so much. I'm so proud of you."

A lot of other kids were standing around, waiting to talk to her, so we said goodbye and walked back to our seats.

Joel and I talked about how we hoped that the Board would say that Ms Finney should stay. We knew Joel's father was for her, but didn't know about the others.

My mother was sitting near us. She was talking to Mrs Sheridan. Even though Mom looked tired, she seemed calmer than she'd been in a long time.

The Board members started to come back. So did everyone else, including Ms Finney. Her face was streaked with tears.

Once everyone was seated, Mr Winston started pounding the gavel again. He looked like a carpenter.

The room hushed. I had all my fingers crossed. I looked over at Joel. His eyes were closed; his fists clenched. I was having trouble breathing again, and my heart felt as if it was going to explode.

Mr Winston stood up and held on to a piece of paper. He looked down at it and began reading. "There is no question in the Board's mind that Miss Barbara Finney has a sincere desire to educate youth. It is also apparent that she has the support of many of the children in her class. We appreciate this, but also wish to state that the majority of the Board does not approve of her stand." He paused and took a sip of water.

I started to cry. It was all over.

He continued. "Although we do not as a group approve, there is a legal precedent to support her stand. We therefore reinstate Barbara Finney to her position as a teacher in our school system."

The room exploded. Everybody started screaming and yelling at once. Joel and I were jumping up and down. I looked over at my mother. She was yelling and clapping her hands. I couldn't believe how happy I was. Everything was fantastic.

All of a sudden, people in the front started sitting down, and you could hear "Shh, shh." I looked to the front and saw Ms Finney standing next to Mr Winston, who was wildly pounding his gavel.

The room quieted down again. Mr Winston said, "Miss Finney wishes to make an announcement."

She stood there, looking very pale.

I thought, You tell them, Ms Finney. Tell those fools off.

She looked very shaky, but then she sort of smiled and said, "I want to thank everyone who has supported me. I've tried always to be all that I tell my students to be. Therefore, I felt it necessary to follow through and take a stand concerning the Pledge. It was important to me that I win, but it is even more important that I can be an effective teacher. This community has been split on this issue so badly that I doubt that I can ever walk back into my classes and be effective. Therefore, I feel that I must resign, effective immediately." Finishing, she turned and ran out of the room. Her friends followed.

I felt as if someone had hit me in the stomach. Stunned, I could feel the tears begin again.

I heard Joel. "That fink. That rotten fink. I hate her."

I turned to him. He was crying. "I don't believe it. Marcy, how can she do it? I trusted her."

My mother called over, "Marcy. Joel. Please come here." Mr Anderson was with her.

"We want to take you both out for sodas and a talk."

"I don't want to go."

"Me neither."

My mother spoke in a voice that I'd never heard her use before. "Want to or not, you must listen to us. There's no use in falling apart. That never solves anything. I've learned that."

So the four of us said goodbye to the Sheridans and Phil and went to a diner.

Joel and I sat across from my mother and Mr Anderson. Neither of us said anything.

My mother began. "I know how you both feel. It's very hard for me to accept. But maybe she was right. It would have been very hard for her to stay."

"True," Mr Anderson said. "It might have been impossible. You know everyone would be watching for her to make the slightest mistake."

"Marcy, look at how much this whole situation has helped both of us grow," my mother said.

I thought about that.

"I hate her," Joel said. "How could she do it."

Joel's father put his hand on his son's arm. "I know this is very hard for you. You trusted her and you feel that she's left you . . . just like your mother did. That's it, isn't it?"

Joel nodded his head.

I looked at him and then at his father. How I wished my father could understand so much.

I thought about what Mr Anderson had said and how Joel must feel. I reached out and touched him too. "Joel, remember when Ms Finney said that we should continue to learn no matter what. That's what we have to do. She cares about us. She just had to do what was best for her."

I thought about what Ms Finney had said about remembering what she taught us. "Hey, Joel. Remember that part in *To Kill a Mockingbird* where Atticus says to Jem that you can't understand someone until you've walked around in his or her shoes for a while. That's what you've got to do."

Joel smiled. Ms Finney had had us write about that, and Joel had written about Mr Stone. He had said that if he walked around in Mr Stone's shoes he'd have a lot of blisters, because everything about Mr Stone rubbed him the wrong way.

"Yeah. Maybe you're right. I'm too tired to think any more about this. I want to go home."

So we all got up and left. Once I got home, I went right up to bed. There was no way I could deal with anything else.

Chapter 18

It's been a month since the hearing, and a lot of things have happened.

My mother is registering for night courses at a nearby college. And she doesn't give me ice cream whenever I get upset.

Joel and I are very close. It's not a romance, but it's a good friendship. You have to start some place.

I no longer think I'm a blimp. Now I think I'm a helium balloon.

I still hate my father. He hardly ever says anything to me any more. He and my mother talk a lot, but he just looks at me and shakes his head.

I'm flunking gym for the year. Our new English teacher is giving us a test on dangling participles.

I still see Mr Stone in the hall. I'd throw up on his head if I were tall enough.

Stuart still has a thing about Wolf. Now he's refusing to go to nursery school unless Wolf also gets registered as a student. I can see it all now. When Stuart graduates from high school, he'll probably have Wolf right beside him. They'll award Wolf a diploma and he'll be elected 'Bear Most Likely to Succeed'.

I'm going to a psychologist. She's very nice, and she's helping me. It's different from Smedley, but I think I'm learning a lot.

Joel's father said that he heard that Ms Finney was going to graduate school to get a doctorate in something called bibliotherapy. That's counselling using books and writing. That sounds good. Maybe someday I'll do something like that.

Yesterday I looked in the mirror and saw a pimple. Its name is Agnes.

There's a Bat in
Bunk Five

To the Weisses –
M. Jerry, Helen, Sharon, Frann,
Eileen and Michael
With love and laughter

Publisher's Note
IT IS NOW ILLEGAL, under the Wildlife and Countryside Act
1981, intentionally to kill, injure or handle without a
licence a bat of any species in Great Britain, or to disturb
bats when roosting, or block the entrance to their roosts,
without consulting the Nature Conservancy Council.

The events in this book take place in the United States.
In Great Britain, none of the 15 resident species of bat is
harmful to people or animals: in fact, as consumers of vast
numbers of insects, bats are a useful friend to man.
Nevertheless, because of various threats to their normal
habitats bat numbers have severely declined, and this has
led to their becoming a protected species.

Chapter 1

If I iron or sew one more name tag on my stuff, I'm going to scream. There are name tags on my jeans, shorts, shirts, nightgowns, pyjamas, sheets, pillowcases, sleeping bag, socks, sweaters, sweat shirts, underwear, and jackets. My mother's having me put adhesive-tape labels on my comb, brush, and flashlight. There's indelible ink on my fingers from putting my name on my sneakers. She'll probably make me carve my name in the soap bars and on my glasses frames.

"Marcy, can't I help you with anything?" My mother sticks her head into my room.

"No thanks. I can do it myself," I say for the eighty-millionth time.

She walks in. "Here. I addressed some envelopes for you with our address on it and put stamps on them. That'll make it easier for you to keep in touch."

"Look, I promise, I'll write. You didn't have to do that." Sometimes they act as if I'm three years old, instead of fourteen and eleven twelfths.

She puts the stationery in my suitcase. "It's the first time you've ever been away for such a long time. I'm going to miss you."

I continue to iron. I know I'm going to miss her too,

but I really want to get away, be on my own. I really want to get out of the house since I'm always kind of tense in it.

She keeps on talking. "I wish I'd had the chance to go away to camp when I was your age. You're so lucky, being part of a creative arts camp, with Ms. Finney as the director."

I nod. I've thought about little else since I got the letter from Ms. Finney asking if I'd like to fill a last-minute vacancy and be a counsellor-in-training, a CIT, at the camp. I've missed her so much. She's the best teacher I ever had, one of the few who really cared about kids. She quit after a big fight with the school administration. We wrote for a while, but I hadn't heard from her for months. Then one day I came home and there was this letter asking if I'd like to work on the camp newspaper and assist in the creative writing programme. I was in shock, so excited I thought I'd die of joy. Overwhelmed.

My father, however, was underwhelmed. It took a long time to convince him I should go. He's always afraid I'm going to be too radical or something. He hated Ms. Finney when she was my teacher. Finally my mother and I convinced him it would look good on my college applications, and it would be better to go than to sit around the house all summer, bored out of my mind.

My mother sits on my bed. "My little girl, going away for the entire summer. I don't know what I'm going to do."

"Maybe you and Dad won't argue so much with me gone. Isn't he always saying you two'd never fight if it weren't for me?"

She sighs. "Marcy, come on. Let up a little. He's had a

rough time lately. He's been trying since we all went for counselling. You're the one who won't give him a chance. Why don't you try to forget the past and live in the present?"

"He wasn't trying last night when he screamed at me for coming in late. That's not the past, is it?"

She sighs again. If they ever hold an Olympics sighing marathon, my mother'd win, lungs down. "He wouldn't yell if he didn't love you. It's just his way. He was very worried. Last night, after we went to bed, he told me he'll miss you."

"Sure." I refuse to listen to the same thing one more time. "If he loved me, he could find better ways to show it. Why did he say the things he did about how I'd be good comic relief for the campers and how I think 'taking a hike' means running out in the middle of an argument."

"Marcy, you're being a bit unfair. He thinks of camps as places for sports, being outdoors. You know those activities aren't high on your list of favourite things." She starts to repack my suitcase, neatening it up. "He just likes to tease. That's the way he tries to show affection. You have no sense of perspective about him. There's nothing he can do that's right in your eyes. You expect perfection from people."

"Well, so does he. How come when I bring home a test with a grade of ninety-seven, he asks what happened to the other three points instead of saying I did well?"

"You should try to understand him before it's too late and you feel sorry."

The same old story. Now I'm supposed to feel guilty. Ever since my father had a heart attack when school began this year, I get scared he's going to die. Sometimes I wish he were dead, I hate him so much. But there's also a part of me that really does love him. My mother should only know how many nights I stay up late worrying and trying to concentrate on keeping him alive.

My mother gets up. "I'm going downstairs now. If you need anything, call."

After she leaves, I continue to iron.

I hate ironing almost as much as I hate taking gym, and that's a lot. Last year I had to take two gym classes to fulfill requirements and make up the one I'd flunked. Ironing and gym should be outlawed. Once my mother began working, we all had to chip in and help out more in the house. The words "permanent press" took on a whole new meaning in my life after that.

I wish I were already at camp. Maybe I can get enough experience there so I can become an editor on the school paper, instead of just a reporter. Then I can get into a good college, study literature, live my own life, and become a writer. I don't care if my father says most writers don't make enough money to support themselves. I want to be a writer anyway.

And I have a goal for camp, a major goal. This summer, I've decided, I'm going to try to be a grown-up, so I'll be able to take care of myself. There's not much that happens that's really earth shattering when you're my age. You've just got to go on living, trying to get through every day. If my life were a novel, it would be one without much plot, just character development. So what I really want to do is develop my character, to try to grow up so that when I'm an adult, I'll be ready for anything.

There's a knock on my door. "Marcy, it's me. Stuart. I want to come in."

He opens the door after I say it's all right. My little brother's eight years old, and he still looks like a baby. At least he's got over his abnormal fixation with Wolf, a teddy bear he used to fill with orange pips. Now he's got this thing about becoming a football player. He wears his football helmet all the time, even to bed. I hope that someone invents a shampoo that can penetrate plastic before his head begins to fungus.

Once he's in my room, he yells, "Lewis has the ball, sports fans, and he's heading into his own territory . . ." Stuart dashes around the room. "No one can touch him. His feet are golden."

He jumps onto my bed. "They try to close in." He jumps off and crawls under the ironing board.

"Hi, Stuart."

He throws his arms forward and touches my feet with the football. "A touchdown, sports fans. Lewis does it again."

I humour him and yell out a cheer that the kids at school do during pep rallies, being careful that the hot iron doesn't fall on his helmet or on my bare foot.

Stuart gets up, dusts himself off, bows, and says, "Thank you. Thank you."

I grin at him. "So what's new?"

"Why can't I go to camp with you?" he asks for the zillionth time. "Just iron a name tag on me and pretend I'm a stuffed animal."

"You know why. I've got to work there, lead my own life."

He crouches into position and yells, "Hike."

"Not that kind of hiking, Stuart. It's a camp for the arts, not for sports."

"But your name's not Art and you are a good sport."

I tap on his helmet. "You're very silly."

"I know, but you like me this way." He stands up. "Marcy, it's not fair. You get to do everything first, just 'cause you're the oldest."

"You're getting on my nerves," I say.

"I'm supposed to get on your nerves. That's what little brothers are for." He grins. "Well, I tried. If I start bugging everyone now, by next summer they'll send me to a camp too." He throws his football into the air, yells, "It's another great interception for Lewis and he's off." He races out of the door.

Quiet. Finally.

Sure I get to do things first, but I have to do all of the fighting to get what I want. Then once I'm all done, he gets things at an earlier age. Being the oldest isn't easy.

I finish packing, fold the ironing board, and take it out to the cupboard.

My father's coming down the hallway. "Marcy, let me help you with that."

"I can do it myself," I say, thinking about how he shouldn't put any strain on his heart.

He frowns. "You never give me a chance to do anything for you."

There's no way to win.

I say nothing.

He says, "Take good care of yourself at camp. Your mother and I won't be around to watch out for you."

134

I nod, holding the ironing board between us, feeling like a lion tamer who's losing control.

"Just be careful," he continues. "Don't try any funny-looking cigarettes or do anything that would make your mother and me unhappy."

I wish he could tell me he loves me, instead of making me feel as if I'm going to screw everything up. I don't even smoke anything. Why can't he trust me?

He leans around the ironing board, kisses me on the forehead, and walks quickly away.

I stare at him as he goes down the steps.

He calls up to me. "Don't forget to set your alarm for six a.m. I want to get an early start."

I don't have to be there until eleven or twelve. The drive from New Jersey to upstate New York should take three hours, at the most. He always makes everyone leave early, to miss the traffic. We always end up hanging around. It's so embarrassing.

I shove the ironing board into the cupboard. It tilts down, hitting me on the head. As I push it back and shut the door, I want to cry—not because I got hurt by the board but because I have a father who just doesn't understand me.

Back in my room, in my own bed for the last time until the end of summer, I feel very strange. This time tomorrow I'll be on my own. Trying to be grown up. Not knowing anyone but Ms. Finney. Being a CIT without ever even having been a camper. Not having a boyfriend back home to tell the other counsellors about. Missing the summer parties back here and the friends I've made. All of a sudden I'm nervous, not sure I'm doing the right thing. I

135

can't believe it. I'm getting homesick before I even leave, homesick for a place I've always said I couldn't wait to leave.

In order to fall asleep, I attempt counting sheep. But it's no use. Not only am I wide awake, but all of the sheep have name tags sewn into their wool and they all know how to act more adult than I do.

Chapter 2

"Rabbit number forty-eight," Stuart yells.

Whenever he sees a van, he yells "Rabbit." It keeps him busy on long trips. Otherwise he spends the entire time asking to stop at bathrooms.

I stare out of the car window.

My father's shut all of the windows, turned on the air conditioner, and lit one of his smelly cigars.

I cough a little.

My mother says, "Martin. Please. That cigar smells like burning chicken feathers—and you know you shouldn't smoke with your heart."

"Stop babying me," my father grumbles. "Anyway, I don't smoke with my heart."

"Rabbit number forty-nine," Stuart yells.

I see the sign. THIS WAY TO SERENDIPITY.

My parents are yelling at each other as we pull into the driveway.

I want to die. What if someone hears them?

The time. It's nine forty, and there doesn't seem to be anyone around. Too early. For once I'm glad, because no one will hear my parents fight.

They continue to yell at each other.

"I hate those cheap cigars."

137

"These aren't cheap."

"Well, they smell like fertilizer."

"Okay, stop it," I yell. "Please, we're almost there. Don't ruin this for me."

My father stops the car in front of a huge stone and wood building, three storeys tall. It looks like a castle owned by a middle-income king. There's grass and dirt and trees all around with huge empty fields, soon to be filled with people. It's definitely not suburbia.

There's no one in sight, and the place looks as if it goes on for ever and ever. There's not a streetlight. I bet there's not a shopping mall for miles.

I don't even see any cabins.

Everyone in the car's still pouting.

Finally my mother says softly, "Martin, I just want you to take better care of yourself. I don't want you to become a statistic."

My father nods. "Smoking is one of the few pleasures in my life, though."

I feel sad for him, all of a sudden. Then I notice it's quiet. Peace. Another truce.

We get out of the car and look around. To the right of the car park there's a tennis court, a basketball court, and an area for volleyball. Oh no. Just like gym.

"Marcy," Stuart yells. "Goats. Real goats."

I look. There really are five goats, standing by a large bell.

"Those are probably the kids assigned to your bunk." My father grins.

Stuart jumps up and down. "Kids—kids are goats—I get it. Very funny."

"Your father likes *kid*ding around," my mother joins in.

Sometimes my family gets very corny, me included. "Sounds like you're both butting in."

Stuart lunges at me, headfirst. "Butt, butt."

I stick my hand forward, to protect myself, and his football helmet bends back my finger.

I yell.

Both of my parents rush over.

My finger's starting to swell.

"Marcy. I'm sorry. I didn't mean to hurt you," Stuart says.

"It's okay," I say.

"Marcy, is that you?"

It's Ms. Finney, coming out of the building with some guy.

I run up to her.

We hug.

She's grinning. "You look wonderful. You've lost so much weight. But then I always thought you looked good."

My family joins us.

Ms. Finney says, "Welcome, everyone. I'd like to introduce you all to my husband, Carl."

My father reaches out to shake hands, saying, "Mr. Finney. I'm Martin Lewis."

"Pleased to meet you. My last name's Klein; Barbara and I've kept our own last names."

"It figures," my father says, sort of under his breath, scowling and backing off.

"I'm sorry I'm so early," I say.

"I'm not," Ms. Finney says. "It'll give us some time to talk before everyone else arrives." She grins.

Mr. Klein says, "Let me get your bags. We can load them into the van now and take them up to your bunk later."

"A van. Where? It'll be Rabbit number fifty," Stuart yells.

Stuart, my father, and Mr. Klein go over to the car to get my stuff.

My mother says, "How are you doing, Ms. Finney? I've often thought of you."

She answers, "I'm doing well, very happy. My master's degree is completed. Carl and I've been married for six months now, and we love working at this camp. We were here last year and have the chance to do lots of new things. It's like a dream come true, to be at a creative place."

"I'm so glad you're at a place where you're not hassled," I say, thinking of the trouble she had at school.

She grins at me and then turns to my mother, "How are you doing?"

My mother says, "It was a little rough for a while, with my husband's heart attack, my job, and taking courses at the local college. But I'm managing. We're all managing."

I think about how well she's done, even stopped taking tranquillisers.

Mr. Klein, my father, and Stuart return, followed by the goats. "The bags are in place," Mr. Klein says. "Barbara, we'd better finish up our work before everyone arrives."

"Carl and I'll be working in the main office, Marcy," Ms. Finney says. "Join us after you say good-bye to your

140

family."

Everyone says good-bye to them and off they go, arm in arm.

I hope that someday I can be just like Ms. Finney, perfect and happy with someone.

We all look at each other.

My mother starts to cry.

Stuart yells, "I don't want to leave. Let me stay here. You can mail my clothes."

"I'll write to you every week," I say.

"You don't have to write to me. I'm staying." Stuart holds on to my legs.

My mother says, "Write every day."

I nod. I'd promise to write every hour just to get all of this over with.

They unloosen Stuart from my kneecaps.

We all stand there.

Finally my mother says, "I guess we should go," and sniffles.

My father says, "Let us know if you need more money."

I feel so mixed up—glad that they're finally going and afraid to be left alone.

Stuart runs toward the basketball court, screaming, "You're going to have to capture me to get me to leave."

With my father racing after him, my mother starts to shout, "Martin. Be careful. Your heart . . ."

Stuart stops short and returns with his head hanging down.

I feel sorry for him.

My father comes up, puffing a little.

"Are you all right?" I'm scared.

He waves away my question. "You worry too much."

Stuart yells, "Touchdown," and runs up as if he's going to tackle me but hugs me instead.

I pat him on his football helmet.

It's time to say good-bye.

My mother hugs me.

My father pats me on my head and says, "I think we'll stop off in Woodstock and do a little sightseeing."

They get into the car and leave, screaming good-byes.

I feel deserted. Now that I'm alone, I'm not so sure I can cope. What if it turns out to be an utter disaster?

I look around the camp. It's beautiful. Any place this great looking can't turn into a disaster. But I bet people said that about the *Titanic* too.

I head for the main building and go inside. It must be the dining hall with all the benches and tables set up. There's even a fireplace.

The goats follow me.

Do goats eat people?

One of them starts to bleat.

Now I've done it.

Ms. Finney bounds down a set of steps on the other side of the room.

A goat rushes over to her.

"Get out. You know you're not supposed to be here."

"I'm sorry," I say. "I thought you said to come in."

"The goats, not you, Marcy." She laughs. "Come on. Let's get these beasts out of the dining room before the Board of Health decides to make a surprise visit."

The goats get turned around and pushed out of the

building. I've never touched a goat before. Ms. Finney obviously has. She's better at it than I am.

Once the goats are gone, I say, "Ms. Finney, I've really missed you. Since you left, there's no teacher I've had who's anything like you. It's so good seeing you, even if I'm expected to touch mangy goats."

"The goats give milk for the children allergic to regular milk. Listen, since I'm not your teacher anymore, please call me Barbara. Everyone else does."

"Okay . . . Barbara."

She rushes on. "I'm so excited about this summer. We'll put on plays, dances, concerts, publish writing, show artwork. It's going to be wonderful."

I smile, thinking of how lucky I am to be here.

She twirls around. "I just can't wait. But now, we've got to finish getting ready. We're stapling papers for the first meeting. Would you mind helping out?"

"Not at all." I feel a little formal, no longer at home, not really a part of this place, even though she's being so friendly and bubbly.

I follow her up the steps and think of what a secret coward I am, how afraid I am of everything.

How the goats will eat me.

How scary it is to meet new people.

It's not easy being so frightened of everything. And when I think of how much I've improved in the last year, I wonder when I'll ever get finished with making changes and be really grown up.

Before I have a chance to think of any more terrors, we're at the top of the steps and Ms. Finney—Barbara— heads into an office, where Carl's running papers off on the duplicator.

"Marcy. Carl." She claps her hands. "Now you'll have a chance to get to know each other."

Another fear. Men. I'm always afraid they're going to yell at me like my father does. Or be as unreasonable as Mr. Stone, my high school principal.

Carl smiles. "Barbara's told me so much about you."

I say, "Nice meeting you," and stare at the floor.

Barbara says, "The others'll be arriving shortly."

"How many?" I ask.

"Thirty-three staff members and one hundred and twenty campers." I knew the campers wouldn't be arriving for another week. "That gives us a chance to do staff training and to set up the camp." Barbara picks up a stack of papers and hands them to me.

I staple them and think about the new staff members, hoping we'll all get along, that everyone doesn't pair up but me. I wish again for a boyfriend back home, so I wouldn't feel so alone. There was Joel for a while, but his father decided they should move to New Mexico. It wasn't a great romance, but it was a good friendship. I miss him.

My mood must show, because Barbara, who has been putting papers in piles, comes over to me. "Are you all right?"

I try to smile. "Does everyone at this place know each other? The staff, I mean."

She smiles back. "Some are returning, some are new. Carl teaches ecology at a local college and gets staff members from there. Some are from other places. Don't worry. I've got a feeling everything's going to be perfect.

We've planned so long, so carefully, so hard, made some changes. Nothing will go really wrong."

Carl says, "Barbara's the eternal optimist, always positive things will be wonderful. Marcy, by the end of the training week everyone will know everyone else. Everything will go well, I hope." He crosses his fingers.

Feeling calmer, I smile a real smile.

We all go back to our jobs.

I staple.

Carl sorts.

Barbara piles.

I look at them. They look good together, happy. Barbara's hair's grown down to her waist. He's got a beard.

I staple my finger.

The points are in my index finger. How gross.

It hurts.

Carl looks up to see why our efficient system is no longer working.

I look at my finger. It's the same one Stuart bumped into.

Barbara comes over.

I still haven't said a word, waiting for the gangrene to set in. It doesn't really hurt much, but I figure that's because it's paralysed or something terrible.

"Oh, Marcy," Barbara says. "Does it hurt much? Let me get some tweezers from the infirmary." She rushes out.

I look at Carl. "You must think I'm awfully dumb."

He shakes his head. "I once slammed my hand in a car door. Things happen."

Barbara returns, pulls out the staple, wipes off the spots of blood with rubbing alcohol, and puts a Band-Aid on it.

"Marcy, I think you're going to live." She grins. "I bet I could have even pulled it out with my fingers."

"No amputation? I'm so glad. I was afraid my writing career was over."

Carl says, "The first casualty of the camp season. I only hope the rest are so minor."

I pull up the Band-Aid and say, "Minor? It looks like a baby vampire has got me."

Barbara laughs. "Or one of the bats that live in the top of this building."

Bats? I never even thought of bats. Now I've got a new fear to add to my long list.

Cars are honking below, suddenly.

"Hip, hip, hurray," Barbara yells, jumping up and down. "Camp's begun."

I follow Carl and Barbara downstairs and wonder whether anyone's ever been sent home for an acute case of stapled finger.

Chapter 3

Everyone's arrived. I've met my head counsellor and seen my bunk. I wonder if it's too late to change my mind and go home. This is a little scary and strange.

I'm stuck with the upper bunk bed. Corrine, as senior counsellor, gets first choice.

Some night I'll probably roll over, fall out, break several bones, and have severe internal injuries and bleeding. Or a rung of the rickety ladder will crack when I'm climbing up, and I'll fall on my head and get a concussion.

Corrine immediately puts a picture of herself and a guy on her cubby.

I put a writing notebook on mine.

As we unpack, I sneak looks at Corrine. She's got curly blond hair, bright green eyes, and an incredibly thin body, fashion-model skinny. I bet she can eat anything she wants without gaining an ounce.

She says, "Barbara tells me that you're a wonderful writer. I'm so glad. This year I want us to help the kids gain confidence in writing. I also want us to help them put out great newsletters and magazines, as well as their individual work."

"Me too," I say.

She continues. "I'm a journalism major at college.

Someday I want to be an investigative reporter."

Funny. I thought sure she'd want to work on a fashion magazine. I've got to remember not to stereotype, not to look at someone and make instant judgments. I hate it when someone does that to me, yet it's something I do, especially when someone's skinny.

A bell rings below.

"We can finish unpacking later," Corrine says, grabbing a notebook. "Staff training's about to begin."

I grab my notebook. "Do we get detention if we're late for the first meeting? Do we have to stay after camp and wash the volleyball court?"

Corrine laughs. "You'll have to follow the goats around, pick up after them, and be in charge of their once-a-year bath."

"Let's get a move on," I say.

We rush out the door and down the steps. Lots of other people are also coming down the hill from their cabins.

Halfway there, someone yells, "Hey, Corrine." Corrine stops. I stop with her. She waves to this absolutely gorgeous blond male who is by the pool, pulling something out with the skimmer.

She yells, "Hello, Jimmy. What did you catch?"

He pulls the skimmer out of the water and comes over to us. "It's a skunk. Want to give it mouth-to-mouth resuscitation?"

Corrine makes a face.

Jimmy turns to me. "Want to give me mouth-to-mouth resuscitation?"

I stare at his mouth.

Corrine says, "This is Marcy Lewis, my CIT. This is

148

Jimmy, camp Romeo."

"Hi," I say.

I want to say: If there are going to be auditions for the person to play camp Juliet, put my name on the list. But I don't have enough nerve. With Jimmy's looks I bet everyone in the world wants to go out with him.

The bell rings again, this time a lot, like someone means business.

"We'd better hurry," Corrine says.

"I'll see you later." Jimmy looks at me.

I try not to stare back at him although I'd love to.

As Corrine and I head down the hill, she says, "I wasn't kidding about Jimmy. He's a bit of a flirt."

I think that I kind of like being flirted with, especially by someone as great looking as Jimmy. He almost makes me want to get over my fear of men.

Everyone's gathered around the bell, the goats included.

It's obvious a lot of people know each other.

There's a lot of hugging and kissing.

I stand off to the side and notice I'm not the only person who doesn't know people.

Someone rushes up, hugs me, and says, "It's so good to see you."

I stare at her, not sure who she is.

"Don't panic. My name's Heidi Gittenstein. I just got bored standing around and not being a part of this."

"I'm Marcy Lewis."

She says, adjusting her baseball cap, "Let's go around and do this to everyone else who's still standing around."

It's a crazy idea. I love it.

I run up, hug someone who's still standing alone, explain what's happening, and then we both go off to hug someone else.

Soon everyone's running around, hugging everyone else.

I have a feeling I'm going to like this place.

Barbara yells, "Everyone inside." We go into the dining room and sit down at tables.

Carl quiets everyone down and announces, "Since this is the first meal of the summer, Barbara and I've decided to give you a special treat—pizza and soda for lunch. Purchased out of our own meagre salaries."

There's wild applause and foot-stomping.

Pizza. I love pizza. Pizza with extra cheese, pizza with mushrooms, with sausage. Pizza with pizza. I've got to be careful, though, not to eat too much of it or within minutes I could probably gain back every lost pound.

I take one piece.

Soda gets passed around. I take a Diet Coke.

I could mug for another pizza slice, but don't.

Once everyone's done and only empty white boxes sit on the tables as evidence, Carl and Barbara stand up and hand out the stapled papers.

"You can read this later," Carl says. "We want to start right in on our training session."

I feel an arm on my shoulder. Looking to the side, I see it's Corrine. She's smiling at me. I smile back.

Corrine seems so nice, I think as I listen to Carl. I wonder why she acted kind of weird about Jimmy.

"I want each of you to pick a person whom you don't know and spend five minutes talking to that person."

150

It's like I'm back in Ms. Finney's, Barbara's, class. She used to do stuff like this.

Jimmy comes over to me and says, "Want to be partners?"

I debate saying, Yes, forever and ever, but instead say, "Sure."

I feel like Queen of the Prom.

We go off into a corner, to the left of the fireplace.

"I hope we get to know each other better," Jimmy says, giving me this sort of sexy smile.

I can't believe it. Here I am, Marcy Lewis, former girl blimp, sitting with this absolutely gorgeous guy who acts as if he really does want to get to know me better.

All my life I've dreamed of something like this.

Nancy, my best friend back home, told me I've really changed a lot in the past year, that I look good, but it's kind of hard to believe after you've spent your whole life resigned to being Ms. Grotesque Lump. But nobody here knows that, except for Barbara.

Jimmy continues. "Don't listen to anything bad that Corrine might say. I think she's got the wrong opinion of me. I'm really a wonderful human being."

"Do you carry around letters of recommendation?" I ask.

He grins. "In my cabin. You'll have to come up and see them sometime."

"I suppose you also do etchings," I say.

"Actually I play the piano."

"And the field too," is the comment of someone who has come over to join us. "Hi, my name is Mel. We're supposed to enlarge our groups."

Mel joins us. So does Heidi, the girl who came over and hugged me. We all talk for a while.

"Two more groups unite," Barbara yells.

Now there are eight of us, all finding out about each other.

"Everyone back together now."

We get back together, only this time we all seem to crowd in closer.

I kind of wish I were sitting next to Jimmy, but he's sitting next to Heidi, looking into her eyes.

Carl points to Heidi. "Who knows something about this person?"

Corrine yells, "She's from Washington, D.C., a senator's daughter."

"She's an artist," I add.

"She wants to be president someday."

"So how come she's at a creative arts camp?" someone wants to know.

Heidi answers, "I want something secure to fall back on if I don't make enough money as a painter. Presidents pull in good salaries."

More people yell out stuff.

I look over at Jimmy.

He winks at me.

Carl points to someone else and everyone makes comments.

He points to me and people say things, all nice. About my writing, my personality, and my sense of humour. What a relief.

No one knows what I was like before. I can be what I want to be, not what people expect or think they know. I always worry that people expect me to be something I'm not when I'm not even sure of what I am.

Finally all staff members are discussed. It's really great. Even though I don't know all of the names, I've got an idea about each person and it's going to be easier to get to know everyone.

"Break time," Barbara yells. "Bug juice."

Everybody stamps their feet and applauds again. I do too even though I'm not sure why.

Gallons of something that looks like Kool-Aid are brought out.

I take a glass. It's sort of like water with a little Kool-Aid sprinkled in.

In her letter to me Barbara mentioned that the camp was not a rich one, but she never mentioned that we'd have to live on coloured water.

I hope my mother can send up a care package of Coke.

I notice that Jimmy's talking to another one of the new female counsellors.

After the break we role play.

The experienced counsellors pretend to be campers with an assortment of problems.

The CITs have to show how to solve the problems.

I get a counsellor named Lori who pretends to be a mosquito-bitten camper and is screaming how she wants to go home.

I pretend to put Calamine lotion on the bites.

"What else?" Barbara asks.

I pantomime putting the cap back on the bottle.

"Scratch them for the kid?" someone yells.

Corrine says, "Hug the kid."

I do.

Barbara nods. "That's it. Just remember that the kids are going to want some attention and will do lots to get it. They'll need a lot of affection. I know that we all do, but remember, the kids come first. I want each of them going back home feeling special."

Role playing continues for a while.

Then Carl and Barbara explain the basic rules. How many days off. Procedures. Responsibilities. How no one is supposed to use drugs or get drunk. What to do in case of emergencies.

Barbara looks at her watch. "Time for general clean-up. Get the cabins ready for the kids. Then we'll have a cookout supper and campfire."

Everyone troops out.

Jimmy and Carl are talking to each other about how to handle the skunk smell in the pool.

As Corrine and I walk back up to the cabin, I ask Corrine what comes next.

"This camp has got to be cleaned up after the winter. We did it before we left last year, but there's always sweeping and stuff."

Housework, actually bunkwork.

We go back to the cabin. I sweep the floor, and Corrine gets the spiders' webs down.

I look down at a corner of the room. There are all of these tiny brown pellets.

"Corrine, what's this?" I call her over.

"Mouse turds," she says.

"Bullshit," I say, figuring it's some kind of curse they say at her college.

She comes over and punches me on the arm. "Very funny, Marcy."

I look at her, then realise she's not kidding around.

They really are mouse turds.

I think I'm going to throw up.

But at least it's mice and not bulls.

I wonder if bats make pellets too.

I feel like Dorothy in *The Wizard of Oz*, when she turns to her dog and realises that she's far from home.

Well, Toto, I guess we're not in New Jersey anymore.

Chapter 4

Camp's wonderful. I only hope it stays that way once the campers get here later today.

I lie in bed, listening for the patter of little mice feet. So far so good. No more pellets. No sounds.

It's quiet outside. Birds singing.

Corrine snores.

The clock says six a.m. I think it runs in my family's genes to be early risers. I decide to go out before work starts.

Work. We've been cleaning the entire camp, getting supplies ready, holding more workshops, playing lots of games. For a camp stressing creative arts, there's certainly a lot of physical activity. Carl says it "enriches the whole person."

My body hurts from all the enrichment. My blisters have blisters.

I quietly climb down the ladder, dress, grab my soap, towel, and blow drier. Corrine's warned me to be silent until she's had her first cup of coffee.

The door creaks when I open it. I catch it before it slams.

No one else seems to be up.

I've got the bathroom to myself. Usually all the females

in camp seem to be using it at the same time. It's as bad as taking a shower after gym.

Finishing up, I go back to the cabin, sneak inside, and put my stuff away.

Corrine's still snoring.

I didn't think skinny people snored.

I grab my notebook and pen and go outside again. It's beginning to get really light.

Two-thirds of the way down the hill, between the cabin area and the main building, there's a good tree to sit under to write the daily letter to my family. The pool's towards the left, the fields are on the right. The main building's down below. I owe four letters. Things are too busy. I can just imagine what it's like at home. My mother will rush every day, anxiously checking the mail. When no letter arrives from me, tears'll come to her eyes. At first she'll imagine the worst. She'll think I've been captured by a band of demon bats or fallen off a mountain. Then she'll get upset and angry. I've really got to make this a good letter to make up for not sending the others.

I write a lot, big, so that it takes up lots of room. It's hard. I'm not sure what I should say. I want to have some privacy, also there's not much to really report. Does she want to hear about my blisters, about my crush on Jimmy, about Corrine's snoring? What do you say about camp to someone who's not there to get the whole experience?

I do my best, filling up four pages and putting them by my side.

There's a goat standing right next to me. It starts to eat my letter. Then it takes off down the hill with all of the pages in its mouth.

Someone behind me laughs. "I've heard of people having to eat their own words, but that's ridiculous."

I turn around and see Ted Chaback, one of the CITs. He's carrying his guitar.

"I bet that really gets your goat." He grins.

Oh no, more goat jokes.

Ted sits down next to me. "Relax. We'll rewrite it. What was it? I'll help."

"It's just a letter to my family. I promised to write every day and haven't. That animal just ate a week's worth of news."

Ted says, "Why don't you start out with: 'Dear Family, I've just met a wonderful human being and while we're not planning to elope, I think I'm going to like going out with him. His name's Ted. You'll love him."

I look at Ted. He's cute, brownish-blond hair, blue-green eyes. He's been in some of my training groups and we've kidded around but never really talked. I know that he's a senior in high school and from Connecticut.

"I think we'd better stick to telling them about the cookouts and stuff," I say. "I'd hate to announce anything prematurely."

"Give it time." He grins again.

We write the letter together, each contributing every other line. It doesn't make much sense, but it's fun to do. Being with Ted is fun. Usually I'm kind of shy around boys, but he's easy to get along with.

People are beginning to go down the hill.

The breakfast bell rings.

Ted and I race down. He beats me, by a lot.

158

I collapse on the grass. "I'm really not in shape for this."

"I like the shape you're in." Ted smiles.

I blush. I'm not used to this.

Jimmy comes up to us. "Ready for the invasion of the campers?"

I nod, still out of breath.

The campers are really arriving today, after lunch.

Jimmy moves on to talk to Ryan Alys, one of the guys on the ground crew.

I stare at Jimmy.

"One of the smitten, I see," Ted says.

I look at Ted.

"It happened last year too. At least half the females fall in love with him."

I blush again.

"You'll develop better taste soon and see that the only person Jimmy loves is himself." Ted raises his eyebrows.

The bell rings again for breakfast, and we go inside.

Corrine and Mark, Ted's head counsellor, are sitting together and we join them.

"Ready? The kids'll be here soon," Corrine reminds me.

"Can't we just keep camp the way it is?" I beg.

She laughs and shakes her head. "The moment of truth, the final camper lists, will be here shortly."

Barbara comes over to our table, says, "Morning. Bunk assignments. Enjoy your day," and hands us the cabin rosters.

Mark says, "No problems evident on my list. Can't wait till the kids get here."

He looks over Corrine's shoulder at our list. "You've got Ginger Simon? What's she doing in with the eleven- and twelve-year-olds? Why are you stuck with her?"

"Sandy said she wouldn't take her again, even if it meant losing her job. You know how Barbara can convince you to try anything. So I said we'd take her, but should be given combat pay."

I sit there listening. How come no one asked me about taking a problem camper? I guess because I don't know the kid. "What's the problem?"

Corrine shrugs. "I'm not sure. I know her parents are divorced and that she's got a real chip on her shoulder. But she's a fine artist. Last summer she did some really nasty things, was cruel to a lot of people, and was a general disturbance. Barbara wants to give her another chance though, thinks maybe we can reach Ginger and help her."

"Barbara's always involved in causes," Mark says. "I don't think this is going to be one of her better choices."

Ted says, "Let me know if I can help."

I have this funny feeling in the pit of my stomach. How can they doubt that Barbara's right? Am I wrong to think everything she does is perfect? Maybe I can show them all and be the one person who is able to reach and help Ginger.

I scrape off the burnt parts from my French toast and cover it with syrup. Calories that will go straight to my hips.

Corrine finishes and says, "I'm going out for a quiet walk. It's probably going to be my last chance of the day. Marcy, I'll meet you back at the bunk to finish getting ready." She waves good-bye.

"Smile, Marcy. Ginger is only one twelfth of the cabin. It'll be all right." Ted pats me on the arm. "And I'll be around to give you a hand."

Mark laughs. "After you finish working with ꜱur seven- and eight-year-olds. That's not going to leave you with much spare time. Although something tells me that you're turning into a charter member of the Marcy Lewis fan club."

It's Ted's turn to turn pink.

Mark looks at me. "You must have some special power, Marcy. This young man was much admired by many last summer but spent the entire time with the kids and working on his music. I've never seen him act like this."

"Man cannot live by guitar alone," Ted says and grins at me.

My turn to blush again. "I guess that makes me your pick," I say. "Guitar pick, get it?"

Everyone groans appreciatively. I guess I'm handling this okay, but I wish I'd brought my brother's teddy bear, Wolf, with me. I could use it now. I bet Wolf would love to be filled with bug juice.

Chapter 5

Countdown. They'll be here any second.

Barbara and Katherine, the nurse, have set up a registration table on the lawn in front of the main building.

Corrine's up at the cabin. I'm waiting to greet our kids and then bring them up to her.

The first car arrives and stops. The parents emerge and try to pull a kid out of the backseat.

He's screaming, "Don't leave me here. I promise to be good. I won't even ask for my allowance. I promise. I'll practice my clarinet at home every day."

I think of Stuart, who'd give anything to be here.

Barbara walks up and starts talking to the kid.

Ted comes up beside me and says, "I bet he's going to be in my bunk. He looks the right age—about eight."

Sure enough Barbara calls out, "Ted, come here and meet Max."

Ted walks over, puts his arm on Max's shoulder, and they go up the hill.

More cars drive up, more parents, more kids.

It's an epidemic.

Counsellors are running up and down the hill, bringing kids and gear to the cabin.

"Marcy, here's someone for you."

Barbara says, "Marcy Lewis, Linda Allen."

I grin and the kid grins back.

Her parents stand there saying things like, "Please, remind her to write to us," and "Make sure she eats her green vegetables."

I nod.

We take her trunks over to the area designated for our bunk so the truck can bring the baggage up later.

As Linda and I walk up the hill, she says, "What's red and green and goes one hundred miles an hour?"

I shake my head.

"A frog in a blender."

Gross. But funny, in a sort of sick way.

"I'm going to be a stand-up comic," Linda offers. "I've come here to try out my material and to learn how to perform in front of groups that aren't my family."

"I hope that you never do that joke in front of a group of ASPCA members."

"What's red, green, and *brown*, and goes one hundred miles an hour?"

I sigh. "I don't know and I'm not sure I want to know."

Linda grins. "The same frog a week later."

It's a good thing my stomach's had a chance to settle from breakfast.

We get to the cabin. I take Linda inside to meet Corrine and then start down the hill again.

Linda yells, "What's green and makes loans?"

"Chase Manhattan Pickle," I yell back.

As I continue down the hill, I wonder whether all of her jokes are going to centre around the colour green and

163

whether her whole family is fixated on that colour. Money, vegetables, frogs, pickles. I bet she's got some jokes about the Incredible Hulk.

By the time I get back to the registration table, there are four campers waiting, saying good-bye to their parents and talking to Barbara.

Three of them are "old-timers": Ellen Singleton, Betsy Zolt, Alicia Sanchez. They tell me I don't have to lead them up the hill, that they know the way and can lead Robin Wiggins, a new camper.

I watch the three go up the hill, arm in arm, with Robin sort of hanging back.

Maybe I should have gone up with them anyway. It's not always easy to know what's the right thing to do.

Ted walks up. "Surviving?"

"Yup. Except for having to listen to some frog jokes. How you doing?"

"Fine. One of the kids is a bed wetter, though, and he brought up a rubber sheet. Some of the guys were making fun of him."

"What did you do?"

"Took the kids who were doing the teasing aside and talked to them. And put the kid with the problem in a bottom bunk. I was told a joke too. What's got a red nose, white face, and lives in a test tube?"

"What?"

"Bozo the Clone." He grins.

I groan.

"Marcy," Barbara calls out.

I run over.

"Marcy Lewis. Risa Hess. Helene Gerver."

164

I welcome them.

Risa's mother says, "Please make sure that she wears her teeth positioner at night."

Her father says, "And that she doesn't lose it. I'm sick and tired of replacing them."

From Helene's mother I hear: "Make sure that Helene gets to bed on time. And don't forget she needs a little night-light."

"Oh, Mom," Helene looks down at the ground. "Stop embarrassing me."

I take out my notebook and write down the instructions.

"Can't we come up and inspect the cabins?" Mr. Gerver asks.

"Sure," I say.

"I'll be all right. Come on. Let me go up without you. Nobody else's parents are going up," Helene begs them.

"We just want to make sure everything's all right."

Helene looks up in the air. "They'll probably want to look at my honeymoon suite when I get married."

Mr. Gerver laughs. "Okay, we won't come up. Kids. They always think we baby them too much." He looks at the other parents.

Helene nods.

I take Helene and Risa up the hill.

We pass Jimmy, who's putting chemicals into the pool.

Risa runs up to him, grabs him by the legs, and yells, "This year I want to be one of your girl friends."

He grins and pats her on the head. "In a few years."

Helene and I just stand there watching.

Risa starts jumping up and down. "I'm so glad you

came back. I was afraid you wouldn't be here, that there'd be no one good to have a crush on. And I'm old enough now. Look, I even got my braces taken off."

She smiles at him.

He examines her teeth.

"She's still got to wear a tooth positioner at night," Helene says.

Risa glares at her.

I laugh. I can't help it.

Jimmy says, "I'll put your name on the list, Risa."

"Use indelible ink," she says.

"What's your name? I'll add yours too." He turns to Helene.

"Zelda Pinwheel."

I've got a feeling I'm going to really like Helene.

As we continue up the hill, Risa yells, "Don't forget, Jimmy. I'm going to be a famous actress someday. You'll be able to say that you 'knew me when.' "

We get up to the bunk.

The old-timers hug each other, and I make sure the new kids are introduced.

Corrine gets them to start making a sign for the cabin.

I leave, head down the hill, and wave back at Jimmy, who is standing in the sun, working on improving his tan.

I wonder if my name's on his list and what the number is.

There are four kids waiting when I get back to the table.

Barbara says, "Marcy, except for Kitty, all of these young women are here for the first time. Be sure to point out all of the important landmarks to them."

I get the names first. Janie Weinstein. Kitty Amoss.

Bobbie Caputo. Stacey Reed, who is carefully carrying an instrument case.

We start up the hill.

"Don't forget the important landmarks," Janie giggles. "I'm from New York City and camp there means something totally different."

I look at her and laugh. "Okay, city slicker, I'll show you the wilds of New York State."

I stop at a tree. "This is a tree. You can tell by the bark, by the leaves on it, and because it grows out of the ground. It's not a counsellor because it doesn't have a whistle around its neck."

"We've got trees in Central Park. Only there's usually a mugger behind them."

We check, discover no mugger, and continue with the tour. "This is a goat."

"I knew it wasn't a counsellor, no whistle." Janie nods.

"It looks like my study-hall teacher from last year," Bobbie offers.

"Who is that absolutely adorable boy?" asks Janie, pointing.

I look up expecting to see Jimmy, but it's Ted. He's holding a crying kid in his arms.

We go up to them. Ted is talking to the kid.

"Alvin, this is my friend, Marcy. Marcy, please tell Alvin that goats don't eat people."

I start to laugh until I take a look at Alvin's face. He's absolutely terrified. Tears are streaming down his pale face.

"They don't bite. I promise. Sometimes they nip, but that's just play. It won't hurt." I figure I've got to tell him the truth. "Just don't leave paper around them."

Stacey tugs on Alvin's sneaker. "Watch me."

She slowly moves to the goat and pets him.

I'm so glad the goat stands there calmly.

She turns around. "See, it's all right. Honest. Let me carry you and show that he won't hurt. Marcy, please hold my flute. Carefully."

I nod and take it.

Alvin clings to Ted for a minute and then goes into Stacey's arms.

He looks so tiny . . . and very scared.

Stacey stands by the goat, not moving.

Alvin's holding on for dear life.

Finally she stoops down and starts to pet the goat.

Alvin keeps his head buried in her shoulder. Finally he turns around and looks at the goat.

Janie whispers to me, "Will they be all right?"

I nod as Ted puts his hand on my shoulder.

Alvin nervously looks and then puts his head back on Stacey's shoulder.

Finally he looks again and slowly puts his hand out to touch the goat.

The goat nuzzles him with his nose.

I relax. I only wish my letter had been so lucky.

Alvin gets out of Stacey's arms and moves closer to the goat.

After a few minutes Stacey takes Alvin by the hand and brings him back to Ted.

Ted says, "You handled that well. Do you know many goats?"

"No, but I've got a younger brother," Stacey says.

Alvin hugs her leg. "Be my friend."

She nods and pats him on the head.

"You were great," I say, handing her back the flute. "Now I think we should head up to the cabin and get settled."

Ted says, "I'll see you later," takes his hand off my shoulder, and grins at me.

As we go up the hill, Bobbie says, "Is that your boyfriend? You sure are lucky."

"Ted and I are just friends."

Why do eleven- and twelve-year-olds ask so many questions?

We arrive just as the truck comes up with all of the suitcases, sleeping bags, and trunks.

A girl from the maintenance staff, Annie, is driving. "All of your kids are here except one and we're not sure she's coming. So we decided to bring this up so the rest of you can unpack."

"Who's the last one?" Betsy asks.

"Ginger Simon," Annie says.

"Oh, no," yells Ellen and pretends to throw up.

Every other returnee has the same reaction.

"How come we're stuck with her? She's supposed to be with the younger kids, isn't she?" Betsy wants to know.

Corrine says, "We've got her. That's enough of that reaction now. People can change. Maybe she has. I want you to give her a chance . . . and I also think you can set a good example since you're older."

"Now you sound like my mother," Risa says.

Corrine continues. "Well, I mean it. We want everyone here to have a good time. We also hope everyone learns how to get along with people."

"Ginger's not people. She's an animal," Risa says.

"Try," Corrine says.

"Okay, okay," the old-timers grumble.

"Let's get unpacked," I suggest.

Everyone brings the stuff inside and puts it away.

The kids look at what each other brought and talk about swapping.

Corrine and I go into our little room.

"I knew it wouldn't be easy when they found out about Ginger." Corrine makes a face.

"Maybe she's changed," I say.

"You're just like Barbara, always looking on the bright side." Corrine smiles. "Well, maybe she has. Maybe we'll get lucky and she'll decide not to come back."

We go out to the kids.

Janie's taking an upper bunk with no one underneath it. "This will be my penthouse apartment. In case the dreaded Ginger doesn't return, I can always turn it into a maisonette, two floors, with the lower bunk for parties."

Corrine returns to our room and comes out again, carrying a bag of lollipops. "Who wants one?"

Almost everyone yells, "Me."

Bobbie says, "Thanks, but I don't eat things with sugar. It's bad for you."

"Me neither." Ellen shakes her head. "And I don't eat meat either."

"Since when?" Risa asks.

"I became a vegetarian last year."

"Ugh," says Linda.

Everyone but Bobbie and Ellen grab a lollipop, yelling,

"I want cherry swirl." "No orange." "No raspberry."

"I can't make up my mind."

"One each," I yell. "Save your appetites for dinner."

Kitty says, "Unless things have changed drastically, I'd rather not. Has the food got any better?"

Alicia giggles. "Oh, Kitty. You always complained about the food and then ate four servings."

Four servings. How can she be so thin?

The door swings open.

"Well, here I am. Bet you were all hoping I wouldn't show up." In walks a frowning kid. Her fringe is practically covering her eyes, and her hair is plaited in pigtails.

"Welcome, Ginger. Have a lollipop." Corrine holds one out to her.

"A bribe? No thanks. I brought my own stuff. If you don't take anyone else's things, you don't have to share your own. Where's my bunk?"

I point to the one beneath Janie.

"I don't want a lower bunk. I was here last year. I should get to choose before one of the new kids."

"Whoever gets here first, gets to pick. You know that," Corrine says.

Everyone's standing around, not saying a word. Standing real straight. Kind of nervous and angry.

Janie's sitting on the top of her bunk.

Taking the lollipop wrapper off, she says, "Oh well, there goes the maisonette."

Ginger turns to Stacey. "Guess you must be one of the scholarship kids. They always let some of you in."

I'm shocked.

Stacey takes a step backwards.

Ginger continues, "I should get your bunk. My father pays full price. I'm not a charity case."

"You're disgusting," Betsy says.

"Thank you," Ginger says. "I just love compliments."

Stacey quietly steps forward.

It's all happening so fast. I don't know what to do.

"Just because I'm black doesn't mean my parents can't afford to pay." Stacey looks like she's going to cry.

I think about how wonderful she was with Alvin. I wonder how Ginger can say something like that.

Kitty tosses her blond hair and says, "As a matter of fact I'm here on a scholarship, and I'm not giving up my bunk for a little creep like you. You were trouble last year and I can see you haven't changed."

Ellen goes up to Stacey and puts her arm around her shoulder. "Don't judge the rest of the campers by this rat."

Alicia says, "Last year she told me I should go back to Puerto Rico and leave America to the Americans. When I tried to explain that we were part of the U.S., she called me a rotten name. Ignore her. She's not worth it. They should never have let her come back."

Corrine says, "Ginger, I want to talk to you privately." Grabbing her by the arm, she takes her outside before anyone else can react.

The room's absolutely quiet. Everyone seems frozen into place.

I try to think of what Barbara would do. "I think we should sit down and talk about our feelings about what just happened."

Everyone looks at each other.

172

Finally they sit down.

"I think we should just totally ignore Ginger, pretend she's not here," Kitty says.

A couple of the kids agree.

"Maybe she's got a lot of problems that make her act that way," I say.

"We all have problems. That's no excuse," Janie says.

"Marcy, you don't know how terrible she can be." Ellen frowns. "Last year they almost sent her home, but they decided to give her another chance, the suckers."

Stacey says, "I don't want you to ignore her because of me."

"If I were you, I'd want them to pour honey all over her and put her on an anthill," Betsy says.

Stacey bites her lip.

Betsy leans over to Stacey and says, "Do you want to swap lollipops for a while? I'm getting tired of this flavour."

Stacey smiles and makes the exchange.

Soon everyone with lollipops is either swapping or licking each other's lollipops.

My mother would die if she saw this.

I trade with Robin.

My mother would make me wash my mouth out with twenty bottles of Listerine. She won't even let everyone use the same bathroom cup.

The bell rings for lunch.

Everyone seems to be in a better mood, in some ways closer because of what happened.

We all rush out of the door.

I can see Corrine sitting under a tree, talking to Ginger.

173

I've got a feeling that it's going to be some summer, that I've got a lot to learn . . . and I'm going to have to learn it quickly.

Chapter 6

Lights out. It's definitely time for that. The campers may not be exhausted, but I am—absolutely wiped out.

It's been a long day, a very long day. The preparation, arrivals, getting them settled, taking them to the pool to be tested, to the showers after swimming, back to the bunk to change and go over the cabin rules, on to dinner (noisier than the school cafeteria ever was), a meeting so that the campers could meet the staff and learn the general rules and regulations.

The campfire. I hope marshmallows come out of hair or else Ginger's going to attract a lot of flies. Somehow, someone managed to drop a freshly melted marshmallow on her head without getting caught. No one would admit to having seen who did it, not even Ginger. She wouldn't let Corrine or me try to help her get it out.

I tried to talk to her, but she turned away.

Now we're back at the bunk.

There's lots of giggling going on. It began as soon as we turned out the lights.

Corrine walks into our room. "I've suggested they all settle down and go to sleep, but I doubt they will. After all, it's the first night, to be expected."

"What should we do now?" I ask.

"Why don't you work on the diary we're supposed to be keeping. Just relax a little."

I get the notebook and look at the first-camp-day assignment. We're supposed to write down first impressions of each camper, a little description of each of them, and my own feelings and perceptions about the first day.

I begin by opening the notebook and staring at it. That's what happens when I confront a blank sheet of paper when I begin writing. I go as blank as the page.

I alphabetise the names then doodle on the margins.

Risa sticks her head in the door. "We're taking a poll to see who in the cabin has already got her period and how old they were when they got it. Do you two want to be part of it?"

Corrine chuckles. "No, and I think you should cut it out. It's time for lights out, and anyway that may embarrass some of the kids."

Risa shakes her head. "The poll's already taken, six yesses, with the youngest age being nine. Four noes. One maybe. And one, 'if you don't leave me alone, I'm going to beat the shit out of you.' "

"Let me guess," I say. "The last one's Ginger."

"It sure wasn't Stacey," Risa says.

"I think that's enough for tonight, Risa," Corrine says. "Lights out."

"We took the poll in the dark. The only light on in this cabin's yours."

Linda sticks her head in the door. "I think this camp's haunted."

"Why?" Risa asks.

176

"Because everyone here keeps talking about the camp spirit."

"Out," Corrine and I yell. "Get into bed."

Risa and Linda vanish, giggling.

Corrine gets out of her bunk and stands up. "Marcy, please watch any comments about Ginger. If the kids think we can't stand her either, they'll just come down harder on her."

I nod. "Okay. I'll try. I'm sorry."

"Don't be sorry. It's understandable. Just don't do it again, if you can help it."

"Okay."

Corrine pretends to pound her head on the wall. "I need a break. First days wipe me out," she says. "Marcy, you're in charge. See you in ten minutes . . . or so."

She leaves. I'm going to have to try harder to be nice to Ginger. Setting an example is hard when you're only a couple of years older than the campers. Being the youngest CIT isn't easy. Still I'm glad that Barbara thought enough of me to ask when they needed a last-minute replacement.

I stare at my notebook for a few minutes and then write.

The day's been really hectic.

Corrine returns. "Your turn to go out."

I yawn. "I'll skip it tonight. I'm exhausted."

She grins, "I ran into someone outside who wants to talk to you."

"Who?" I ask, jumping out of my bunk without even using the ladder.

"It's Ted. I'm glad you got over your crush on Jimmy,"

FIRST DAY IMPRESSIONS- Marcy Lewis

	NAME	# of years	Impressions
1.	Linda Allen	0	cute, short, brown hair. BAD JOKES! Wants to be a comic-actress.
2.	Kitty Amoss	3	Medium height, blonde, stood up to Ginger-no sugar. WRITER
3.	Bobbie Caputo	0	Tall, curly brown hair, kind of quiet, no sugar. artist.
4.	Helene Gerver	0	long straight brown hair, great looking, green eyes, seems quiet but has sense of humour-actress.
5.	Risa Hess	5	curly short brown hair, talks alot, flirts, a leader. actress & writer.
6.	Ginger Simon	2	brown hair, fringe, pigtails, awful. THE PITS!!! artist.
7.	Stacey Reed	0	corn-rowed brown hair cute, nice to little kids MUSICIAN
8.	Alicia Sandez	3	brown hair, bi-lingual, assertive, nice, DANCER.
9.	Ellen Singleton	3	Tall, very thin, vegetarian ARTIST (pottery)
10.	Janie Weinstein	0	curly brown hair braces on teeth, funny, bright. Maybe person who dropped marshmallow on Ginger. Wants to be writer, dancer, MUSICIAN, artist.
11.	Robin Wiggins	0	very quiet. Don't have clear picture of her in my mind.
12.	Betsy Zolt.	5	Good at getting kids together, watches a lot. DANCER.

A B C D
E F G H i
J K L M N O
P Q R S
T U V
W X
Y
Z

CAMP IS FUN, TIRING, AND CONFUSING!

she says while I put on my sneakers. "I didn't want to butt in before, but I know what he's like. I went out with him once last summer. It's just not worth it. You spend the entire time listening to him talk about himself."

She crawls into bed. "I feel much better now that I told you. I feel like you're the little sister I never had, but always wanted."

"I'm glad you've adopted me. I always wanted an older sister."

She grins. "Now go outside and say hello to Ted. And Marcy, don't do anything that I wouldn't do."

I wave and walk outside.

The kids are still giggling and talking to each other in their beds.

Ted's standing near the cabin, looking at the sky. It's glorious in the country. Clear. Stars. There's even a full moon tonight.

I come up behind him, tap him on the shoulder, and say, "Pardon me, sir. Is this space taken?"

He turns around, smiles, and says, "Hi, Marcy."

After that wonderful start I've got no idea what to say next.

"I just wanted to see you, find out how your first day went. I hope I haven't disturbed you." He looks a little uncomfortable.

I hear giggles from the direction of the cabin. We move to a more secluded area, where we won't be the cabin's late-night show.

We sit under a tree.

I slap at my arms, killing the mosquitoes who think I'm the local blood bank.

"So how did your first day go?" I say.

"Fine. And yours?"

"Okay."

"This is a wonderful conversation," Ted says. "For two people who were hired for their creativity, this is really dull."

I giggle. Giggling must be catching. "I'm sorry. I guess I'm just feeling a little overwhelmed . . . by camp."

"Not by me?" Ted grins. "Well, good then. I can handle that as long as I know that the diagnosis is overwhelmed due to occupational hazard."

As we sit there, I see Jimmy walk by with one of the girls who is on the grounds crew. He's got his arm around her waist and he's pointing something out in the sky.

I'm glad that's not me. Tonight at the campfire Jimmy asked if I wanted to go back to his room later to look at the newspaper clippings he's got about his sports triumphs. He asked while we were trying to deal with the marshmallow in Ginger's hair. I said no. Risa volunteered to go in my place, but Jimmy just looked at me, said, "Your loss," and left.

Ted pinches me on the arm and says, "Marcy."

I look at him.

"I don't think you've heard one thing I've said for the last four minutes."

"Oh, Ted, I'm sorry."

He shakes his head. "You were too busy looking at Jimmy. I can't believe you could be turned on to that creep. I thought you had better taste." He stands up. "We'd better get back to our cabins."

I jump up. "It's not the way you think it is. Don't be

mad at me."

He says, "I'm not . . . Well, maybe I am. I don't really know exactly what I'm feeling. I just think you're special and it makes me angry to think you like Jimmy better than me."

"But I don't," I say and realise that it's absolutely true. "I do care about you, not him. I'm just a little confused."

"Marcy, I want us to be friends. At least friends. Probably more."

At least friends. Probably more. This thing with Ted isn't a crush. It's something more for me too, only I'm not sure. What if I let myself start to care and get hurt? I'm not sure I can survive a broken heart. I get hurt so easily anyway, so I've never let myself get too close to a guy, not that there have been that many opportunities. I'm scared. What if it turns into a real relationship and it's as bad as my parents' marriage?

I look at Ted. He's bright and fun and very cute. He's one of the nicest people I've ever met. He likes me, obviously a lot, and he's not afraid to let me know.

I push the hair out of his eyes and say, "Friends. At least friends."

He puts his arms around my waist.

I bet he's going to think I have no waist at all, that I'm just a puffball. Then I remember, I'm not fat anymore.

I put my arms around him.

A mosquito's draining all of my blood out of my right arm, but I decide now is not the time to slap it.

We kiss.

It's wonderful.

We kiss again.

182

It's still wonderful—until the large flashlight beams on us, we hear a cough, and separate.

It's Carl and Barbara, who are smiling.

I could die of embarrassment.

Ted says, "We're on a ten-minute break. The cabins are supervised."

Carl says, "We're just doing our nightly check of the areas, to make sure everything's okay."

"Everything's okay," I say.

"So I noticed." Barbara smiles.

I blush.

"About time to get back, isn't it?" Carl says.

Even though our parents aren't around, I've got the feeling that Barbara and Carl keep an eye on things.

I'm not so sure that's bad.

As Carl and Barbara go off to check out the camp area, Ted puts his arm around my shoulder and we walk back to the cabin.

I feel good. A little nervous but good.

We stand by the cabin for a minute.

I hear muffled giggling.

So does Ted because he leans over and gives me a fast kiss and whispers, "I'll see you tomorrow."

As I walk into the cabin, there's applause and a lot of voices start singing:

MARCY AND TED, SITTING IN A TREE
K-I-S-S-I-N-G;
FIRST COMES LOVE
THEN COMES MARRIAGE
THEN COMES MARCY WITH A BABY CARRIAGE.

Corrine's standing there, singing with the kids.

I look at everyone, wave as if I'm a queen greeting her subjects, and walk into my room as everyone applauds again.

Chapter 7

Two weeks of camp gone already.

Linda and Risa organised a midnight raid on the kitchen.

Kitty's been taking extra food from the dining hall and hiding it under her bed, in case hunger strikes late at night. We found a mouse under her bed. Stacey brought it to the nature shack.

Crying a lot from homesickness, Bobbie said she's allergic to bug juice and wanted to leave. Now that she's having fun, her allergy has disappeared and she's consuming large quantities of bug juice.

Alicia's teaching everyone to swear in Spanish.

Ellen's circulating a petition, protesting about the amount of meat served. She wants a choice for vegetarians.

Ginger's been brutal. I tried to talk to her one day and she told me to "bug off". Another time I put my hand on her arm and she pushed it away. Only once was she ever friendly, the time that I suggested that she do some drawings for the camp magazine. When I asked her about the artwork later, though, she said, "Who wants to work on that lousy magazine, anyway?" So I gave up.

I hardly have any chance to be alone with Ted. Camp's

been in session for two weeks and while it's mostly fun, Corrine and I've been run ragged.

We've just called a bunk meeting.

Barbara's on her way up the hill right now to be part of the meeting.

The kids are sitting around, not saying much, playing jacks, writing letters, practicing dance steps.

I look over my notes about what we're going to cover at this meeting.

Barbara arrives. "Hi, gang. Let's get started." She smiles.

Everyone looks at her.

"Why don't we hold the meeting under a tree outside?" Corrine suggests.

"Good idea," Barbara says.

Outside we go.

Barbara takes out a clipboard. "I understand some of you want the chance to air your feelings. Well, let's do it."

The girls look at each other.

"I don't think it's fair that we have to go swimming," Janie says. "I don't want to learn. It's impossible."

"But it's good exercise," Barbara answers.

"Not when Jimmy's had to rescue me twice," Janie says.

"Lucky." That's from Risa.

Ellen raises her hand. "I think the food here is nutritionally bad, too starchy, too much meat. Meat makes people act like animals."

"I like meat," Kitty says. "Just because you don't, doesn't mean the rest of us have to live on rabbit food."

"I'll give you my spinach," offers Linda.

"Sugar's bad for us. There's too much sweet stuff given out." Ellen won't quit.

"How come there's a rule that we can only get two candy bars a day from the canteen?" Janie makes a face.

"How about some rice and beans?" Alicia asks.

Barbara says, "I want all of you to notice the differences of opinion here and see how hard it is to meet all of the individual needs."

"You end up meeting no one's needs," Robin says, pulling bark off a twig.

Sighing, Barbara says, "We try."

Stacey says, "Someone put bubble gum in my flute. No one's been caught."

"And someone cut the strings on my guitar."

"My sculpture got destroyed." Ellen is angry.

Corrine says, "It's hard to prove who's responsible."

Everyone stares at Ginger.

"I get blamed for everything. I don't have to take this." Ginger sticks out her tongue. "And I have a complaint too. How come you won't let me bring up my portable television? I'd rather watch that than have to be part of all the stupid group activities around here."

"No TVs allowed. You know that." Barbara stares at her.

"Rules are made to be broken," Ginger smirks.

"No they're not." Barbara shakes her head. "Not the rules here. They're for your own good."

"You've broken some rules in your life," Ginger says. "So don't play Ms. Perfect with us."

"Ginger," I yell. "Stop that."

"It's all right," Barbara says. "It might as well be out in

187

the open. I've been hearing a lot of that lately from a few people. It's better to get it all straightened out."

She looks very tired but continues. "I know I've taken some stands that don't go along with everyone's wishes. But I want you to realise, Ginger, that I felt that there were some very important issues at stake. It wasn't done lightly or without a lot of careful thought. That's different from the way that you've been acting, Ginger."

"I don't see the difference."

"Well, that's what we've all been trying to help you see."

"Why don't you just leave?" Janie says. "Good riddance to bad rubbish."

"No name calling, please," Corrine says.

Ginger says, "Someday I'll be gone and then you'll all be sorry."

"I doubt that," Betsy says, speaking for the first time at the meeting.

Everyone looks at her.

She shrugs. "Well, it's true. None of us would be sorry if Ginger left. I know she's the one who put peanut butter in my sleeping bag . . . the crunchy kind."

Barbara says, "I really hope you can all learn to get along."

"Dream on." Kitty makes a face.

Linda says, "We're making it sound like camp's terrible. I don't think it's that bad. I'm having a lot of fun."

Of course she is, I think. She loves camp and kidding around. The other day someone told her that if you put a sleeping person's hand in warm water, that person would think she wet the bed. This morning I woke up with my hand in warm water.

"I like camp too. I just want a vegetarian diet," Ellen says.

"I don't want to find bubble gum in my flute again, but I like it here," Stacey says.

The kids continue to talk.

I keep waiting for Barbara to come up with the magic solution, the thing that's going to make it all better.

It doesn't happen.

What does happen is that everybody gets a chance to talk out what's bothering them.

Barbara takes some notes and promises to consider the suggestions.

The meeting ends, and the girls go on to other activities.

I'm not sure what's been accomplished, except that I'm going to try again to reach Ginger, to do something no one else has been able to do.

Barbara puts down the clipboard. "What a week. I'm exhausted."

"It'll be okay," I say.

She smiles. "Carl would say you're beginning to sound like me, always sure that everything's okay."

"That's what I tell her," Corrine nods. "Barbara, are you getting discouraged?"

Barbara nods. "I figure that we've got a great place here—creative, open, sensitive to the individual—and still, people complain. Not only that, but we've had to send home two staff members for breaking the rules, smoking grass in their cabin. It's not been easy."

"But think of all the good things happening here." Corrine puts her hand on Barbara's shoulder.

"I'd like it to be perfect. How are we going to work all of this out? Where are we going to get the money to afford all these different foods? Vegetarian? Ethnic? No sugar? Some sugar?"

We sit quietly for a minute.

She speaks again. "Is Ginger getting any better? Do you think she's responsible for all those problems?"

"Most of them." Corrine nods.

"Maybe I made a mistake, letting her come back." Barbara puts her head into her hands.

"You wouldn't do anything that's not right," I say. "Somebody may be able to reach her."

"Marcy, stop making excuses for me. It's getting a little hard for me to be the perfect example that you want me to be. I'm really getting tired of it."

"But . . ."

"Just get off my back," Barbara says, standing up. "I'm going for a walk."

She leaves.

I feel stunned.

I really hurt.

The tears start.

I'm glad the kids aren't around.

Corrine says, "Marcy, she didn't mean to hurt you. People sometimes say things without meaning them."

"But she's really mad at me."

"She's upset and just took it out on you. Marcy, you really do expect her to be perfect. You don't think that the people you care a lot about can make mistakes or be human. That's a heavy load to lay on someone."

"I'm sorry," I sniffle.

190

"You don't have to be perfect either. I know I'm not."

"Sure, you are." I smile at her.

"I snore. That's not perfect." She's grinning at me.

"How do you know you snore?" I ask. "You seem to sleep right through it."

She grins more. "I've had some comments and complaints."

I grin back. "Well, your snores are perfect, just the right decibels and very even. When I grow up, I want to snore just like you."

"Surprise, my dear, you do snore."

"Really? Nobody ever told me that before." I'm surprised.

"That's because you usually don't sleep with anyone."

I get up. "I guess I'm just not as worldly as you are. Have you had *many* complaints about your snoring?"

"Nosy," Corrine says, getting up. "I'm not going to answer that on the grounds that it might incriminate me. Look, don't you have the afternoon and evening off today?"

I nod, drying my tears.

"And a date with a very nice young man named Ted?"

Again I nod.

"So go and get ready. And cheer up. It'll work out. I'll come in to talk to you after I check on the kids."

I go back into the cabin and think about what's been said. Maybe I do expect too much of everyone. My mother tells me that a lot.

I start to pick out what I'm going to wear.

There's a knock on the door.

"Come in."

It's Barbara. "Marcy, I'm really sorry."

I stand there, holding a shirt.

"It's been a little rough lately. I'm sorry I blew my top."

"It's all right." I'm just relieved she's not mad at me.

"I want you to know the reason I got so angry is that I think sometimes we're a lot alike. I want too much perfection from myself and others too. There are lots of good ways we're alike and some not so wonderful ways. So I guess getting angry at you is a little like getting angry at myself." Barbara plays with her hair, twirling some of it around her hand.

"I can think of worse things than to be like you," I say. "But I do understand what you're saying."

"Good," Barbara says. "I'm glad we can talk about it."

"Instead of yelling," I say, thinking about how my father reacts.

"I'll see you later. Have a nice day off," Barbara says. She smiles, waves, and leaves.

Being close to other people isn't always easy, but it's worth it.

Vacation. I need a vacation. All of this dealing with feelings. Working. Living with thirteen other people in the same small area. Being helpful. I'm wiped out. If I've got to finish off one more lanyard, I'm going to scream. Swimming. Hiking. Working on the camp paper. Cookouts. Getting ready for the talent show. Trying to keep the kids from killing Ginger when I'm not sure that I really want to stop them. Thinking of ways to try to reach her even though I'm afraid to try because she'll be mean. She's only ten, but she can be deadly. At night I'm so exhausted it's hard to fall asleep. The kids giggle. Corrine snores. I stay awake waiting for the sound of rushing mice feet and the swoosh of bat wings. I'd almost like to go off somewhere alone and sleep my time off away.

But I'm going to Woodstock with Ted. He's managed it so that we've got the time off together, and he's even arranged to borrow a car. A date with Ted, the use of the car. I wish everyone back home could see me now.

Corrine walks in while I'm getting ready. "Marcy, why are *all* of your clothes on your bed? Are you planning on running away and can't decide on the proper wardrobe for your flight? Please don't desert me."

I grin. "I can't decide what to wear."

"It's Woodstock. Denim," Corrine says. "Wear blue jeans or something like that. You're not going to a prom."

"I've spent the entire time up here in blue jeans," I say. "I want to wear something different. After all, it's my day off."

"You just want to show Ted how pretty your legs are," Corrine teases.

Janie runs in. "Would one of you please remind the powers that be around here that I'm going to take the next bus back to New York City if they don't stop bugging me about learning to swim. If I were meant to be in water, I'd have been born with gills."

Corrine says, "Marcy, it's your time off. I'll handle this," and she takes Janie outside.

I think about going to Woodstock. For years I've heard about it and I saw the film about the rock festival, which wasn't even held there. I've always wanted to go. It's supposed to be this special place for the arts, for all different kinds of people. And now I'm going . . . and with Ted. I'm so excited that my stomach hurts.

I decide on my denim wraparound skirt, a light blue blouse, tights.

I grab my bag and walk out of the cabin.

"Stockings." Corrine raises an eyebrow.

Janie looks at me. "You look nice. Big day off, huh? Bet you're going out with Ted. Be good. And if you can't be good, be careful. . . ."

I can't believe she said that. When I was her age, I knew nothing. As a matter of fact I still don't know much.

Risa and Linda come running up to us. "Did you see Nick? Did you? Did you?"

We shake our heads.

They're all out of breath.

We assigned them the job of camp gossip columnists, and they take their jobs very seriously. Only they spread the word before it's printed.

"Some of the kids bet Nick he didn't have enough nerve to shave his head. Now they've got to pay up."

"You mean Nick, the counsellor, or Nick, the kid in bunk nine?" Janie wants to know.

"The bunk nine Nick."

The bunk nine Nick is coming up the hill, surrounded by a bunch of kids. Only now he's the bald bunk nine Nick.

"I only hope his parents aren't coming up on Visitors' Day," Corrine sighs.

I look at my watch. "I'll see you later. I've got to go."

I'm glad everyone's paying attention to Nick. Now I can make a fast getaway without any more comments.

194

Ted's waiting in the car park.

I get into the car.

He looks different, a little less like camp, a little more dressed up. Blue jeans, just washed and even pressed. A short-sleeved T-shirt with the insignia from his sister's college, Princeton. Even his sneakers look like they've been washed.

Neither of us are wearing the usual layer of camp dirt that seems to collect on us as soon as we've been out for an hour.

"Did you see Nick?" I ask.

He nods. "I'm afraid of what he'd have done for twenty bucks."

Ted starts up the car and heads out of the driveway.

We're on our way.

Chapter 8

Woodstock, only eight miles from camp. Here we come.

"Do you have to sit all the way at the other side of the car?" Ted asks. "I promise to keep both hands on the steering wheel."

I move closer to him and look at the scenery.

He says, "I think you're going to like Woodstock."

"Corrine says there are some great places to shop. Do you like to shop?"

"Sometimes. When it's places I want to go and my mother's not along telling me what I should buy."

I continue to look at the scenery.

"So what do you really want to be when you grow up?" I ask and giggle. Giggling's truly catching. A regular plague. By the end of the summer I'll probably turn into a laughing hyena.

He says, "A set of Tinker Toys. And what do you want to be when you grow up?"

"I want to be a kumquat." I don't even know what a kumquat looks like. I just like the way it sounds.

"Are you sure?"

I nod. "But if the job market's tough and there are lots of kumquats out looking for work, I guess I'll be a novelist."

"I want to be a doctor, if I can't be a set of Tinker Toys. And no matter what, I always want to be able to play music."

We grin at each other.

Getting into town, I see how small the shopping area is. I'm used to the shopping malls around my house. Ted parks behind the bank, and we walk to Tinker Street. There are lots of people around. Folks are sitting on the village green, talking, playing instruments, looking around, resting. Some of them look like pictures of the sixties, long hair, headbands. Some are wearing jeans, long skirts, dresses, shorts. It looks like anything goes when it comes to dress. Everyone looks summery. Comfortable. No one is wearing a prom dress. Corrine was right.

Ted holds my hand. "Come on. Let's start at the library and work our way down."

We walk along, swinging our hands and looking at everything.

The Woodstock Library is a wonderful little building, one storey, made of wood. It looks like a house that elves could live in.

"Let's go in," I say. "I love books."

"Me too."

We walk up the path. People are sitting all over the lawn, reading and talking.

We enter. It's great, really homey with librarians who smile and offer to help.

"I wish I had a card here, even though I don't have much time to read," I say.

"There's a bookshop farther up," Ted says. "We can

stop there."

As we leave, I hear one of the librarians talking to someone about the fair that's going to be run later on in the summer. Jumble sale, games, plays, good stuff like that.

We walk up farther.

There are lots of great shops, beautiful jewellery, clothes.

"Here we are," Ted says. "The Golden Notebook."

In we go. I love the place. It's got natural wood, books all over, piled up on the floor, shelves practically up to the ceiling. By the nature section there's even a real spider weaving a web. I point it out to Ted.

"They probably pay it to be there," he says.

"Maybe it's going through an identity crisis and thinks it's a worm—a bookworm" is my comment.

I feel like a little kid in a toy shop. All those books. I've always wanted to be a writer, but before Ms. Finney, Barbara, I was afraid to tell anyone. I think it's some kind of miracle that all we have to work with is the twenty-six letters of the alphabet. And they turn into words, sentences, paragraphs, chapters, books, conversations, plays. It's just incredible to me.

I buy three books. So does Ted.

We go through more shops.

"Here's one of my favourites," Ted says, stopping in front of a house. Rainbow Shop, it says.

We walk in. The place is filled with rainbows, stars, moons, unicorns. It's like being in a fairy tale.

The guy standing there smiles. He's wearing all this rainbow jewellery. He's even got an enamelled tooth with a star and rainbow on it. If I saw him walking down the street in my home town, I'd be a little surprised, but here it seems perfectly natural.

A woman walks up to us and hands us a piece of paper. "Here's your rainbow."

"Thanks." I want to hug everyone in the world.

Ted starts to ask the Rainbow Man some questions, about the shop, about how he got started. I think it's wonderful that Ted's not afraid to talk to people.

The Rainbow Man's telling him about the time he said, "I wish I had a quarter for every person who comes in here," and then decided to charge admission.

"I refused to work until he cut it out," the woman who gave us the rainbow said. "I went into the back room until he quit doing it."

Everyone's smiling at everyone else.

I pick out a pair of rainbow earrings for me and a copy of *The Rainbow Book* for Stuart. I want to share this with him in some way. After all, he's stuck back home, and I just want him to be part of this somehow.

As I take the things up to the cash register, the Rainbow Man says, "Would you like me to autograph the book?"

It dawns on me. He's the one who did the book. The real-live author. I'm in shock. A real-live author. And he seems like an ordinary person.

He signs the book.

As we leave the store, everyone waves good-bye.

Ted hugs me. "Happy?"

"Very." I hug him back.

He kisses me right there on the street in front of the world.

I'm too busy kissing him back to notice the world's reaction.

If my father could see me now, he'd probably lock me up in my room. But he's not here.

We stop kissing because I've dropped my packages and have to pick them up.

Pizza next. The bulletin boards in the restaurant are full of news of upcoming concerts, plays, and art exhibits.

Next comes Rock City Rags, a place for T-shirts, where you can have anything printed on them.

"Let's get matching shirts," Ted says. "To always remind us of today."

He's not afraid to say things like that. I come from a family that finds it hard to show feelings. It's so nice to be with someone who isn't.

We pick out the shirts. White. With the "I Love New York" emblem put on it. Ted has his name put on the back with black lettering.

I say, "I think I take a medium or a large, and I'd like 'Marcy' put on with glitter letters."

The saleswoman looks at me. "Medium or large? I think you'll need a small. In fact, I'm sure of it."

She and Ted are looking at me.

I can feel myself blush. Always blushing. It's disgusting. And it embarrasses me to have them look. Don't they know that blimps always take big sizes?

She puts a T-shirt up to me. "I bet you've lost a lot of weight. People who do never have a really accurate picture of what they look like."

The small shirt fits.

One of these days, when I grow up, I'm going to learn

who I really am, what I really look like. But it sure isn't easy.

Even when I was heavier, I wasn't as bad looking as I thought I was. People usually aren't. But it's not an easy lesson to learn.

We leave the store.

Ted's got his arm around my shoulders, and I've got an arm round his waist.

All of a sudden I feel something weird around my hips, under my skirt.

It's my tights. They're starting to roll down.

I stop and pretend to look in a store window.

I put my hand into my skirt pocket and grab on to the tights to stop them from continuing the roll down my body.

We continue to walk.

One hand's holding on to my packages, the other's trying to hold up my tights. The hand that's trying to hold them up is attached to the elbow that keeps hitting Ted in his side.

Finally he stops and whispers in my ear. "Want to tell me what's going on before I end up with a bruised and battered body?"

I whisper back, telling him.

He starts to laugh and can't stop.

I start to laugh too, dropping my packages, and try to hold up the tights with both of my hands in my pockets.

He just stands there looking at me.

"We have several choices," I say. "I can let them roll down and die of embarrassment. But then they'd have to find a new CIT and it's sort of late in the summer for that. Or we can find a place with a toilet."

Ted picks up my packages and says, "There's a place farther up where we can get sodas. They have a toilet."

"Sounds good to me."

We walk along. Actually Ted walks and I sort of hobble, legs close together, hands in pockets.

Finally we're there. It's a sidewalk café, and we sit down at a table.

Ted orders Cokes.

I creep into the toilet, take off my sandals and tights. Shoving the tights into my bag, putting my shoes back on, I imagine what it would have been like to have my tights roll down to my ankles in front of everyone. It's too awful to even think about.

I come back to the table.

Ted looks at my face and then down at my bare legs. He starts to laugh again.

So do I.

By the time we calm down, the Cokes have arrived.

We sip them and look at all of the people walking around. I love sitting in an outside café. I love Woodstock. I love the world. I love Ted.

I love Ted. Terror . . . happiness.

We finish the sodas and walk across the street.

Candlestock. The whole place is filled with all of these different kinds of candles. It's hard to make a choice.

I pick out a candle. Actually it's a beautiful bowl with a candle in it, one that can be refilled.

Ted's by the cash register, talking to the two guys there.

I continue to look around, at the sign on one of the shelves that says, SHOPLIFTERS WILL BE PROSECUTED BY THE LORD and at the candle that's taller than I am. Actually it's one that they keep adding to.

As I pay for my purchase, Ted introduces me to the two guys, Dennis and Martin.

Everyone's very friendly.

When we get outside, I hand the bowl with the candle in it to Ted. "I want you to have this. It'll always glow, not melt down and be gone."

He doesn't seem at all embarrassed by the gift. "It's symbolic, like us, huh?"

"Writers are known to deal in symbolism," I say.

We take the packages back to the car and then continue walking around town.

Then Ted and I drive all around. I sit in the car, daydreaming about what it would be like to spend the rest of my life here, the rest of our lives. I even have the names of our two future kids picked out. Heather and Dylan. Dylan because it's the name of one of my favourite poets, Dylan Thomas, and also the name of Bob Dylan, the singer who once was part of Woodstock. Heather because it just seems right for this place.

We stop by a stream, get out of the car, and go down the banks and sit there.

For a long time we talk. It feels so comfortable. So right to be there with Ted. So this is what it's all about. Being in love. I don't want it to ever end.

We get back in the car, head back to town, and then sit for a while in the car holding hands and talking.

Dinner. Then a movie. It's fun, but I want to be alone with Ted, without other people around.

By the time we get out of the movie, it's very dark. There aren't any street lights.

"I guess we've got to go back," I say.

Ted nods. "Yeah, but I don't want to. Do you?"

I shake my head.

Another kiss. I think I've been kissed more times today than the total of all the times I've ever been kissed before.

This time, when I get into the car, I sit right next to Ted. It's really dark on the road.

We drive along. My head's on Ted's shoulder. I put my hand on his knee.

He gives me a kiss on the top of my head and says, "Watch it. I've got to keep my mind on driving."

I take my hand off his knee and move away.

"I didn't mean you had to leave. Are you always a person of extremes?"

I nod, move back, and just sit there.

We pull into the camp car park. Ted stops the engine, turns off the headlights, and puts his arms around me. "Now I don't have to keep my mind on the driving."

Reading books never really prepared me for how I feel. It's one thing to read about love and caring and wanting to hold someone and be held, but this is one time that the twenty-six letters don't come close to the real thing.

"Making out" is such a dumb expression for something so special.

Finally Ted says, "This steering wheel's really uncomfortable. Why don't we find somewhere else to go? Like the back seat?"

I shake my head. "I don't think that's a good idea."

"Afraid?"

I nod.

He kisses me. "Okay. Let's just sit here a few minutes and relax." He leans back.

I think about how wonderful he is. How I've always heard that lots of guys won't take no for an answer. But Ted's really nice. And I'm not ready yet. I know that. It's not just the question of what's right or wrong about sex. I know that right now it would be more than I could handle to actually "go all the way" as the kids in the cabin always say.

I put my hand on his knee and say, "I really care about you."

He takes my hand off his knee and says, "That's not going to help me to relax, to have you do that right now. I'm glad you care. I do too."

More kissing.

"Want to reconsider your decision about not moving to the back seat?" he asks, touching my face.

"I keep reconsidering it, a lot. But no," I say.

"Okay, then I think we should go back," he says.

"Are you mad at me?"

"No. I just think it's best for us to stop now, if we're not going any further. Otherwise it's going to be very hard for me to maintain my reputation with you as 'nice.'" He pats my hand. "Come on. Let's get going."

As we walk up the hill, he says, "Tomorrow morning I'll talk to Carl about giving us the same days off again for the next time, if you want that."

I nod. "I want that."

We get to the cabin. Just as we start to say good night, we hear a lot of screaming coming from the bunk.

We rush inside.

There's a bat in bunk five.

Chapter 9

There's a bat in bunk five!

It's flying all over the place.

I duck and feel like throwing up. What if it swoops down and its wings touch my face? Even worse, what if it bites me?

The kids are screaming, crying, and running.

Corrine's trying to kill it with a dust mop.

Ted grabs a broom.

One of my worst fears is coming true. There really is a bat. Just when things are going well, something happens to ruin it. It's like I'm being punished for being happy and doing what I want to do. That's why I'm so scared much of the time. Either things are going badly or they're going well and I expect disaster to strike.

The screams are getting louder. I think I'm one of the people screaming.

It's bedlam, absolute craziness.

Corrine trips over Robin, who's in the middle of the floor, curled up in a ball shape.

Stacey yells, "Don't kill it. Let's try to catch it and make it the bunk mascot."

Someone throws a Frisbee.

A Paddington bear flies through the air.

Ellen's trying to get it with her tennis racket.

Ted gets the bat.

Wham.

It falls to the floor.

He finishes off the job.

Crunch.

"I think I'm going to be sick. And they say New York City's rough. I'd rather have a cockroach than a bat any day," Janie yells and heads outside.

Stacey starts to cry.

Ted comes over to me. "That was some BATtle, huh?"

Carl and Barbara rush in.

"What's the problem?"

Corrine gets off the floor and points to the mangled bat. "Ted got it."

"Good job, Ted," Barbara says.

"I just happened to be in the neighbourhood and came to the rescue." Ted bows.

"My hero!" I say. "Perhaps I should be BATting my eyes at you."

"I'll dispose of this," Carl says, pointing to the bat.

"We've got to give it a funeral and bury it." Stacey's still crying.

"I think its last wish was to be cremated," Ted says.

"Bat killer," Stacey says and steps on his foot. "I'm never going to talk to you again."

Barbara explains to her about how bats may carry rabies and that Ted did the right thing.

Ginger interrupts, "And it might have been a vampire and sucked out someone's blood and driven that person insane. The person would then have brutally murdered every other person in this bunk and then committed suicide by throwing her body on a newly sharpened marshmallow stick."

"Warped. You're absolutely warped. Look, let's have the funeral and get some sleep. It's after midnight."

Ginger continues anyway. "The bat's brother and sister vampires are probably going to come here and try to avenge its death. They'll probably get all of us and we'll leave here with fangs."

"I wonder if my orthodontist has ever made braces for fangs," Risa says. "Come on, Ginger. You're just being obnoxious, as usual. Isn't she?" She looks around, waiting for someone to say yes.

Barbara says, "Ginger, I think you could put your active imagination to good use. Why don't you write some of this fiction down and submit it to the magazine."

"She'd rather try to scare everyone," Alicia says.

I think of how in the beginning I wanted to help her but haven't. She's so difficult. I don't think she knows when to stop, what's a joke and what's cruel. That makes me nervous.

Corrine brings out a shoe box and shovels the bat into it.

We all grab flashlights and go outside.

Everyone shines her flashlight on one spot, and Ted makes a hole in the ground with the broom handle. Then he puts the box into the ground and says, "Now, somebody's got to say a few words."

"Me," Risa yells and begins. "Dearly beloved, we are gathered here . . ." begins Risa.

"That's for weddings, dummy," yells Ginger.

"No name calling," Barbara says softly, putting a hand on Ginger's shoulder.

I expect Ginger to pull away, but she doesn't. In fact she places her hand on Barbara's.

Risa starts over. "We are here this evening to mourn this dearly departed bat."

"He's not dear," Bobbie says.

"Well, he is departed. That's for sure." Risa continues. "While we did not know him for long, he will leave a memory in our minds."

"Not in our hearts," Helene says.

Janie pretends to cry. "He looks just like he did when he was alive."

"Except that he's squashed and dead," Betsy says.

Risa continues, ". . . so we hope that he rests in peace."

"Or pieces," whispers Ted, coming up behind me and putting his arms around my waist.

The girls all start to go back into the bunk.

Bobbie says, "I think we should bury the broom too. I'm never going to touch it. It's disgusting."

"We'll wash it," Carl says. "Now, those of us who live in other bunks should think about going back to them. It's really late."

"I guess he means me, since they've got a house and I'm the only other person not assigned to bunk five," Ted says with a smile. "Carl, don't you think I should get special visiting privileges since I saved the day?"

"Back to your bunk or I'll have you arrested for hunting out of season." Carl points toward the boys' bunk area.

"And for carrying and using an unregistered broom," I

210

add.

Ted gives me a quick kiss good night and says, "I'll see you tomorrow."

Barbara turns to me. "We're still friends, aren't we? You're not still upset about this morning, are you?"

I shake my head. "No, I'm trying to learn that we've all got the right to be human and less than perfect."

"Except for me. Remember that I'm perfect," Carl says.

Barbara shines her flashlight in his face. "Okay, Mr. Perfect. Then how come you left the coffeepot on tonight, forgot about it, and burned it out?"

"A momentary lapse." He shines his flashlight into her face. "Let's go home now."

She nods and mumbles something about practice making perfect.

Corrine and I go into our room.

The girls have all quietened down and seem to be going to sleep.

As we change into our pyjamas, Corrine says, "Boy, am I glad you two arrived when you did. Did you have a good time in Woodstock?"

"Wonderful." I must have said or thought "wonderful" a million times today.

We climb into our bunks.

I tell her about our day and how my tights rolled down. After we finish laughing about that, I ask, "Corrine, how old were you when you fell in love for the first time?"

"Oh, it's that serious, huh? Well, the first time I was eleven and he was my fifth-grade teacher. The first time the love was mutual and serious was when I was fourteen.

Boy, was that great . . . and very confusing, ending when his parents decided to move to Ohio. We swore our undying love but it's hard from a distance. After that, I fell madly in love with John, but he broke my heart. I still think about him sometimes, but it wouldn't have worked out in the long run. Now I'm in love with David. I really miss him. He's in France. We decided we needed some distance, some time apart. This love I hope is going to last forever. I even have the names picked out for the kids we'll have someday."

I think of Heather and Dylan . . . Ted and my future kids.

I also think of the comment that Heidi once made about how she doesn't want any kids. But I do, I think. But not until I'm older, about twenty-seven, and have had a chance to do a lot of stuff.

Corrine says, "I really think Ted's great. I'm glad you and he hit it off." She turns out the light.

"Just remember that camp's going to be over and both of you live in different places."

That's something I don't want to think about, not now, not tonight.

There's a lot more I want to ask Corrine, about being in love and sex, but I'm too shy to ask and I don't want to seem like a dumb kid, especially when she's treating me like an adult. It's hard to know who to talk to. I've never been able to talk much to my mother about it, even when she sat me down and told me the facts of life. Somehow that was hard because I kept thinking she and my father must have done it since Stuart and I are here, but it's weird to think of your parents having sex.

I'm not just shy, I'm tired, very tired. It's been a long day.

I'm almost asleep when I hear screams of "raid" and someone playing a trumpet.

Suddenly the whole bunk is filled with kids from the boys' intermediate cabin.

The girls are screaming again.

I quickly jump out of bed.

Corrine grabs her dressing gown and puts it on.

I grab mine and do the same.

Opening the door, we get bombarded with water balloons and shaving cream.

Rolls of toilet paper are flying.

The trumpet's still playing.

Pillows are being thrown. Feathers are flying.

As quickly as it began, it's ended.

Bunk five's a disaster area. It's filled with toilet paper, water, and shaving cream.

There are also frogs running around, obviously collected and saved for just this occasion.

"Someone stole Paddington," Stacey yells. "He was my favourite stuffed animal."

"I managed to bite one of them," Ginger calls out.

Alicia curses in Spanish.

"Get those frogs out of here before I die," Linda yells.

"Try catching them and putting them in a blender," Helene yells back.

"Not funny." Linda stands on her bunk. "Please, if you catch them, I promise I'll never tell those two jokes again."

The frogs are caught—I hope we got all of them—and

taken outside.

"Everything okay now?" Corrine checks.

"Someone stole my bra," Robin says.

"Don't worry. You don't really need one anyway," Ginger says. "A Barbie doll's got bigger boobs than you do."

"I'm going to kill her," Robin yells, lunging at Ginger.

Corrine holds her back, while I say, "Ginger, apologise."

"Robin, I'm sorry you don't really need a bra."

"That's not what I meant."

Ginger sneers. "Sorry."

Some of the girls give Robin a hug and say things like "Don't let her get to you," and "We should have made her eat those frogs."

Corrine looks around the room. "Let's get this all cleaned up and then we're going to have to go down to the showers to clean off."

We clean up.

We troop down to the showers.

I'm past being exhausted. I'm not even sure I'm alive anymore.

Everyone looks the way I feel.

Finally we all go back to bed.

It's finally quiet.

I wonder what Ted's doing right now.

The sheep I try to count are all jumping over rainbows. Frogs are hopping under those rainbows.

Someone from the bunk yells, "Revenge will be ours."

I hug my pillow, pretending the pillow's Ted, and fall asleep.

214

*　　*　　*

Reveille.

Someone should shoot the kid with the bugle. Or at least put a muzzle on him.

I'm tired. The only reason I can think of for getting up is to see Ted at breakfast.

That's enough of a reason.

I jump out of bed.

Giggling. I hear giggling. How can anyone be alert enough to coordinate their giggling mechanism after all of last night's disturbance?

I'm almost afraid of what I'm going to find when I open the door.

I peek out, into the righthand part of the cabin.

No one's there.

They're all on the left side.

"What's going on?" I ask, wiping the sleep out of my eyes.

All of the girls, except Ginger, are sitting together, looking guilty.

I repeat my question.

Risa says, "We were just practising kissing."

"Each other?" I ask.

"No, ourselves. Look." She shows me her arm.

I look.

She's given herself a love-bite, a big red mark on her arm.

The rest of the girls hold out their arms. They've done the same to themselves. All of them have love-bites, red turning to purple.

"I didn't do it," Ginger says. "For once, I'm the good

one."

Corrine comes in.

"You two do it too," Risa says. "Then we'll all be alike, except for Ginger, and she doesn't count anyway."

Ginger stomps off.

Corrine looks at their arms and then at me. "Marcy, I have a feeling that today's going to be one of those days when I wish I'd taken another kind of job."

I nod. But that's not really true. There's no place in the world that I'd rather be than Camp Serendipity.

"Okay. Get ready for breakfast," Corrine says.

The girls try to convince us to give ourselves love-bites.

When we won't do it, they all sing, "Every party has a pooper, that's why we invited you, party pooper."

Finally we go to the dining room.

The girls are trying to give love-bites to all the boys in the bunk that raided us last night.

Corrine's right.

It's going to be one of those days.

Chapter 10

Where's the time gone?

I feel like I've just got to camp and now it's half-way over.

The hiking. I don't think I've ever walked so much in my entire life. Back home, everyone walks to and from school and sometimes over to friends'. Other than that, our parents take us places in cars.

Not here. We walk everywhere. And as if that's not enough, Carl's some kind of nut about going on hikes. There have been three of them since the night that the bunk was invaded by the bat and by the boys from the intermediate cabin.

And the overnight. Some of the kids were terrified. And those who didn't start out scared got that way after two hours of ghost stories.

Visitors' Day. Parents taking kids off the grounds, talking to us, making sure that the kids are having fun.

The swimming. Even Janie's learning to swim. And it's Ginger who taught her. Amazing. I still can't reach Ginger. I tried once more to be nice, but she told me to go away.

There's been kind of an uneasy truce for a while, ever since Corrine and I've been holding daily bunk meetings.

I only hope it lasts.

And in another week it'll be time for carnival and the talent show . . . both on one day.

Ted and I are still "going together." That means the few minutes that we have free, we spend together. It's not really like back home where people get to go out on real dates. It's more like when people in grammar school and junior high went out (I always heard about it, but it never happened with me). People "hang out" together, and everyone says they're a couple.

So now I'm part of a couple and I love it. It's not always easy, though, because sometimes I would like to spend more time with other people, and there just isn't enough time.

Especially with carnival and the talent show coming up.

It's been so busy here that there was barely enough time for me to even remember my birthday. That's why it was such a wonderful surprise, the party that Corrine and Barbara threw for me.

And the magazine. That's coming out this weekend too. With the hour and a half each day that the majors (dance, music, writing, art) have allotted, we've been getting the magazine ready, as well as the daily newsletters.

I'm watching the kids practice the bunk skit for talent night. They've put it together so that it's a showcase for their individual talents.

It's about a magic kingdom (only they've made it a queendom) where everyone is allowed to have one special talent and what happens when the people want to branch out and have more than one talent. The wicked witch casts a spell. They are, individually, unable to break that spell until they discover that as a group against the wicked witch, helping each other, they can make things end "happily ever after."

Risa says the skit's going to be a real show stopper.

Ginger says the only way it's going to be a show stopper is so that everyone can take time out to throw up. She's got the part of the wicked witch. I tried to talk to the kids about changing the script, but Ginger said she loved her part.

Oh well, you can't expect miracles.

I watch the kids practise as I work on the costumes.

Heidi Gittenstein stops by the cabin. "Hey, Marcy, we've got permission to go into Woodstock after dinner to pick up some stuff for carnival. Want to come? It'll be you, me, and Sally.'

"I'd love to."

"Great. We'll meet right after dinner." She goes down the hill.

Great. It'll give me a chance to spend some time getting to know her and Sally better.

I continue to sew and try to remember if Ted and I've made any plans to be together after dinner. I doubt it, not formal ones. I don't think he'll mind though. It'll give him some time to practise his guitar, since he's always saying he doesn't have the time.

Ginger comes over. "I've got some time free until I have to do anything again. Can I go brush my teeth? I've got some corn from lunch caught in my teeth."

"Sure," I say.

She rushes into the bunk for her stuff and runs to the bathroom.

Either she really is getting better or I'm getting used to her.

She comes running back, yelling, "I'm going to kill someone."

I rush over. "What's wrong?"

She's angry. "Someone put a pinhole in my toothpaste tube. When I went to use it, the gunk slopped all over me."

"Calm down," I say.

"I don't want to calm down. I've had it. Last night when I got into bed, someone made me an apple pie bed, and now this."

"Why didn't you mention that at a meeting?"

"I didn't want to tell tales, but too much is happening."

"Look, Ginger," I say, "I'll talk to Corrine about it after dinner and we'll try to work it out."

She looks at me. "Promise."

"Sure," I say, thinking that maybe now she'll be easier to reach. I would really like to be the one who helps her.

She joins the skit and I go back to sewing.

The other girls act like they're not responsible. I wonder who is.

Corrine's at the office, getting the literary magazine put together. I'll have to discuss it with her later.

The afternoon goes well.

Time to go back to the bunk so that everyone can write letters. Once a week every kid has to write a letter home and present the sealed message to the counsellor before dinner. That way we can see that mail is being sent home so that no parents complain.

The dinner bell rings.

Corrine comes up to me. "I'm going to skip dinner tonight. I've got a fever or something. Do you mind?"

"I was supposed to pick up some stuff in town for carnival. Should I cancel?"

"I just want to rest for a while. I'll be fine after dinner."

The kids are all kind of quiet at dinner, but I figure it's because they're all tired out from practising.

After dinner Ted comes over to me and says, "Want to go for a walk after the tables are all cleared?"

I nod.

Heidi comes running over. "Ready? Barbara says we can go now."

I forgot.

I turn to Ted. "Ooops, I've got to go shopping. Okay?"

"Does it matter if it's okay with me? Looks like you've already made your choice." He shrugs.

I want to be with him. But I promised to go. And I do want to get to know Heidi and Sally better. It's confusing.

"See you around sometime," he says in this really cold voice I've never heard before.

I start to say something but he's already turned away.

I watch as he goes over and starts talking to Betty, one of the other CITs.

That hurts—a lot. She's been after him, ever since camp began.

Heidi looks at me. "Wow. I didn't realise this was going to cause any trouble. Would you rather stay here?"

I'm not sure of what I want to do. Part of me wants to

cry. Part of me wants to strangle Ted. How can I be so angry at someone I love so much?

Heidi turns her baseball cap to the back and says "Would you rather stay here, really? I'd understand."

I look over at Ted. He's put his arm around Betty and they're laughing about something.

That does it. "No, I want to go."

We get into the van and Sally drives into town.

I try to put all thoughts of Ted and Betty out of my mind and concentrate on talking with Heidi and Sally.

After a while it becomes easier to join in their conversation.

I can even laugh a little.

Neither of them mentions what happened with me and Ted.

I'm glad because I might say something I would regret.

I remember that I'm supposed to talk to Corrine about what happened with Ginger. Oh well, I can do that when I get back, or Ginger'll probably tell Corrine herself.

We pick up lots of stuff and then go over to a café, sit on the patio, and have Cokes.

"Do you play pinball?" Heidi asks.

I shake my head. In my home town the only kids who play are the kids who cause trouble.

"Want to learn? It's fun. We've got one at home," Heidi says.

Pinball in the house of a U.S. senator. I guess it's okay to play then.

We go into one of the rooms.

Pinball machines.

There's a little kid playing.

Heidi, Sally, and I go over to one, Close Encounters of the Third Kind.

They're really good at it.

I'm not.

But it's fun. I love the flashing lights, the sounds it makes, and the way you don't think about anything personal when you're playing.

We play eliminations. I lose. They play for the championship.

I practice on another machine, feeding it quarters.

There's someone tugging on my Camp Serendipity sweat shirt. It's the little kid.

"Lady, want to play?"

Lady, he thinks I'm a lady. He's seven or eight so I guess he thinks I'm a grown-up. The little kids at camp are the same way.

A little kid. I bet I can beat him. He doesn't look tall enough to see over the machine. Maybe I've got a chance.

He continues. "Loser pays for both games, after the first one."

"Sure." I'm sure I'll win, but even if I do, I won't make him pay for the next game.

We play.

Final score—320,840 for him to 16,500 for me.

I've been hustled.

"Where'd you learn to play like that?" I ask.

"Tom's Pizzeria in New York City, near where I live and go to school. I play there a lot." He grins. "My name's Paulie. What's yours? Your turn to pay."

I put in the quarters. "I'm Marcy. How about teaching me?"

We play.

I pay.

He teaches.

I think Ted and I'll have to come here sometime and play.

Then it all comes back to me. Ted's mad at me, out somewhere with Betty. I bet he never talks to me again.

Heidi and Sally come over. "We'd better get back. It's getting late."

I wave good-bye to Paulie, who's getting more quarters from his parents.

He waves back.

By the time we get back to camp, it's dark.

We all go over to the staff recreation room. There are some people there, but no Ted and Betty.

Sally and Heidi go over to talk to somebody.

Jimmy comes over to me. "Looking for Ted?"

I say nothing.

"I saw him go off with Betty. Why don't you and I go off for a walk?" He lifts one eyebrow.

"Thanks, but no thanks. I'd rather be alone," I say and walk away from him.

I wave good-bye to Heidi and Sally.

Heidi comes over and whispers, "Want some company?"

"I think I'm going for a walk. Thanks anyway."

She nods. "Just remember—the path of true love never runs smooth, or something trite like that."

Once I get outside, I think about Jimmy's offer. Maybe I should have taken him up on it. That would teach Ted. But Ted probably wouldn't even care.

I feel as if someone has ripped my heart right out of my body.

I go off to the area where there are swings.

Corrine's on duty so I don't have to go right back to the bunk. I'm glad. I don't want anyone to see me right now, not when I feel like I'm going to split in two and want to die.

Sitting down on a swing, I start to cry.

It's all so confusing. I love Ted. He used to say he loved me.

Life can get pretty complicated, growing up. I used to think that if I were in love with someone who loved me, everything would be absolutely wonderful.

But it's not working out that way. It's so confusing.

I like being with Ted, having him hug and kiss me, hugging and kissing him. Sometimes I get nervous because I like the feelings so much and then I get scared that I'm not sure I'm making the right decision. But mostly I just like it.

Now, though, I feel as if I'm never going to stop crying, that all of the water in my body's going to exit through my eyeballs.

Someone sits on the swing next to me.

It's Barbara.

I try to stop sobbing but can't.

She says, "Want to talk about it?"

I nod.

She waits for me to say something.

"I feel so dumb . . . and I'm trying so hard to be a grown-up. It's terrible." I continue to sob.

"I know it's hard," she says softly.

I tell her everything. How much I love Ted, how I set the goal for myself to be grown-up, how hurt I am because Ted went off with Betty, how I'm trying so hard to do everything right with the kids that it makes me nervous, how confused I am.

"You shouldn't be so hard on yourself. It's difficult growing up. Carl and I always talk about what we want to do and be when we're grown up." She smiles.

"You do? But you are grown-ups," I say, wiping my eyes.

"Marcy, I'm not even sure what it means to be a grown-up. Everyone has moments when he or she doesn't feel adult. We're all concerned about doing the best thing and we've all had times when we're confused confronting new situations. You've really got to learn not to be so tough on yourself, to realise that lots of other people have the same problems. That doesn't mean that your problems aren't important, you've just got to learn to put them in perspective. You should try to progress at a comfortable rate without worrying about being perfect."

"It just doesn't seem fair. I do the best I can. And still things don't work out. I feel as if I'm being punished all the time."

"But you're not. It's life. Things happen." She shakes her head. "You know, Marcy—an example—I know there are times you hate your father. But he really does care about you. When you hadn't written to them, he sent me a note asking if you were all right, just so they didn't have to worry. So you see he does care, even if you think it's unfair that he's not perfect."

"How come you never told me?"

226

"He said not to. He figured you were busy, but your mother was 'driving him nuts' with her nervous concern about you. And he didn't want you to think that he thought you were incompetent. You know, Marcy, he doesn't. He sounded very proud of you in the letter. So you see, you've got to learn to look at the whole situation. Did you do that with Ted, take his feelings into account?"

Thinking back, I realise I didn't, that I figured that he wouldn't mind—that I didn't have to check it out with him.

"Did you always have an easy time when you went out?" I ask.

She laughs. "No. I made lots of mistakes. Maybe that's why Carl and I do so well together. We've both made mistakes and learned from them. Now we try hard to understand each other and listen."

"I wish there was a magic pill that would make everything all better," I say.

"But there isn't, and pills are not the answer. Working on things is."

"It's scary."

Barbara nods. "It's the only way, and it gets less scary as time goes on. You've got to allow yourself the chance to work things out. You'll survive it. And there are some very good times to be had, just remember that."

"Probably not with Ted. He hates me now." I start to cry. "Could you talk to him for me?"

"No." She shakes her head. "So many people make that mistake, trying to get a friend to be in the middle. You've got to confront him yourself."

"I can't."

She frowns. "You're feeling too sorry for yourself. Of course you can. Look at how far you've come in the time I've known you."

She's right. I used to be scared of everything when we first met. I can even deal with bats. Now I'm just scared of some things.

We sit and swing back and forth while I think about all that's been said.

All of a sudden I hear Carl yell, "Come on, Ted. Let's see how high they can go."

I feel someone pushing me higher and higher.

Barbara's swinging higher and higher too.

"Are you okay?" It's Ted's voice that I hear.

"I want to get down. It's too high." I slow down.

He helps me to stop the swing. I was a little afraid he was going to keep me swinging until I flew over the bars.

Barbara's stopped too.

She gets off and hugs Carl.

I get off and look at Ted.

We just stand there.

I want to yell, So, where's Betty? Where were you? But I don't scream. In fact, I don't say anything.

We stare at each other.

Carl says, "Barbara and I'll be over at the volleyball court setting up. Be there in a few minutes. We're playing your team for the championship."

Team. I'm not even sure we're talking to each other.

They go off, arm in arm.

Ted and I just look at each other.

I think about what Barbara said.

"Ted, let's try to work this out. I'm sorry I didn't

explain that I was going into town. I guess I just didn't take your feelings into account. I should have talked to you about it."

He looks at me. "I'm sorry I walked away like that. I know you've got a right to do things with other people. It's just that all day long, the kids were driving me nuts and all I kept thinking about was that I'd feel better when I could be with you for a while. And then you were going off. I really wanted to be with you, to be with someone special, someone who didn't keep asking me to tie shoelaces or scream 'There's a Fungus Among Us.' Someone who didn't pretend to pull cooties out of my hair. I just wanted to spend some time with you."

"You didn't even give me a chance to explain, to talk it out with you. You went over to Betty."

He nods. "I know. That was lousy . . . to you . . . to me . . . to Betty. I wasn't being fair to anyone. Look, Marcy, I just walked her up to her cabin and then came right back down again to talk to Carl."

"Honest?"

"Honest."

I hug him.

He kisses me on the top of the head and then on my mouth.

When we stop, he says, "I think we've got a volleyball game."

"I hate volleyball," I say. "I like kissing better."

"Me too," Ted says. "But they've challenged us to the championship."

"Do you think we can change it to a kissing championship?" I ask and grin.

He grins back. "They might win. I think they've got more experience."

"We could practice a lot."

He takes my hand, and we go over to the volleyball net.

It's very dark. There were lights by the swings but not here.

Barbara and Carl are pretending to serve.

There's no ball.

Ted and I get on the other side of the net.

"Ready," Carl yells.

"Serve," Ted and I yell.

I pretend to hit it back.

Barbara slams "it" down over the net. "Our point."

"Cheat," I scream. "Your hands were over the net."

I can't really see but it doesn't matter.

We argue about that for a while and then decide to give them half a point.

We then get half a point for a disputed ball.

Another serve.

A return.

"It bounced twice," Ted yells.

I can't believe it. It's pitch dark and we're playing volleyball without a volleyball.

Final score: $21\frac{1}{2}$ to $21\frac{1}{2}$.

No one loses.

We're all winners.

Game called on account of mosquitoes.

Chapter 11

Four days after the volleyball game and I'm in charge of bunk five.

Corrine got poison ivy.

Bad.

Her face's swollen to twice its normal size. There's a rash all over her body. She's got to wear mittens so she won't scratch.

At the infirmary right now Corrine's getting Calamine lotion poured all over her body.

I'm watching the final dress rehearsal of the skit before the talent show.

Ginger walks by.

"Hi," I say.

She ignores me.

"What's the matter?"

"Do you care? You won't do anything about it anyway." She looks at me.

I never did talk to Corrine. With everything else that's happened, I've been so busy, I forgot.

"Ginger. I'm sorry. How's everything going? Really. I promise we'll have a talk as soon as carnival and the talent show are over. I thought everything was going better."

She shrugs. "Don't bother. It's not worth it. Who

cares?'' and she walks away.

The girls finish up the skit and hang out in front of the cabin.

Ginger sits by herself under a tree and draws. Risa and Linda go into the cabin.

A few minutes later they start to scream.

There's a bat in bunk five.

Oh no, not again.

Corrine's in the infirmary.

No one else is around but me.

I've got to deal with it even though I'm scared.

I can do it. At least I think I can. I'm learning that things happen that aren't always wonderful, but I can handle it. It's not punishment for being good or bad, a success or a failure—it's just life. Scary, but I'll survive . . . That's what I'm learning this summer, not to take everything so personally. The bat didn't wake up this morning and say, "Oh goody, I'm going to get Marcy Lewis today."

I can survive—and more than that, I can live my life. I've always been so afraid that I couldn't do anything on my own. Now I can do lots of things. And what I can't do, I can try to get help with.

This bat, however, is not going to help me out. It's up to me.

I thought bats only came out at night.

A bat. An ugly, vicious bat. It's probably dripping with rabies.

Linda taps me on the shoulder. "Marcy, you've got to do something. It's flying all over the place. Our clothes are probably covered with bat turds."

I grab a broom that someone's left on the front porch.

232

"Don't go," Kitty yells.

"Don't kill it." That's Stacey.

Everyone's upset except for Risa and Linda, who look like they're trying to keep from laughing.

It seems fishy to me.

Opening the door slowly, I look inside.

"It's in your room," Risa yells.

Linda's rolling on the ground laughing.

I'm going to be brave.

I open the door.

On the floor of my room is a baseball bat with a sign on it: "AUGUST FOOL!"

That's it. That's the bat in bunk five.

I pick up the bat and pretend that I'm going to clobber Linda and Risa.

I put down the bat when I realise that I really do want to clobber Risa and Linda.

Someday this is going to be very funny, but right now I'm just trying to get my heart to stop pounding so fast.

Everyone starts laughing.

Even I begin to see the humour in the situation.

There's a knock on the cabin door.

It's Carl. "Marcy, the magazine's ready, all put together. How about you and the girls coming down to the office to put the finishing touches on it?"

"There's a bat in bunk five," yells Risa.

Carl looks at me.

I grin. "In my room, take a look."

He does and comes out laughing.

I can't believe I used to be afraid of him.

We all go to the office to work on the magazine. It

looks great. I'm really proud of it.

Corrine walks in and calls me over to the side. "Marcy, I'm going to stay in the infirmary for a day or two until this clears up. I feel terrible. I can't believe it. Would you be in charge of the candy floss machine tomorrow for the carnival? Barbara says it's all right, that someone will show you how to work it. I can't. It's hard to twirl paper cones with mittens on my hands. Also I think the Board of Health would view it as a health hazard to ooze poison ivy onto candy floss."

"Sure," I say, seeing how bad she looks. "Do you want me to do anything else?"

She hands me an envelope. "Here. Katherine wrote this list for me of the stuff I need from the bunk. Would you please have one of the kids pack a suitcase for me and deliver it to the infirmary?"

I nod. "Want me to walk you back?"

"No thanks. I just had to get out for a minute before I went stir crazy."

She leaves, and I give Betsy the list so she can get Corrine's stuff.

Lunchtime.

It starts to rain. Oh no, the dreaded downpour. That's one of the worst things that can happen at camp, having everyone closed in for a long period of time.

Everyone remains in the main house after lunch.

One of the upstairs rooms is set up with arts and crafts supplies.

Another is turned into a rehearsal room for skits practice.

Most of the kids stay on the ground floor, running,

yelling, and joking around.

Someone lets the goats in.

The campers have a great time rounding them up, pretending it's a rodeo.

Once the goats are outside again, we push aside the tables and chairs and set up a kickball game. Ted heads one team and Sally heads the other.

I referee.

The noise level's high. It sounds like a rock concert.

I hope the rain lets up soon.

Heidi comes over. She's wearing an orange hooded rain poncho with the baseball cap on top of it. "I hope this clears up and the sun dries everything out. It'd be awful if carnival had to be postponed. The kids are really looking forward to it."

Ted's team is up to kick and it's his turn.

I watch as he kicks and rounds the bases.

"I'm glad you two got everything straightened out," Heidi says. Then, "I kind of wish I'd met someone here. Oh well, I suppose I could always take Jimmy up on his offer and go look at his newspaper clippings."

"You're kidding," I say.

She grins. "I'm kidding. I'd rather be alone than with someone just to be with someone. If they learn how to clone people, I'd like to have one made from Ted."

I tell her the Bozo the Clone joke.

We laugh.

It's good to have a friend who isn't jealous because you're doing something she's not. I really like Heidi.

Finally the rain stops and we can go outside.

Back to our regular activities.

Then on to dinner. A lot of camp seems to centre around the dining room. I hope I'm not gaining weight. But I don't think so. My clothes still fit, and I'm getting lots of exercise.

Then we have a campfire, only we have to hold it inside, using the dining room fireplace because the ground's still wet from the rain.

A special treat. Hot chocolate with marshmallows. And Somemores, graham cracker sandwiches with melted marshmallows and a piece of chocolate inside. For the kids who don't want sugar, there is a special package of nuts and raisins.

Then it's off to bed.

I'm in charge and nothing's gone wrong. What a relief. I'll be glad when Corrine feels better and comes back. I miss her.

Sleep, then reveille. There's definitely a pattern to camp.

Carnival's to begin just before lunch, a break in the pattern.

Chapter 12

The big field, next to the dining hall, is ready.

The staff's really busy.

We've set the booths up.

The sun, thank goodness, is shining.

Some of the staff is roaming around, making sure the bigger kids don't try to take the rolls of tickets away from the little kids. The tickets have been given out so that the kids can "buy" things. Each kid gets the same amount of tickets with certain categories printed on them. That's to make sure not all of the tickets are used just for one thing—all food . . . or all games . . . or all pony rides.

The camp's really gone all out on this.

There are booths where the kids can paint themselves with body paint. Others where they can batik cloth, do water gun painting; there's even a dunk-the-staff member booth, lots of booths.

I go over to the candy floss machine.

Ted's got the booth right next to mine—toffee apples. I think he swapped with someone to get it.

We're both wearing the T-shirts we bought in Woodstock.

"Ready?" he asks.

I nod. "Corrine explained to me how it works. It

would be just my luck to break a rented machine."

"I'll help." He comes over and puts his arm around my shoulder.

We look at the machine.

"Shouldn't be too hard," I say. Since I've been at camp, I'm not so scared to try out new things.

We turn the machine on, pour sugar and food colouring in, and like magic, spun sugar starts to collect on the sides of the machine.

I grap a paper cone and twirl it around the machine.

Ted turns off the machine while we look at the first cone of candy floss. It's lopsided, but it'll do.

Ted takes a bite out of it and then gives me a kiss.

"Sticky lips," I say.

He grins.

Ellen comes over. "Traitor. How can you two work at these things? Candy floss and toffee apples. I'm going to put up a sign telling kids to boycott this junk."

We let her. I'm not sure that she's wrong, but it's going to have to be something each kid decides for himself or herself. Ted goes back to his booth.

Ellen's sign, POISON, with a skull and crossbones, doesn't seem to be stopping a lot of the kids.

They've been let loose and are all running around, with long lines at Ted's and my booths.

Alvin comes running up with his tickets. "I want a candy floss and a jelly apple."

"Don't forget to get a hot dog or hamburger," I say.

"You sound like my mother," he says. "This is camp. Give me a break."

I give him the candy floss and take his ticket.

238

There's a long line.

The candy floss is a real mess to make. How come it always looks so easy when other people make it? The stuff keeps globbing up on the sides of the machine, and I have to keep stopping and scooping all the goop off. I'm covered from head to foot with candy floss.

Ted looks my way. "What a sweet person you are. Sugar and spice and everything nice, that's what little girls . . ."

I walk over to him and cover his face with candy floss. "Sweets for the sweet, you male chauvinist."

Alvin runs up, crying. He shows us his toffee apple. One of Alvin's teeth is attached to it.

I don't think it's the right time to say I told you so.

Sally runs over to me. "Marcy. I'm here to relieve you. It's time for you to go to the dunk-the-counsellor booth."

I look at Alvin.

"It's okay. I can take care of him," Ted says, pulling candy floss off his face and sticking it down my back. "Just remember that the next time you're tempted to call me a male chauvinist."

I give them both a kiss and go take my place on the "dunking board."

It's set up by the pool.

I have to sit down on the diving board, fully clothed.

A target area's set up nearby. If someone throws a ball through the middle of the target, someone behind me pushes me into the water.

Kitty aims and misses. She tries again. Safe. She's got really bad aim.

So does Risa.

And Linda.

Stacey's been practising. She gets the target twice.

I'm pushed into the pool twice.

Soaking wet.

Bobbie aims and gets me.

I'm in the water again.

The water's made the mess from the candy floss even worse.

Alicia, Ginger, and Janie throw together. One ball hits me and the other hits the target.

Down and wet again.

Betsy and Robin miss.

A breather.

Some of the kids from the writing group get me.

"Isn't my time up yet?" I yell.

"Not yet. Our turn." It's Barbara, Carl, and Ted.

"But I thought you were my friends," I say as I go down again.

Finally my time's up and it's Ted's turn.

I get him.

I wave good-bye, go up to the bunk, change, and go back to the candy floss machine.

By the end of the afternoon I'm exhausted and it's not over yet.

The talent show. All of the bunks perform. Then the individual kids perform. Then some of the counsellors. There's a lot of talent at this place.

Then there's a campfire and everyone sings.

By the time we finally sing, "Day is done, gone the sun," it's very late.

We help carry the little kids who've fallen asleep up to the bunks.

The kids crawl into bed.

They're exhausted too.

I do a bed check and then go to sleep.

Camp's three-quarters over.

Next weekend's Visitors' Day.

It's going too fast.

That's the last thing I remember before I fall asleep.

I'm awakened in the morning by Janie.

She hands me a piece of paper with writing on it.

It's from Ginger.

She's run away.

Chapter 13

Ginger's gone.

I read her note over several times. Each time my stomach turns more.

> Dear (ha!) Bunk Five,
>   I'm gone. Who are you going to pick on now? Nobody pays any attention to me anyway. It'll probably be the last day of camp before you even notice I'm gone. I was in your dumb skit even though no one hung out with me at the carnival or sat with me at the campfire.
>
>   I hate you all.
>   *Ginger Simon*

"Did anyone hear or see her leave?" I ask, feeling like my insides are going to erupt out of my body.

The girls crowd into my room.

No one did.

Betsy says, "Marcy, what are we going to do?"

"I don't know. I wish Corrine was here." I'm beginning to feel numb. "I feel so guilty."

"It's not your fault," Helene says.

"It's all our faults," Risa says.

I try to figure out what's best, even though it's hard to think. "Someone get dressed fast and take this note to Barbara and Carl."

"I'll do it," Robin says, taking the note and rushing out.

I jump out of bed. "Everyone get ready. Check out the bathroom and around the cabins. Then meet me in the dining room."

I throw on clothes and rush to the dining room, remembering how I said I was going to help her and then pretty much ignored her.

By the time I get there, Barbara and Carl are waiting by the bell.

"I'm sorry," I say. "I didn't know she was this upset. It's all my fault. I should have listened to her."

"Let's worry about whose fault this is after we find her. When did she leave? Did she take her clothes or anything with her? Does anyone have an idea of what she could be wearing?" Carl is holding the note.

"I don't know." I look down at the ground.

Robin offers to go back to the bunk to check out Ginger's clothes. She runs back up to the bunk.

A lot of people are arriving for breakfast.

Soon everyone knows what's happening.

Jimmy walks up. "The other day Arnie was taking Polaroid pictures by the pool. I think he's got one or two with Ginger. Maybe that'll help if we have to call the police."

The police. Oh no. This is really serious. What if something terrible happens to her? What if she falls down and gets killed? I'd never be able to look at myself in the mirror again.

"Let's stay calm," Barbara says. "It won't help if we look upset. That'll only make the rest of the kids more upset."

"I'll help search," Jimmy says.

Maybe he's not so bad after all.

Ted comes over. "What can I do?" He puts his arm around my waist.

I stand there thinking about all of the time I spend with Ted. I should have spent some of it with Ginger.

"We can all go inside," Carl says.

Robin reports. Some of Ginger's clothing is gone.

Once everybody goes inside, breakfast is quickly served and the meeting begins.

"Attention," Carl says. "We've got to have silence in order to discuss this."

It quietens down immediately, and Carl asks if Ginger had confided to anyone about running away.

She hadn't.

He explains that running away never solves anything because you take your problems with you.

Barbara tells everyone that the camp activities for the day will revolve around the pool and sports areas. That'll free a lot of staff members to look for Ginger. She calls out the names of the staff who will search.

My name's not on the list.

After everyone goes outside, except for the searchers

who are awaiting instructions, I go up to Barbara.

"Please let me look," I say. "It'll make me feel better."

She shakes her head. "It may make you feel better, but I don't think it's what's best for the rest of the kids in the bunk, Marcy. You'll be more useful here being with them."

I go outside, feeling awful.

Sandy, the counsellor who refused to have Ginger in her bunk, comes up to me. "Marcy, I'm sorry this had to happen. I warned Barbara. Ginger needs more than we can give her."

"But I thought maybe I could reach her." I shake my head. "But I didn't do enough, actually hardly anything. She was nasty whenever I attempted to talk to her."

"Look, you tried. She's really manipulative. She's done just about everything to get attention. This is her latest. I only hope she gets some help before she really hurts herself."

I stare at the ground. "Thanks, that makes me feel a little better. I just hope they find her and she's all right."

I look up to check on the rest of the girls in bunk five. They're all sitting together, under a tree.

Saying good-bye to Sandy, I walk over and join them.

Kitty says, "We should have been nicer to Ginger."

I think about what Sandy just said. "Maybe. But I think none of us could've given her all that she wants or needs. Don't blame yourselves."

"She was getting a little better. She only called me a moron once in a while instead of every few minutes." Ellen arranges rocks in a pile.

"She taught me to swim," Janie cries.

That makes me wonder more about Ginger. She's so hard to figure out.

Alicia shakes her head. "I hope Ginger's okay, but we've got to remember that she's done lots of bad things to us. She started it. How long do we have to turn the other cheek?"

They all start to talk at once.

"She used a lanyard stitch on the laces of my ballet slippers," says Betsy.

"And she licked all of my stamps so the glue's gone and they're hard to use," Ellen says.

"What about the time she told one of the little kids that eating the bark of the tree would help him fly? That kid could've died if the counsellor hadn't pulled him out of the tree."

"I should have listened to her when she wanted to talk," I say.

"One of the goats should've eaten her," Helene says.

"Look, everything will work out," I say to reassure them. "Now, I think it would be a good idea for all of you to take part in some activity. Okay?"

They get up and go over to the basketball court, to play "horse." That's the game where you've got to make the basket the way the person in front does, if the basket's made. Missing means getting a letter. If you keep missing and get all five letters, you're a "horse" and you're out.

I sit on the sidelines, watch the game, and keep hoping Ginger will turn up.

Linda comes over and sits down.

"You out already?" I ask.

"I'm just HO, but I thought I should tell you something. Ginger once bragged she had some extra money hidden—about twenty dollars—that she didn't turn in at the canteen like she was supposed to do."

"Are you sure?"

Linda nods. "Yeah. She showed it to me and bragged that her father sent it to her. She kept it in her baseball mitt."

"Please, Linda, go up and see if it's gone."

"Okay, but you've got to take my turn at basketball."

I nod and go over to play.

Linda rushes back in a few minutes, out of breath. "It's gone. So's the mitt."

"Please go tell Barbara."

"First tell me how many letters I've got now that you took over."

"HORS."

As she runs off, she yells, "Change the game to 'horsie.' I'll be back in a minute."

When she returns, I gladly get out of the game.

Barbara and Corrine come over.

"I know it's too late to apologise, but I want you to know Ginger did try to talk to me a while ago, but I was too involved with other stuff. And then, last morning, she was mad at me, and I don't think I handled it right." I have to confess.

Barbara frowns. "Marcy, I know I told you you didn't have to be perfect, but this time I wish you were. But I'm not sure that anyone could have known what the best way to handle the situation is."

Corrine starts to scratch. "Dumb poison ivy. I could be out there looking for her right now if . . ."

Barbara says, "Half the camp's looking. So are the police. It's okay that you can't search."

"Have you heard any news?" I want to know.

"Carl and Ted just called in. I told them about Ginger's twenty dollars. They're going to check out the bus stops in Woodstock and Kingston."

"If she left here in the middle of the night, she could be long gone to anywhere," Corrine says.

"Well, we've contacted both of her parents. Since they're divorced, she may go to either one of them. They're awaiting further word from us, and they'll let us know if she runs to them. Somehow I doubt it though. I don't think she likes either of them very much." Barbara shakes her head. "I don't think Ginger's had an easy home life."

I'm so nervous. I feel as if my head's going to explode and my stomach hurts all the way to my legs. The only other time I ever felt this bad or felt so helpless was the night my father had the heart attack and the ambulance took him away.

Finally it's lunchtime. Everyone comes in for a quick meal and goes out again.

Still no word.

The crafts teachers bring down rolls of lanyard materials and hooks.

Soon a lot of the kids have put the hooks on trees and are working on the lanyards. It looks like the kids are attached to the trees. I wonder what the kids do with all the lanyards when they get home. Probably they give them to their parents as presents. I can just see an executive going to work with a lanyard and a briefcase.

Maybe it'll become a new fashion fad.

Some of the searchers return to say they've had no luck.

We're in the middle of the woods. I don't know where she could have gone.

More searchers return.

The police check in.

No luck.

It's enough to drive someone crazy.

It's almost dinnertime, and they still haven't found her.

One of the goats comes up and sniffs at my sneaker. Maybe the goats can be trained as police goats, sniff an article of clothing, and find a missing person.

Finally Katherine, who's on phone duty, sends a messenger out to us.

Carl and Ted have called in.

They've found Ginger on the village green at Woodstock.

They're on the way back to camp.

Relief.

Barbara rings the bell to let everyone know.

I start to cry.

So do a few other people.

Now I know how my parents felt the time I was five and got lost at Disney World. I want to hug Ginger. I want to kill her.

But most of all I want to understand why she did it.

Chapter 14

"How about some food? I only had one slice of pizza and a soda all day." Ginger sits on a chair in Carl and Barbara's living room.

Corrine, Carl, Barbara, and I look at each other.

Ginger continues. "My parents paid for my meals. You owe me three."

Barbara says, "And you owe us an explanation."

Ginger looks at her Woodstock purchases.

We all stare at her.

She smiles, says nothing, and continues to take things out of bags.

With the amount of money that she obviously has spent, she couldn't have been planning to take a bus anyplace. I bet she had no intention of staying away longer than for the day.

I could murder her.

Barbara looks ready to explode. "You're very pleased with yourself, aren't you? Well, I've had it. We keep giving you chances and you keep holding out. Don't you realise what could have happened, running away? Hitch-hiking? I don't know what to do anymore."

Ginger says, "I thought you never gave up."

Carl takes Barbara's hand and pats it. "Ginger, do you

want to tell us why you ran away?"

"No." She gives him a wide grin.

He shakes his head. "I wish you would. Then we might be able to help you."

I want Ginger to talk, to explain. It's so hard to understand her.

"Your parents have been called and are on their way up," Barbara tells her.

For the first time Ginger's not smiling. "No. I don't want to see them."

"They're on the way up," Barbara repeats.

"No." Now Ginger's yelling. "I don't want to see them. Call them back and tell them not to come."

"We've got to have a conference with them," Carl says.

Ginger stands up and tries to run out of the room.

Carl stops her.

She kicks him and tries to get away.

He holds on to her.

She kicks and screams for a while and then goes limp and sobs.

Carl lifts her up and sits down on the chair, holding her.

Barbara goes over, stoops down, and strokes her hair.

Ginger continues to sob.

The tears start to stream down my face. I'm not even sure why I'm crying.

Corrine's staring at her mittens, her face still swollen with poison ivy.

No one says anything for a few minutes.

Finally Ginger looks up. "Please don't make me go home with one of my parents. Let me stay."

Carl says, "I don't think we can help you enough."

Ginger looks at me. "It's Marcy's fault. I wanted to talk to her, and she didn't have time."

I feel as though I've been shot through my heart.

Everyone looks at me.

"You should send her home too," Ginger says. "If I have to go, so should she."

I panic. Maybe they will send me home. Maybe I should be sent home. I'm probably the worst counsellor-in-training ever.

Barbara shakes her head. "Ginger, you're still trying to run things your way, blaming everyone else. Marcy's not the only person to talk to, and anyway, I know that she did try to talk to you in the beginning, and you made it impossible."

"She likes everyone else better than me. So does Corrine. So do you. So does everyone." Ginger starts to rock back and forth in Carl's arms.

Carl shakes his head. "You can't treat people the way that you do and expect them to take it."

Ginger continues to cry. "I'll apologise to everyone, tell them I'm sorry. Corrine, I'm sorry that I rubbed wet poison ivy all over your sheets. I won't do it again."

I look at Corrine.

She looks like she could kill Ginger.

Barbara gets up. "I think Corrine and Marcy should go now."

The three of us walk outside.

"I'd strangle that monster if I weren't wearing mittens," Corrine says. "I really hate her."

"She is rather hard to love," Barbara says. "I don't know what to do anymore. I really thought that I could

252

help her, but she's too much for me. I'm going to recommend that her parents get professional help for her."

I think of the counselling that my family got and hope that it works for Ginger too.

I used to think that things were the worst in my family. Now I can really see that other people have problems too.

We all stand in front of the house for a few minutes, saying nothing.

Finally I speak. The suspense is killing me. "Are you going to send me home too?"

Corrine says, "Please don't. Marcy's a really good CIT."

"I know that." Barbara looks at us. "Who died and left Ginger in charge?"

"I was going to try to reach her," I confess. "Then I got all tied up with other things."

"I know." Barbara nods. "Part of camp is your own growth and experience. I'm not sure that any of us are aware of what Ginger's going through. Look, I'd better go back inside and make sure that she and Carl are doing all right."

She returns to her house.

Corrine says, "I'm going back to the infirmary for more Calamine lotion. You'd better go back to the bunk."

I nod and start to go up the hill.

"Marcy." Corrine runs up to me. "I just want you to know that I think you've done a good job but I also want you to think about how much time you've put into getting your own head together and your relationship with Ted and how much time you've spent getting to really know the kids."

"Do you think I've been bad?" I ask.

She shakes her head and smiles. "Not bad. Human. You've really got to stop seeing things as all bad or all good. And you've got to learn that just because someone tells you something that you don't want to hear, doesn't mean that person's out to get you."

I nod. My mother tells me that all the time, especially when I'm angry at something my father's said. Somehow it's different when you hear it from a friend, not a parent.

She says, "We're still friends, right?"

I nod again. "We could even become blood sisters, like the kids did the other day."

"Not till I get rid of this poison ivy. That's all we'd need, to get it into cuts." Corrine smiles.

We wave good-bye.

I think of Ted. I really want to see him, talk to him, have us hold each other.

I also want to see the kids in the bunk, find out how they're doing.

I finally understand what my parents mean when they say that there aren't enough hours in the day. I used to get so jealous when they wanted to spend some time alone together and I wanted to be with them. I think that a day should be at least thirty-five hours long.

I'm beginning to realise that it's like my glasses have been focused inwards on me and not outwards to see the rest of the people in the world. I wonder if my eye doctor can help make me a special pair of glasses so that I can see the right amount inside and outside.

I decide to go back to the cabin and see Ted later. That's what I was hired to do, to be with the kids. I knew when I signed up that it wasn't a nine-to-five job.

There's laughter coming from the bunk.

As I walk in, Linda says, "Marcy, how many counsellors does it take to change a light bulb?"

I sigh, "How many?"

"Only one, but the light bulb really has to want to change."

I laugh.

Ginger. The joke makes me think of her. Maybe that's why Linda told me the joke.

Heidi's with the kids. "If everyone in the United States owns a pink automobile, what would the country be called?"

"A pink carnation."

Groans.

Risa yells, "What's green and hangs from trees?"

No one knows.

She yells again. "Giraffe snot."

People throw pillows at her.

Finally it quietens down.

"So what's happening with Ginger?" Helene asks.

Everyone's staring at me.

"Her parents are coming up to discuss things."

"I hope that they take her home," Betsy says.

Alicia nods. "They'll probably get into another fight like the one they had Visitors' Day."

I remember. Everyone's parents came up and were standing around talking when Mrs. Simon yelled at Mr. Simon for not sending child-support checks. It was absolutely awful.

"I bet neither of them wants to take her home." Alicia makes a face.

Heidi shakes her head. "I know it's been difficult to have Ginger in the bunk, but I think you've all learned something from this."

"Yeah, what a creep she is." That's from Ellen.

Heidi shakes her head. "No, that it's not always easy to get along with everyone but that you should try to understand his or her problems."

"You sound like Barbara," Stacey says.

"That's not a bad thing." I come to her defence. "She only wants what's best for all of us. She doesn't have to be perfect."

"That's what my parents always say when I complain about something. That they are doing their best. But that doesn't stop them from being pains," Janie says.

"Well, they may be pains, but I think you should try to see them as human beings," I say and think of what my parents' reaction would be if they could hear me say that. They'd probably have me write it down, sign it, and get it notarised.

Heidi says, "My parents are always saying, 'How much longer must we be punished for the things we did that we thought were right?' Maybe we should all swap parents for a while and see if it's any different."

The girls talk about that for a while. They decide to write to their parents and tell them about how when camp's over, everyone in bunk five's going home with a different family.

"Are you serious?" I ask.

"No," Risa says. "You're so gullible."

"I kind of thought it would be a good idea." Janie smiles.

"Who should I ask to the Sadie Hawkins' Dance? That's more important right now," Linda says. "I don't want to go with Howard anymore."

I didn't even know that she was going with Howard. That must have been the shortest "going together" in the world.

It's kind of hard to know who's going with whom. At camp all of the kids past a certain age seem to pair up. "Going out" means walking together to meals and sitting together at campfires.

The girls all discuss their choices.

With summer almost over they've really changed, become a group, developed more of their individual personalities. I think that camp's a place to try out new behaviour, see what works, discover who you are in relation to other people. And that is, I'm learning, not just true for campers. It's also true for counsellors. And directors. For everyone.

I'm not sure what's going to happen to Ginger.

Or with Ted and me once camp's over.

Or with my parents when I return home feeling as different as I do.

It's really strange. I don't want camp to ever end and yet I can't wait until I get home to experience new things. It's all kind of funny and sad and joyful and exciting at the same time.

It's kind of like what I've always thought, that my life goes on like a novel with lots of character development. But there is a change. There is a plot.

I can hardly wait for the next chapter.

Can You Sue Your
Parents for Malpractice?

When I teach people, I marry them.
Sylvia Ashton Warner, Teacher

Some days I wanted a divorce.
Paula Danziger

This book is dedicated to all my students, ever, especially:
Lincoln Junior High School, West Orange, N.J. 1977–8

PERIOD 2

Wes Arlein, Jamie Batterman, Marc Begun, Michael Bruno, Renée Feldman, Beverly Fong, Andrew Gaynor, Steven Gerber, Ellen Gordon, Jon Herbst, Traci Husid, Tom Ippolito, Stephen Judd*, Laura Juliano*, Heidi Ladell*, Cathy Lee, Lynne Lenkowsky, Maureen Mason, Scott Nelson, Ilyse Odesky, Patti Russo, Andi Sable*, Michelle Skarbnik, Mitchell Sussis

PERIOD 3 Journalism: *The Lincoln Log*

Linda Baker, Julie Bossie, Laura Fajvan, Elyssa Kolin, Wendy Juliano, David Manspeizer, Vincent Pallito, Abby Sarret, Jay Scharer, Eric Schondorf, Jeanne Senney, Marvin Silverman, Marla Zimring

PERIOD 4

Gail Broad, Judy Bromberg*, Michelle Butensky*, Mark Davis, Ilene Davison, Mitchell Gervis, Linda Grossman, Angie Jones, Adam Kaletsky, Monica Kaszerman*, Bill Kievning, Wendy Kolton*, Laurie Kopp*, Gail Levine, Donna Molinaro, Nancy Nolan*, Pat Phalen, Mike Pitch, Bonnie Quinn, Max Silverman, Dale Sippel, Lauren Weiss

* Also on *The Log*

PERIOD 5

Raymond Beck, Scott Cabe, Danny Distasio, Dianne Hendriksen, Danny J. Kaylor, Kara Luisi, Elaine Mijailidis, Michael Neglio, Jean O'Neil, Sam Rockaway, Todd Ruja, Paul Slivka, Andy Tulli

PERIOD 7

Maria Armenti, Debbie Calimano, Tom Commandeur, Donny Dalgauer, Ronnie DeAngleus, Patti Dugan, George Falus, Pete Feinblatt, Jackie Geswelli, Chuck Helfeld, Jill Henning, Lee Herman, Liz Holstein, Mark Kelly, Lisa Kuhlmann, Michael Parlin, Ed Pringle, Bonnie Raskind, Lisa Renna, Lee Sherwood, Andrea Weisbard, Paula Whittington, Joan Zink

Also Betsy Gaynor, Joci Krasner, Mark Licht, Anthony Picillo, Tommy Popple, Leslie Schwartz, Rusty Wagner, Andy Weinstein, Ian Ziering

And to the Memory of His Principalship, O. Stanley Stonesifer, a truly fine educator and human being.

Chapter 1

"Lauren, why was the skeleton afraid to cross the road?"

I pretend I don't hear Linda.

She keeps talking anyway. "Because he had no guts."

It's hard coping with a ten-year-old sister who wants to be a stand-up comic and treats the family as a captive audience for all her routines. It's especially hard while I'm trying to get over a broken heart.

"Look," I say, "would you please go away? I've got to study my Spanish. There's a quiz tomorrow. I flunked the last one and I've got to get an A on this one, or else."

"Just one more. Please, Lauren, then I promise to go."

I wonder how many other fourteen-year-olds in the world have to deal with a younger sister determined to take her show on the road. It's not that I don't like her, it's just that my mind's on other things right now.

She looks so hurt.

I say, "Oh, OK. But just one more. I really do have to study. You'll see what it's like when you get to ninth grade and have to worry about grades to get into college."

She grins. "Did you hear the one about the rodent who almost drowned and his brother had to give him mouse to mouse resuscitation?"

"Out," I yell. "Enough is enough."

Linda goes, "Da da di da da da," and tap dances out of the room.

I laugh at the dumb joke after she leaves, and shake my head. She's got a right to her dreams. It's just that my mind's on other things right now.

My special elective class, "Law for Children and Young People," is about to start. And I definitely have lots of questions. It's a good thing the school started it just in time for everything I have to ask. The first one's going to be "What are the grounds for justifiable homicide?" Can I kill off one or more of the following: an older sister who gets her own room and ends up with all the beauty genes in the family? A mother who lives in a fantasy world always dreaming about winning the lottery or some big prize so we can all live happily ever after? A mother who's always writing letters and going to tryouts for quiz shows? A father who constantly complains about how hard it is to sell insurance and to support a family in this day and age? Sandy Linwood, who stole my boyfriend because she goes further than I do?

It's absolutely disgusting being fourteen. You've got no rights whatsoever. Your parents get to make all the decisions: Who gets the single bedroom. How much allowance is enough. What time you must come in. Who is a proper friend. What your report card is supposed to look like. And what your parents don't tell you to do, the school does. What section you're in. What's good literature. What courses you have to take to fulfil their requirements. The worst thing is that the more I realize what I want to do, the stricter everyone becomes.

The school started all sorts of new electives this year, based on what teachers want to teach and what they think we want. Last year no one wanted to run for PTA president and when Ms. Corday finally said she'd run, everyone voted for her because she was the only one. She's turned out to be radical, which is great for the kids, since she wants all new things tried out. And the school's always trying to please the PTA, so we got some great things. One of them is "Law for Children and Young People." It's so popular they had to put all the names of students who wanted it into a bowl and pick out thirty names. I got chosen, which is lucky because it's my only chance before I graduate and go over to the high school. And since I've decided to become a lawyer, it's very important to me.

I guess the big tragedy in my life, at the moment, is that Bobby Taylor jilted me for Sandy Linwood. It's hard to lose your first real boyfriend because he wants to do more than you do. Just because he's two years older than I am he said things like what a real child I am, a late bloomer. Can I help it if I've been taught that virginity's important? Can I help it if Bobby prefers Sandy, who probably has "Lust Is a Must" and "Chaste Makes Waste" as mottos? She's a cheerleader. They ought to have rules against cheerleaders doing that sort of stuff. It would serve her right if she had to turn in her pom-poms and megaphone. I just hope that they both get some terrible disease and rot away. It's going to be really hard to ever trust a man again. There's not much chance that I'm ever going to get involved again. It hurts too much. Anyway, there's no one else I'm interested in.

There's a knock on the bedroom door.

"Lauren, O K if I come in?"

"Sure," I yell. Melissa's not so bad for an older sister except that she gets everything, like her own room and no curfews and clothes before they become hand-me-downs. She's also my father's favourite, although he'd deny it and say he cares about all of us equally.

She floats in. Other people walk; not Melissa. She's got a special style.

She sits down on Linda's bed and says, "Think I could borrow your lumber jacket? I'm going to a concert tonight at the college and they're holding it outside in the amphitheatre."

Remembering the plaid poncho she lent me for my first date with Bobby, I say, "Sure."

She says, "Thanks," and starts brushing her hair.

"Melissa, when you go out with Mike, how far do you go?" I ask, trying to sound nonchalant.

"What?" She drops her brush on the floor and looks for it under the bed.

"I said, how far do you and Mike go?" I think that for someone who is nineteen, she's losing her hearing awfully quickly.

"Lauren Allen, that's really none of your business. Do I ever ask how far you go with any of the pimple-faced kids you hang out with?"

Hang out is right. That's all it ever was 'til Bobby. And then it wasn't much. At least he didn't think so.

Personally I think men should be willing to love women for their poetic qualities. And I think the comment about pimples isn't very nice. Ms. Clear Skin shouldn't make fun of people who have a few zits. The only guy I've ever known with skin problems that were major was John Hiller, and he went to the dermatologist and looks fine now.

"When I was your age," Melissa goes on, "I never asked anyone how far they went. So you're just going to have to keep wondering. I have a right to my own life." She sticks out her tongue at me.

I never give up that easily. Future lawyers have to be relentless in their questioning. And even though I've sworn off men, I can always use any information to store away in case I have to defend some women in court cases concerning males. "All those times you say you're staying with Cindy in the dorm, do you really? Come on, you can tell me. I won't be a stoolie."

She laughs. "Cut it out. Ever since you were a baby, you've asked a million questions. You're impossible."

"How else am I supposed to learn?"

"Don't they teach you anything in health class?" She's still brushing her long hair.

"Sure they do." I think about Miss Crawford, not Ms., Miss Crawford, who's about ninety-two and tells us that if we're going to sit on a boy's lap, we should put a telephone book on it first. "But I'd rather hear it from someone who's had field experience, not from someone who says, 'it's a wife's duty.' "

"Crawford always was warped, but she's got tenure

and they can't do anything about her," Melissa says. "Lauren, why don't you do your own fieldwork? Does this have something to do with the breakup with Bobby? Do you want to talk about it?"

It's just too embarrassing, so I say, "OK, you win. Let's change the subject." Sometimes I'm sorry that my best friend, Bonnie, ever fixed me up on a blind date with him.

Melissa puts down the hairbrush. "Are you sure? I know it's impossible to get Mom to talk about sex. With three daughters, you'd think she'd be able to say more than 'We'll discuss this when you decide to get married. Just don't do anything before then.'"

I smile. "That's the line I got when I tried to ask her a question when I was a little kid. Then she told me about the birds and bees. I wanted to hear about humans."

Melissa giggles and puts down her hairbrush. "It's hard at your age. I guess it's always hard, but I think junior high's the worst. It was for me. So if you want to talk, just let me know."

I think about how mad I get at her for getting her own room, more privileges, and more new clothes, and then feel guilty when I see how nice she can be.

I change the subject. It's difficult sharing real feelings with anyone. "My elective begins on Monday. I'm so excited. I got the law course I wanted."

"Matthews is teaching it, right?" she asks.

I nod.

"He's just gorgeous. Practically every female I know had a crush on him when he arrived. I never did get his

270

history class, though. Just used to drool every time I saw him in the hall. You're going to love him."

Fat chance. Men have no place in my life. I've loved and lost and will never love again. The hurt is too much to bear. It just isn't worth it. "Not me. I just plan to learn as much law as I can."

"We'll see." she grins.

I ignore her know-it-all attitude and change the subject. "Where's everyone?"

She says, "Mom and Dad went over to Sears to price a new washing machine."

Thank goodness. When the washing machine broke down and the repairperson told my parents to hold funeral services for it, I was afraid we'd have to do our clothes with a washboard and tub, like in the pioneer times. I was afraid it was going to be like the dishwasher. After Linda accidentally put the liquid detergent in the dishwasher, instead of the regular stuff, and it foamed all over the kitchen, our parents decided it was too expensive to fix. Now we have to take turns with the dishes.

"You and I are here," she says. "That's four so far. And Linda's telling jokes to Gopher."

Now that's a captive audience. My weirdo sister's telling jokes to a dog who's tied up in the cellar due to an unfortunate encounter with a skunk—who won.

She looks around the room. "I can't believe how you and Linda have such different taste. This room looks like it's been split down the middle. Couldn't you have at least agreed on the same bedspreads?"

I look at the room. She's absolutely right but I wanted

271

the bright-orange bedspread and Linda wanted a plaid one and neither of us would give in. So Mom decided to let us each decorate our own side of the room the way we wanted.

"And doesn't it drive you nuts, being such a neat person with Linda such a slob?"

There are books all over the floor on Linda's side . . . and stuffed animals on the floor and clothes on her bed.

"Some people," I say, "are lucky and don't have to share their room with anyone else so they can develop their own sense of style. And do you have any idea what it's like to be in the ninth grade and have to share a room with someone whose idea of a good time is pretending that her Ken doll is taking her Barbie doll out for a pizza?"

She keeps brushing her hair. I watch and am jealous of her long frosted hair. My mother says I can't bleach my hair until college. Doomed to a high-school life of turd-brown curls that won't be controlled. And freckles to match. Gross.

"Look, I'm sorry I mentioned it. If I had my choice, you know I'd move into the dorm immediately and you could take my room. But as we are told constantly, Dad can't afford it and he makes too much for me to get financial aid, so I'm stuck commuting to a state college while all my friends get to go out of state. Think I'm happy about that?"

I stand up on the bed. "Well, I'm going to law school. He's had to pay for braces for you and they're going to get them for Linda. He should put the money he saved on my straight teeth into a special college fund just for me so that some day I can be a super lawyer." I jump up and down on my bed. "I plan to preserve truth and justice and the democratic process—to help the poor, the maltreated, the innocent." Then I do a forward flip on the bed and land on my back.

She laughs. "You're crazy, but then that seems to run in this family. I think I'm the only sane one."

Sane. Sure. I consider reminding her of the time people asked her to run for homecoming queen of the high school. She said no and then tried to get a write-in campaign to make Gopher the queen. Her slogan was: "Elect a real dog. Beauty is only skin deep and these contests are sexist, anyway." Mary Anne Lothrop beat Gopher out by only about ten points. And Melissa thinks she's cornered the market on family sanity.

I stare at the ceiling. "Why couldn't we have been born rich instead of middle class?"

"It could have been worse. But that would be nice. Then Mom wouldn't always be dreaming of winning prizes. If only Dad didn't think it's awful for women with a family to work, then maybe she could go to work and not be so bored."

Gopher bounds in and jumps on my bed. I guess he had to escape from listening to Linda's monologues, or someone took pity and untied him. The dumb mutt smells like a combination of Eau de Skunk and tomato juice. He starts to lick my face. Grossness.

Melissa holds her nose and says, "Mike's picking me up in a few minutes. OK if I take the jacket out of the closet?"

"Sure." I fend off Gopher with a pillow.

She gets up to leave. "And if you ever want to talk about what happened between you and Bobby, maybe I can help."

"Not unless you want to be an accomplice to the murder of a sixteen-year-old creep," I say, trying to sit up with our monster of a German shepherd jumping all over me.

She shakes her head.

I watch her leave and start to say something. Gopher licks me in the mouth. Yeech!

I lie down on my bed and stare at the ceiling again. When the new elective starts, I'm going to find out if it's possible to sue Sandy Linwood for alienation of affection.

Chapter 2

The weekend at last.

Linda and I are alone in the kitchen. My parents, after much discussion and comparison shopping, have gone back to Sears to buy the washing machine.

My turn to clear the table and wash the breakfast dishes. Linda dries and puts away. Only she's too short, so I end up putting the stuff into the cabinets. Life just isn't fair. Everyone should have equal responsibility. But no. Melissa's out. Dad says that as breadwinner, his job is finished once the groceries are paid for. Mom says that once the meal is cooked and on the table, she's done. It's just not fair. Fourteen and fated to a life of dishpan hands. I wish Linda had never messed up the dishwasher. So does she, now that we're stuck with this job. I tried to explain to Mom, but all she did was go out and buy a new detergent supposed to keep hands youthful. How kind, how thoughtful. What ever happened to child labour laws? Minimum wage? That's why I'm going to become a lawyer to see that kids get an even break.

"Lauren?" Linda says.

"Yes?" I wonder why people don't just keep talking once they've said the name.

"Did you hear the one about the guy who only works on Saturdays and Sundays because he's a candle trimmer and they only work on wick ends?"

"Linda, cut that one from your act. That's awful," I say, trying to get a glass clean.

She smiles and dries a saucer.

"Lauren."

"Not another one. Please. I can't take it."

"No, this time I want to ask you something." She blows a very large bubble. She can do that because she always puts the whole pack in her mouth at once.

I'm tempted to smash it all over her face. Not to be mean. Just because it's there.

"This is important to me," she says.

There's bubble gum on her lips from where she's popped it inward.

She stays quiet for a few minutes and then very softly she says, "How old were you when you stopped wearing a vest?"

I want to laugh, but I remember how wearing a vest was once the grossest thing in the world for me. So I say, "For my eleventh birthday, Mom bought me a training bra."

She giggles. "Like a training bicycle, with wheels for extra support?"

I can't help laughing now. "Kind of. Keeps you on balance, psychologically. Listen, why don't you talk to Mom, tell her you want a bra?"

"I did. She said to wait 'til something starts happening or until I'm eleven, whichever comes first. But that's not for nine whole months and Judy's mother just bought her one."

It's tough when your friends start developing first, even though I remember how weird my friend Bonnie felt when she was the first one in the class to wear a bra. I guess there's no way of winning. "Don't worry. It'll happen to you."

"Every day I check under my arms to see if hair's growing. Nothing. I'm probably going to be in the Guinness Book of Records. Latest developer in the world." She looks absolutely miserable.

I want to hug her but my hands are covered with dish suds. "Lin, honey, you know what? I bet I still have my training bra someplace. I was going to bronze it like Mom did with our baby shoes but I decided that they probably wouldn't bronze padding. After we get done here, we'll go look for it."

"You're the best sister in the whole world!"

I look at her and wonder if she'll remember that the next time we have a fight about the room. Being a sister is not always the easiest thing in the world, but sometimes it's pretty good. Especially when you know it's so hard to trust people in the outside world. Especially heartbreakers.

She's smiling. "Lauren, do you know what the best medicine is for a pig with a sprained ankle?"

Oh, no. The kid never lets up.

"Oinkment. And when is a pig like ink?" she asks. "When it's in the pen," she answers herself, and then takes a bow even though no one's clapping.

I accidentally drop the Brillo pad into the soapy water

277

and have to find it, so I can ignore her.

"How can you tell there's been an elephant in your refrigerator?"

"By the footprints on the jelly," I say. "Linda, come on. Cut it out."

She dries a glass. "What's yellow, has four wheels, and lies on its back?"

She's got me on that one.

"A dead school bus."

"My turn. Whose initials are L.A. and will not be given my training bra if she doesn't quit driving me nuts?"

"Don't you think I'm funny?" she asks.

I think about it. "Sometimes. But sometimes it gets on my nerves."

"Oh, O K. but I have to practise. What am I going to do if some big entertainer gets sick and they need a last-minute replacement?"

"How are they going to know to call you?"

She smiles. "I wrote to all the big nightclubs and television shows telling them I'm available."

It really must run in our family. My mother's always writing letters, asking to be put on some big quiz show, and they always write back and tell her that she's on a long waiting list.

"We'll worry about that later. Now let's finish up and go look for the training bra. Then Bonnie and I are going shopping."

While we're finishing up, I think about Bobby and how much he hurt me. I wish there were a novocaine to numb my heart. That's why I'm never going to love again. You get hurt and don't get over it. I'm glad that I learned this in the ninth grade so that I won't ever go through it again. I'll just devote myself to law. I just hope that some day Bobby realizes what he gave up. I may not be that great, but Sandy's no bargain. It takes all her brain power just to remember the cheers and cartwheel at the same time.

We go upstairs.

I look in my mirror. Five feet four inches. Same long dull brown frizzy hair. Greenish-blue eyes. Probably the best thing about me. Freckles. Too many of them. An OK body, could probably lose about five pounds.

I think about what Linda's going through at her age and what she's got ahead. Maybe she'll be lucky like Melissa: able to get over heartbreaks and go out and find someone as nice as Mike. Maybe she'll be like me and never get over it. It's a rough road ahead.

I turn to Linda and say, "Come on, Munchkin. Let's look for the bra. I think it's in a shoe box."

That's where we find it, under my bed. With only one closet for two people, there's never enough room. The shoe box has the bra, a dried-out corsage from my eighth-grade dance, a broken guitar string rumoured to have once been used by a Beatle, and a six-foot-long chain made up of Juicy Fruit wrappers.

Linda jumps up and down, grabs the bra out of my hands, and rushes into the closet, shutting the door behind her.

"What are you doing?" I yell. "You've never got dressed in a closet before."

Her muffled voice comes through the closet door:

"Yeah, but I never had to put on a bra. It's different with vests."

She emerges holding her T-shirt in front of her from the waist up.

"Come on, let's see," I say.

She blushes and drops the shirt.

I loosen the straps so that the bra's not so close to her chin.

"It's fine," I say.

She puts her T-shirt back on. "Are you sure?"

She throws back her shoulders and looks at the mirror. There's a grin on her face. "I have to call Judy to tell her I got a bra, too. Thanks. I just hope she doesn't get her period first."

She starts to walk out the door.

We can hear my mother coming up the steps, yelling, "We're home. Where is everyone?"

Linda throws herself on the bed, chest down.

My mother comes in. "Well, we got one. At the price of washing machines, I'm not sure gold wouldn't be cheaper. I just wish I had got on a quiz show so we wouldn't have had to spend all that money ourselves."

She starts to straighten up the clothes on Linda's side of the room. "Come on, Lin, get up and give me a hand."

"Can't I just lie here for a few minutes? You don't have to do that, Mom. I'll do it when you go downstairs."

At first I can't figure what the problem is. Then I catch on. The training bra. Mom said no and Linda got one anyway. I wonder if I'm going to be in trouble, the party of the second part, helping the party of the first part, or something like that. I wonder whether giving her the bra is legal. Oh well, it's important to her.

My mother says, "Get up, now. What's going on?"

"Look, Mom, I'll help her clean up. You don't have to."

"Now I know something's going on here. A mother always knows. Lauren, you never offer to help her clean up. You just complain about it."

Linda sits up, with her shoulders rounded.

"So that's it. Do you have a bra on? Did you get it from Lauren or buy it while we were out? You know I told you to wait."

Linda starts to cry. "But everyone in the whole world has one but me . . . and Michelle Haley."

Michelle Haley lives next to us and is six years old. I think Linda's carrying this a little too far.

My mother walks over to her and says, "Stand up straight, Linda Allen."

Linda does.

"Well," my mother says, "I don't like the fact that you disobeyed me, but I guess this is very important to you, so all right. But I don't like it. You don't need it, first of all. And second, I guess I don't like to see my baby growing up."

"It's O K, Mom. I'm still not all grown up."

My mother sighs. "I feel like I always stay the same but my girls are constantly changing. You wearing a bra. Melissa's stopped wearing one. I guess that's part of the deal when you're a mother. At least it is for me."

I think of my friends' mothers and how that's true for

some of them and different for others.

"And what about you, Lauren? Is there anything new that I should know about you?" she asks.

I shake my head.

She says, "Would you girls like to do something after lunch? Your father's watching the football game on T.V. How about going shopping with me, to the supermarket?"

"Sorry, I've already promised Bonnie I'll go to the shopping centre with her," I say.

"I'll go with you, Mom," Linda says. "But first let me call Judy."

My mother nods and heads for the door. "I'll meet you downstairs."

As she leaves, Linda says, "I guess she's not as mad as I thought she would be. At least she didn't kill me. Do you think Dad will?"

I think back. "No, he'll just pretend he doesn't notice. That's what he did with Melissa and me."

She giggles. "Then I guess I made it. Wait 'til I tell Judy."

She goes out to make her phone call.

I lie down on my bed and think about how important all that used to be. Sometimes I wonder if there's ever going to be a time when there aren't things to worry about.

Chapter 3

Allowance. Saturday ritual. My father hands it to me as if he were giving away a million dollars.

I have to interrupt his precious football game to ask him for it.

He's sitting in his chair, the chair in which no one else can sit when he's around. He's drinking a can of beer, eating a hamburger, and watching two teams of grown men carrying a stupid ball, trying to break each other's bodies. I hate it. It's so awful. And Sandy Linwood cheers for stuff like that.

"What do you want, Lauren? Can't you see that I'm busy?"

"I just want my allowance. Please." I feel as if I have to beg for it, even though I do work around the house. Maybe I should do what Beverly Wells does, get a paper route. Then I won't have to ask him for the money. But I'd still have to help around the house. And if I had a paper route and it rained, I'd have to be outside and my hair would get even frizzier. So I guess there's just no way out.

I'm lucky. He's into the game, so he just says, "Don't spend it foolishly. You know how hard it is for me to earn it and to keep this family going."

I'm very lucky. Usually I get a much longer lecture, about how prices are inflated, how high the family dental bills are, how ungrateful children are.

I take the money and say, "Thanks."

He turns back to the game.

With this money and the rest that I've saved up, Bonnie and I can go ahead with our plan.

I grab some lunch, go back upstairs and call her. "Hi, it's me. All set?"

She says, "Sure."

I say, "Are you sure you want to go through with this? My parents are going to kill me when they see it. And you know how I hate the sight of blood."

"Don't weasel out of this one. Don't even try," she says. "You promised. We've talked about this for years."

"But what if I faint?"

"Look, you're only going to get your ears pierced, not have your appendix taken out." She laughs.

"But your mother won't kill you. My father once said he thought it was a barbaric practice. And I know he'll kill me for spending the money."

She sighs. "Well, if you don't want to get it done at the jeweller's, Marla said she'd do it for us. She did Andrea's and the holes are only a little lopsided."

The thought of a needle and an ice cube are more than I can bear. I give in. "We'll go to the jeweller's. You only live once."

"How soon can you get over here?" she wants to know.

"Ten minutes."

"See you then and, Lauren, don't worry. If you faint, I'll pick you up."

I go into the bedroom and look at myself in the mirror. I stare at my naked earlobes for the last time. Then I think of Jill Renna, who has two sets of holes and has lived to tell about it.

I think of all the excuses I can give my father. That it'll be cheaper because then I won't lose earrings anymore. That Bonnie gave it to me as an early birthday present and I gave it to her as a late birthday present. Maybe that'll work.

I sneak out of the house. No need to, but it'll be good practice for sneaking back in with my pierced earlobes.

My father's still got the television on. As I close the door, he yells, "Don't slam it. Do you think you live in a barn?"

By the time I get to Bonnie's, I know I'm going to be the first person in history to die of complications caused by ear piercing.

Ms. Alda's at the door, in her tennis outfit and her fur coat. Bonnie's mother definitely has a style of her own. She's also got a licence plate with her name on it.

"Have fun with your ear piercing, Lauren." She grins.

"Thanks, and have a nice time," I yell as she gets into her Mercedes.

She waves and drives off.

Even though Bonnie's my best friend, I get jealous sometimes because she's got so much money. I happen to live in the poorer section of the rich side of town. Some

285

days, it seems like everyone has more than I do. People get to go on these great vacations and I just bet no one else gets as much grief as I do about how much I spend. I wonder if Melissa ever felt as strongly about it as I do, but I hate to ask her. She feels bad enough about having to go to a state college. She thinks that most state colleges rot.

Bonnie comes to the door. She's carrying her favourite stuffed animal, Moose. Moose was given to her by an old boyfriend. While she can't stand the guy anymore, she still has this thing for Moose. Being an only child does that to people sometimes.

"Hi, you ready?" I say, secretly hoping that since our phone call, she's contracted some minor disease that will keep her from leaving the house.

"In a minute. Just have to put on my boots." She pushes her fringe out of her face.

I come inside.

She yells from her room, "Come on in. Follow me."

I do and sit down on her bed. It's a giant room, with two closets. All for one person. I always want to ask if she'll trade Moose for one of my sisters, but somehow I don't think she would.

I lie down on her bed and watch as she puts on her boots. "Do you think it's going to hurt much? You know how I am about needles."

"We've been through this before. They use a machine like a hole puncher. It's real fast. Everyone says you don't feel a thing. You've just got to remember to keep using the peroxide so that it doesn't get infected. It's a breeze."

I stare at her ceiling. It's so high, and I love the mobile

286

hanging from it.

"O K, ready or not, here we go." She's putting on her coat.

I debate throwing myself on her mercy and begging that we just go to a movie instead, but decide against it. I really do want to have my ears pierced. And the worst thing that can happen is that my parents will kill me. I guess I can live through that.

I get off the bed and start out the door with Bonnie.

We catch a bus to the shopping centre.

The mall is an absolute zoo of people. It's almost impossible to get through the crowd even without the craft fair that's going on in the middle of everything. I stop at a table with handcrafted jewellery and think about how soon I'll be able to wear all the earrings that I like— the unusual kind. Well, not all, because they're not cheap, but some of them.

"Come on." Bonnie grabs my hand and pulls me to the front of the jewellery store.

I stare at all the stuff in the window, trying to stall for time.

She pulls me inside.

Maybe I should faint before I get it done. That way they can do it while I'm unconscious.

We go into the store.

"May I help you, girls?"

"We're here to get our ears pierced," Bonnie says.

The woman nods. "We do free ear piercing, as long as you purchase a set of gold earrings. They're over here." She leads us to a counter.

So many to choose from. They're beautiful. I just hope that the ones I choose aren't much more than ten dollars or I'll have to spend my milk money for the week.

Bonnie picks out a pair of plain, small gold balls.

I pick out ones that the lady says are Florentine and cost ten dollars, plus tax. So far so good.

Then she takes us to the man behind the counter and tells him that we're going to have our ears pierced.

He takes us to a room in the back of the store. There's a door, a back exit. I guess that's where they take the bodies when they make mistakes.

"Now, who wants to go first?" he asks.

I step forward. I've got to get it over with before I have a heart attack.

He sits me down on a stool. I close my eyes and try to think of pleasant things, like school being called off because of snow.

He makes me open up my eyes so I can check to see if he's putting the hole where I want it.

I nod and look at the thing he's got in his hand. It does look like a hole puncher, only with a spike in it.

I close my eyes again and count to ten. I feel the thing go in and then I say, "Is it over?"

He hums and says, "The earring's even in. Now that wasn't so bad, was it?" and does the other side.

A snap. I get up and Bonnie walks slowly over and sits down on the stool.

I'm so busy looking at my ears that I don't even watch him do hers. At least not until I hear him say, "Put your head between your legs and sit there for a while. The dizziness will go away in a few minutes."

I turn around and see that Bonnie's incredibly pale. I walk over to her and hold on to her shoulders. "Are you OK?"

She says, "Just a little dizzy."

The man comes over and breaks something in front of her and puts it by her nose. "Smelling salts. You'll be all right in no time. I haven't lost a customer yet."

Bonnie's head comes up quickly. "Wow. Yeech! I'm OK now. No more of that."

We pay for the earrings and walk out of the store.

"Lauren," she says, "if you ever tell anyone that I almost passed out, I'm going to kill you."

"I promise. But don't forget how you made fun of me for being scared."

She giggles and apologizes.

I keep staring into store windows, trying to get my reflection so that I can see the earrings.

As we're about to go into a coffee shop for soda, this guy comes up to her. It's the new kid I've seen in the halls.

"Hi, Bonnie. How are you?"

"Oh, hi Zack. Fine. And you?"

He nods and looks at me. He's got a wonderful smile. Bonnie says, "Zack, this is my friend, Lauren Allen. Lauren, Zack Davids. His mother and mine went to high school together. He just moved here from California at the end of last marking period."

I say, "Nice to meet you. I've seen you in the halls."

Zack says, "I already know who you are."

Before I have a chance to ask how, Bonnie says, "We

289

just got our ears pierced. Do you like them?"

What a spot to put him in. Why does she always do stuff like that?

He looks at our ears and says, "Fantastic. I really like the blood that's gushing down your left earlobe, Bonnie."

Quickly she opens her purse and pulls out a mirror.

"Got ya," Zack says.

He and I both laugh.

He's very cute. He's got sandy brown hair, dimples, great cheekbones. I'm an absolute nut about cheekbones. Bobby has great cheekbones. Bobby. Men. I remember my vow never to be interested in one again and look away.

"Well," Zack says, "I've got to run an errand for my mother. Lauren, it was nice meeting you in person." He takes off.

I say, "Bonnie, do you think he's seen me in the halls? Is that what he means?"

She shrugs. "I don't know. He's awfully nice, though. Our mothers had us meet one day when he first moved here. He's only in eighth grade though, so I didn't want to hang around with him."

In our school, it's living death for a ninth-grade girl to be seen with an eighth-grade guy. People just don't do it.

We go in and have a soda.

Bonnie continues to talk. "His older brother's away at college. Zack and his mother moved here after his parents got a divorce. My mother and Ms. Davids were once really close. They've become friends again. Since they're both divorced, they go to some of the same places."

290

Divorce. It seems like everyone I know has parents who have split up. Some kids even have a real father and a couple of stepfathers. And one mother and a couple of stepmothers. Melissa says it's like some kind of suburban virus and that she wants to make sure it never happens to her. I guess even though things aren't always wonderful at home, at least it's good my parents stay together and try to work it out.

Bonnie says, "Hey, you seem a million miles away. What are you thinking about?"

"I don't know. Divorce. Cheekbones."

She laughs. "You and those cheekbones. Zack does have a nice face, doesn't he. He's cute. An eighth grader, but cute. Look, Lauren, aren't you over Bobby yet? Why don't I fix you up with someone again? Dave's got a lot of nice friends."

Yeah. And Bobby's one of them. Ever since Bonnie and Dave have been going out, she's been after me to go out with his friends so we can double. Well, I did it with Bobby and I'm not going to do it again.

"Thanks, but no thanks," I say. "Let's finish our Cokes and go home. The waitress keeps looking at us like she wants to fill this table with people who are going to have more than Cokes."

Waitresses never seem to like kids. Not when there aren't parents around to leave big tips.

We finish up and catch the bus back.

I sit there quietly and try to imagine what it's going to be like when I come into the house with pierced ears.

My father will probably cut off my allowance and tell

me how barbaric it is. I'll tell him I think football's really barbaric and we'll have a major fight.

Linda will want me to help her get hers done. Put a training bra on the kid and she thinks she's ready for anything.

Melissa will like them. If she's ever around to see them.

My mother will try to maintain the peace and tell me privately that it looks nice but that I shouldn't do things that upset my father.

By the time we get to Bonnie's house, her mother has returned from the tennis lesson. She keeps telling us how wonderful we look and then goes upstairs.

"She really is nice," I say.

Bonnie nods.

Ms. Alda comes back downstairs. "Here's a present for each of you." She holds out two sets of loops. They're just beautiful.

"Bonnie, your pair once belonged to your grandmother, your father's mother."

"They're gorgeous," Bonnie gushes.

Her mother nods. "I'll probably give you most of her jewellery. I really don't feel comfortable wearing it since the divorce. But I know that your father and she would be pleased for you to have them."

Bonnie's parents still get along even if they aren't together. Her mother and stepmother even get along. It certainly does seem strange to me.

"And the pair for you, Lauren, I bought with my first paycheck after the divorce. My first purchase on my own for the first time in years. I used to call them my

292

independence earrings. I'd like you to have them."

Not just any pair of earrings. A special pair. For me.

I lean over to Ms. Alda, give her a kiss, and say, "Thank you."

She smiles and says, "Whenever you want to do something very brave, wear those earrings. I used to do that and it helped me through some rough spots. That's why I want you to have them."

I think about that. What a wonderful idea. What a very nice thing. She knows a lot about my family life. I bet that's why she did it. Now when I put them in, I can think about independence and that there's someone out there who understands my need for it.

By the time I leave Bonnie's house, it's almost time for me to be home to set the table. I'm nervous, knowing that I'm going to be killed. Maybe my long hair will hide them forever. But if they don't find out right away, I'll have to stay scared until they do find out. I'll be the first person on my block with pierced ears and a nervous disorder. So maybe it's better to get it over with as soon as possible.

I walk into my house. Linda and my parents are sitting down in the kitchen.

"Guess what?" Linda yells. "Mom got a letter. She's going to be on a quiz show. She made it through the interviews. The one you like. The one where you can win up to twenty-five thousand dollars."

I sit down, making sure my hair is covering my ears. "That's wonderful. When?"

My mother says, "They'll be taping it in two weeks. Then it'll be on in about a month. Isn't that exciting?"

I nod. "That's wonderful."

"Wonderful," my father says sarcastically. "A chance to look ridiculous in front of millions of people. Folks are going to think I can't take care of my own family without sending my wife on one of those dumb shows."

My mother makes a face at him. "Well, Jack, maybe I'll do badly and only get a consolation prize. Would that make you happy?" She sighs. "I just don't understand why you think this is so awful. It'll be fun for me, something different. Even if I lose. But I'm going to try to win. If I did, we could do so much with the money. Send the girls to college. Go on a trip."

"You'll have to go yourself. I want nothing to do with whatever you win. We'll take a trip with my money, from my salary." He storms out of the room.

Linda says, "Why's he so angry? I think it's just great."

My mother shrugs. "He's just in a bad mood. He'll get over it. Why don't you two set the table? I'm going upstairs and rest for a while."

Linda and I get the dishes on the table.

"Did you hear the joke about the bed?" she asks. "No? Well, it hasn't been made yet."

It figures she'd think that one was funny. Hers hasn't been made in two months.

I decide to change the subject. "Hey, Linda. Guess what I did. But you've got to promise not to tell Mom and Dad."

She immediately comes over to where I'm standing. "Promise."

"I got my ears pierced." I lift up my hair and show her.

294

"Oh, wow, do you think I can get mine done too?"

Just then my father walks in and looks at us.

I drop the hair down, back over my ears.

Too late.

He starts yelling. "I thought I told you not to do that. Doesn't anyone ever listen to me any more? How much did that cost you, young lady?"

I yell, "I paid for it out of my own money. I can do whatever I want with it. I have my rights."

"Don't you yell at me in my own house. I won't have it. When you start to pay rent here, you can do whatever you want. Until then, I'm still the boss."

The same argument. "That's it," I yell back. "I've had it. I know what I'm going to do. I'm going to sue you for malpractice, because you're such a lousy father."

My mother rushes in. "Can't I get any rest around here? What is it this time?"

My father and I both start yelling again at the same time.

He tells her how I never listen, how he told me not to get my ears pierced.

I scream that I never get to do anything I want to—not without a fight.

My mother says, "Both of you calm down. Really, there's absolutely nothing wrong with Lauren getting her ears pierced. Everyone's doing it."

My father shakes his head. "It's not right. You always side with the girls. I'm sick of it."

Sick of it. He should look at himself.

I run upstairs, leaving them to the fight that's

beginning.

I lie down on the bed and think about it all. Can you sue your parents for malpractice? I'm sure going to find out when the new course starts on Monday.

Chapter 4

I check my earlobes out to make sure that they're not infected. I must have cleaned them out at least eighteen million times in the past two days.

I wish I could clean up the mess at my house. All the fighting is driving me nuts.

I haven't said a word to my father since the fight. I'm waiting to find out what my rights are in the new law course.

Morning announcement over the loudspeaker. "Will all teachers please check their phones. If they don't work, call the office immediately."

I look at Bonnie, and we crack up.

The bell rings.

Everyone rushes into the hall, past Ms. Lawrence, who is frantically trying to communicate with the front office on her defective phone.

Past Mr. Baxter and Ms. Daniels, who always look ready to hide out in the supply closet. Rumour is that he left his wife for her. And they always think kids don't know anything.

"Do you believe that idiot announcement?" Bonnie asks. She touches her fringe to make sure it's hanging down in her eyes.

"Typical," I say.

Finnegan, the Faculty Freak, is patrolling the halls, as usual. He takes hall duty very seriously. "OK, girls, move it," he bellows. He acts as if God personally directed him to get students to class on time.

As usual, we ignore him and go on in to biology class. My worst subject. It's a terrible way to start the day.

Erik Marks is standing at the door, pretending to look at his notebook. He's got this tremendous crush on Bonnie, but she prefers older men.

"Hi," Erik says and smiles. A rubber band from his braces shoots out of his mouth.

It's tough not to laugh, but he's a nice guy so I don't. Poor Erik. The same thing happened last year during his bar mitzvah. I hope his parents own stock in a rubber company.

We stand at the lab table.

Ms. Solomon passes out the frogs.

I want to puke.

I hate dissecting.

I hate frogs.

I hate the smell of formaldehyde.

I hate Ms. Solomon for screwing up my average.

Last marking period it was worms. Gross. Some of the boys used to put the spare parts in girls' pocketbooks.

"Now, class." Ms. Solomon raps on her desk with a pointer. "We've graduated to frogs. Isn't that exciting?"

No, I think. The only thing I'd like to dissect is Sandy Linwood. Her brain is probably smaller than the frog's.

"Put on your aprons now." She smiles.

I put on my puke-green lab apron. Robots. That's what we are. Robots.

Ms. Solomon comes over to our table, plops down a frog, and says, "I'm going to have to split the two of you up if you don't stop socializing this term."

It's kind of weird to wonder what a biology teacher who is obsessed with dissecting means when she talks about splitting you up.

I think to myself, "Big deal. Can I help it if guidance makes me take this because I'm college prep?" But I just stand there trying to look good.

She moves to the next table.

Some day she's going to be sorry. She'll have this awful lawsuit brought against her by the Frog Lovers of America and she'll need a good lawyer. She'll come to me begging forgiveness. I'll remind her of the C that she gave me and turn her down. She'll beg. Weep. Kiss my feet. But I won't change my mind. They'll put her in jail for life.

Bonnie interrupts my thoughts. "Let's name him Ferdinand."

I nod. It's as good a name as any. Ferdinand the Frog. Last marking period the worm was Winifred.

Ms. Solomon says, "Now quietly copy down the diagram on the board."

I whisper to Bonnie, "Got an extra pen? Forgot mine."

Ms. Solomon says, "Lauren, detention for talking. I warned you."

I say, "But I just asked for a pen to . . ."

She marks it down in the special book where she keeps track of offenders.

I mumble, "It's not fair."

"Two days detention." She smiles and makes another mark in her book.

I want to scream but I know she'll make it three.

Erik sneaks me a pen. He whispers, "Here, keep it."

Ms. Solomon doesn't give him detention. She thinks he's wonderful because he wants to be a doctor and has this fantastic brain. The type that always ruins the curve on a test. It's a good thing that he's nice. I'm grateful for the pen.

I look at the pen. It has some writing on it:

Brush Your Teeth
Wear Your Elastics
Wear Your Headgear
HAPPY HOLIDAYS
from your
FRIENDLY ORTHODONTIST

No wonder he doesn't want it any more.

Bonnie and I examine our frog.

Slime.

Disgust.

It's got beady eyes.

I hate it.

I only hope I don't get so sick that I have to go to the nurse and get sent home and miss the law elective.

I make it through the class.

I make it through the day until seventh period. Finally, the elective. I'm so lucky to be in the first group.

I rush off to the class. Bonnie rushes off to yoga. I take a seat right up front. Zack walks in and sits down next to me.

"Hi," he says. "Isn't it great, getting this course?"

I nod and try not to stare at his cheekbones. His eyes aren't bad either. Brown. Why must he be here?

The teacher walks in. Melissa's right. He's gorgeous. Blond hair. Blue eyes. The longest eyelashes I've ever seen on anyone (except Señora Schwartz, our Spanish teacher—and she glues hers on every day). He looks like he could win an Olympic gold medal in dimples.

He opens his mouth. "Welcome, class. I assume we're all here because we want to be. I've asked to teach this course. You've taken it as an elective. The reason that I am so pleased to teach this course is that I have been going to law school at night for several years. If any of you have similar plans to be lawyers, I hope this will help you decide what course to follow. Some of you may be here because you want to know what your rights are. I'll tell you from the beginning that great strides are being made in that direction, but there is still a long way to go. But you will learn things here that will help you to determine your own destiny."

Determine my own destiny. I love it.

He continues. "Laws are constantly changing. You are all going to have to become avid newspaper readers, if you aren't already. That will be an important part of this class. I also want you to know that I don't know everything, that we will all have to do research."

I decided then and there that I will do anything he asks. I think he's wonderful.

He says, "Let's go around the room. Give your name and tell why you took this course. It will help us get acquainted, and I'll learn more about the needs of the class."

A teacher who cares about our needs. I bet he wouldn't make me dissect a frog.

Ed Harmon starts. "I want to know my rights in case I ever get busted. I'm Ed Harmon. I want to know what the drug laws are and how to get around them."

Typical. Ed thinks he's the sharpest person around. I bet he doesn't even smoke grass or anything. He just thinks saying that will make him sound like a Big Shot. Even if he does, I don't think that makes him a big deal. He's so obnoxious hardly anyone can stand him.

A couple more kids speak.

Then it's Zack's turn. "My name is Zachary Davids. My friends call me Zack, but they're back in California. I'm here because I want to find out exactly what rights I have, whether I can go back on my own. I want to know if just because of a divorce, I've got to stay with my mother in New Jersey."

He says "New Jersey" as if it's the armpit of the nation.

I look at Zack while some of the other kids are speaking. Actually, I kind of look sideways so he doesn't know I'm checking him out.

He's chewing on his eraser as he listens to the other kids speak. Sandy brown hair. Brown eyes. Those cheekbones. Blue jeans. A rugby shirt. He looks older than he is.

I think about Bobby and wonder what he's doing over at the high school. Probably making out under the bleachers.

All of a sudden it's my turn. I try to look intelligent to impress Mr. Matthews, and say, "I'm Lauren Allen. I want to be a lawyer and change the world." I decided not to mention malpractice suits right away.

He nods and then the rest of the class do their introductions.

At the end of the period, he says, "There will be a major class project. Either working alone or in groups of no more than three, I want you to specialize in one part of the law affecting children and young people. I also want this class to publish fact sheets informing the entire student body of their rights."

The bell rings.

Zack turns to me and says, "Maybe we can work together on the project."

I start to say no. I mean he's just an eighth grader. Then I think about how he seems so nice and all his friends are back in California, so I say, "I'll think about it."

I rush out to meet Bonnie at her locker.

Later on I see Zack. There are a lot of eighth-grade girls hanging around him.

I guess I shouldn't worry so much about whether he needs friends. He seems to be doing all right.

Detention with Ms. Solomon. I wonder how many years I'd get for slipping some arsenic into her Thermos of coffee.

By the time I get home it's time to set the table again. I feel like I spend half my life setting the table.

My mother's all excited. She's just bought the dress that she's going to wear for the television programme.

"Oh, Lauren. Do you want to take the day off and watch it being filmed? If I win, you can all come running on stage to congratulate me. It'll be the most exciting thing that's happened to me in years." She's smiling. "And you know what? I've been thinking. Maybe I should start substituting in the school system. After all, I did teach before I was married, and I'm sick and tired of being home all the time. Even if I do win all the money, I've got to do something more with myself. I know your father wants me to stay home, but you're all growing up so fast. I realized it the other day when I saw Linda with the training bra. You don't need me so much anymore. You're all growing . . . and I'm not."

"But Mom! Subbing? The kids are animals to subs. And I'll just die if you come to my school."

"You won't die. Your father didn't die when you got your ears pierced. You won't die if I come to your school."

I think about that. Maybe I am being selfish, and she looks so happy with her decision.

"Oh, OK," I say. "But you're going to be sorry. They tear most of the subs to shreds. Once one quit by third period. Just walked out of the building and never came back."

She smiles. "I'll do all right, and if I don't like it, I don't have to do it. But I want to try. Your father and I discussed it last night and that's what we decided. He doesn't like it much, but he realizes how important it is to me. And it'll be good to have more money coming into the house. It'll make your father less anxious."

"I don't want to talk about my father. I'm going to sue him for malpractice. I told him that the other day."

She smiles. "So I heard. Lauren, you've always been such a strange child." She's teasing me now. "Please try to remember we only want the best for you. I bet we can even prove that in court."

"Don't worry," I say. "I'm not really going to do it, sue you I mean. Well, at least not you."

She said, "Knowing your father, he'd probably countersue. Watch it."

"But I'm a model child."

"Trust me. We have evidence, too." She smiles. "Remember the time you filled his pipe with incense? And the time you cut one of his ties in half because you thought it was ugly?"

I remember. I was ten and he was wearing it and I walked up to him in front of company and cut it off at the middle. It was for society's sake that I did it. It was a crime for that tie to be seen in public.

She continues, "And the time you hid play money in the lamp and it caught on fire? And the time you made him feel just awful for running over the doll you left in the driveway?"

"But I didn't mean anything bad."

"The defence rests," she says. "He doesn't either. Try

getting to know him. I'll talk to him again and see if I can get him to lighten up on you. Give him a chance."

Linda walks in.

"Melissa just called," she announces. "She said to tell you that she's staying at the dorm tonight with Cindy to study for an accounting test."

My mother frowns, but doesn't say anything.

Linda says, "If you win a lot of money, will you buy me some joke books?"

My mother hugs her. "Honey, if I win, I'll buy you a good comedy writer."

I hope she wins.

Chapter 5

My mother doesn't win. She comes close but this guy from Hoboken, N.J., does. He's a free-lance writer so I guess he can really use the money, but it would have been nice if Mom had won. Then maybe we could have got the attic fixed up and I could have had my own room. And Linda could've got her comedy writer.

Now my mother's decided to sub for sure. Once she gets her papers in order, she's going to start.

At least I got the day off from school. No frog cutting for the day, and I did have fun thinking about what I'd do if she won. How I'd run up on stage, jump up and down, hugging her and yelling. How some Hollywood producer would be home with a cold, watching the tube, and discover me. But that didn't happen.

My mother did get some consolation prizes. The case of dog food would have been wonderful if Gopher weren't so particular and hadn't refused to eat it. The vacuum cleaner would be OK if we didn't already have one that works, one of the few appliances that does. The year's supply of Pampers is useless to our family. How gross to think of my mother having another kid at this point. With my luck, she'd put it in Linda's and my room.

The other consolation prizes were equally wonderful . . . two cartons of popcorn, and floor wax.

Now I'm back in school, and the day's started off badly.

I cut the frog's heart in half by mistake. When will this unit end?

Lunch was terrible, fish cakes and something masquerading as creamed corn. For dessert there were two pear halves in a paper cup.

By the time I get to law, I'm disgusted.

Zack says hello to me.

I smile at him but not too much. I don't want him to get the wrong idea. Sometimes I look at him and wish that he were in the ninth grade, but then I remember how I've sworn off men so I'm glad he's not.

Mr. Matthews is talking. "I want all of you to be on the lookout for proof that children are or are not granted rights. You should observe what's going on around you and read the newspapers daily. You've all got to be well informed if you are to be certain of your rights."

I think about how I have no right to refuse to work on the frog and wonder if the Supreme Court would rule in my favour. Allen vs. Frogface Solomon.

The class is given some free time to try to come up with some good ideas for the newsletter that we are going to put out.

I work with a group of ninth graders.

Every once in a while I sneak a look over at Zack. He's really excited about the project. His group looks like it's having more fun. The kids in my group, because we're all ninth graders, spend a lot of time trying to impress each other with how much we all know about things like drugs and sex and stuff like that. Half the time I don't think most of the people know what they are talking about.

When the bell rings, I rush out to meet Bonnie. She's going to get her hair trimmed and needs me along for moral support.

She's always sure she's going to ask them to trim off an inch, and they're going to make her look like a Marine.

We walk to the beauty parlour.

Bonnie says, "If it looks like they're going to cut off too much, promise me you'll scream."

I nod.

She always goes through this. Once when she was eight, someone cut off a little too much, and since then she's had this thing about getting her hair cut. It's ridiculous. She's the kind of person who could have her hair messed up and half the kids in the school would rush out and have the same thing done to their hair. That's because, no matter what, Bonnie always looks fantastic.

She says, "If it's even a slight bit too much . . ."

"I promised. You know I will."

She grins. "I know. Look, Lauren, are you over Bobby yet? Dave says he thinks one of his friends would like you. We can fix you up and double."

Fix me up. It sounds like she's going to call in a cosmetic specialist.

"No thanks." I shake my head. "I keep telling you, no. Last time you did that, I ended up with Bobby. Never again."

She looks at me. "He wasn't so terrible. Come on."

Our only major argument. I don't see why my social life is so important to her.

I change the subject. "Mr. Matthews said to be on the lookout for any examples of kids not being allowed certain rights. Can you think of any?"

"You're changing the subject as usual," she says.

I nod.

"Oh, OK. I won't ask you to meet any of Dave's friends, at least not this week." She grins. "I've seen Zack looking at you. I think he's got a crush on you."

"Don't be ridiculous. He's just a nice kid," I say.

She's still grinning. "Sure."

"Look, why do you have to make something out of something that's not real?"

She shrugs.

We near the beauty parlour. She gets that terrified look on her face.

"It'll be OK. Just tell them you only want a trim. I'll watch."

She gets very quiet as we walk in.

They take her immediately. They know her and what a nervous wreck she is until it's over. I watch to make sure she doesn't end up with a crew cut.

I really wish my hair were absolutely straight. Once I even tried to iron it, but it got singed and I ended up smelling like a charred lamb. It's just no use.

I sit there and think about what she's just said. Maybe I should go out with one of Dave's friends. That way if Zack does have a crush on me, he'll know it's no use. I really don't want to hurt his feelings. He seems so nice.

Bonnie's hair looks perfect, as usual.

We leave.

"Want to go for a soda?"

I shake my head. "Got to get home. Mom said she was going over to the Board of Education to register to sub."

"She's really going to do it?" Bonnie groans. "Couldn't you talk her out of it?"

I shake my head. "It's going to be gross. I know I'm going to die if she ever subs for one of my teachers."

"Didn't you tell her what the kids did to Ms. Koster?"

Ms. Koster gave the kids an assignment and someone set fire to the garbage can. Then the next class turned all the desks upside down when she stepped out of the room. When she came back they pretended nothing was unusual. By the time she got to her study hall, she was just about finished off. When they started to chant, she went nuts. She just sat there and cried for the rest of the day. Finally, they sent her home and had regular teachers cover the classes.

I nod. "I tried to tell her but she says she wants to try."

"Maybe if she'd won the quiz show, this wouldn't have happened. She'd stay at home and not sub."

"Don't think so. She's going crazy at home. I think she'd do this anyway."

"I hope she survives." Bonnie tends toward the dramatic sometimes.

"Me too. Look, we've got to rush. I promised to set the table."

We do rush. But by the time we split up and I go into

the house, my mother's already there.

The table's already set.

"Mom, I'm sorry I'm late."

She says. "So am I. What's going to happen when I go to work? You are all going to have to pitch in and help more."

I nod. There's not much I can say. When I know I'm wrong, I find it best to just keep quiet about it.

She says, "You can finish up. There will be only four of us. Melissa's staying at school again to study. Only pour the iced tea for the four of us. Your father should be home any minute, so get a move on."

"Where's Linda?"

"Upstairs practising something for a variety show her class is putting on. She set the table before she went up."

Guilt. I always end up feeling such guilt when my mother is calm and doesn't yell when I do something wrong. She's got a way of doing that. Maybe it's something that comes to mothers easily . . . being able to make their kids feel awful without raising their voices.

I try to change the subject. "Isn't Melissa going to be around any more? I never get to see her."

My mother looks at me. "Melissa's an adult now. She's got to lead her own life. Anyway, college is different She's got a lot more work to do. And I don't want you to bring up that subject in front of your father. You know how upset he gets about it."

I agree.

My father comes home. He's in a pretty good mood. Insurance sales were good today. That makes him happy.

312

We get through the meal without a fight. The only time it's a little uncomfortable is when my mother talks about going to the Board office. But my father says something about how the whole thing's a passing fancy.

Linda tells four new jokes—bad ones.

After dinner I clear the table, do the dishes to atone for not setting the table.

Then I go to my room to think about Bobby. It's not that I miss him so much. It's just that sometimes it's nice to know that someone cares especially for you, someone who's not your family. I guess I wish there were someone like that for me, someone I was sure wouldn't hurt me.

The phone rings. It's Melissa.

"Lauren. Hi, how are you? Listen, tell Mom that there's someone on the phone. Don't let Dad know it's me. He'll only get on the phone and yell at me for not coming home for dinner."

I say, "Sure," and get my mother. I tell her to come upstairs. She does without asking why. I guess she'd heard the phone ringing and figures out what's going on.

I wish I were more sure of what's happening. When Melissa and I were really young, we fought a lot, but when we got older, we got closer. Now that she's been going out with Mike, she seems really distant. I think sometimes I'm jealous of him. She never used to act this way with any of her other boyfriends, but now that she's at college, she's different.

I try not to eavesdrop while my mother's out in the hall talking to Melissa. Sometimes I think my mother likes Melissa better than me.

313

She talks for a while and then goes back downstairs.

I was kind of hoping she'd come in and tell me what's going on. No such luck.

The phone rings again. This time I don't even get up.

Linda calls in, "Lauren. For you. A boy."

I go out. "Who?" What if it's Bobby, all kinds of sorry for what he did? If it is, I'm just going to hang up on him.

She shrugs and goes into our room. I bet she'll eavesdrop.

I pick up the phone. "Hello."

"Hi, Lauren. It's Zack."

Zack.

He says, "Hi, you still there?"

"Sure. What's happening?" I feel like an idiot, not sure of what to say. Why do I feel so dumb? He's only an eighth grader. Why do I feel so shy?

He says, "I've been thinking about the project Mr. Matthews assigned. I plan to do it on child abuse and want to know if you would too. I mean, when we discussed it in class, you said some good things and I figured we could do a good job on it together. It's a lot of work and I know you do well and take the class as seriously as I do."

I listen. He sounds older then he is. Older, more mature than most of the kids in my grade.

He says, "So what do you think?"

I don't know. "Let me think about it. I'll let you know tomorrow. That sounds like a good subject to me, but I'm not sure."

"Oh, O K." He sounds very disappointed.

"I promise. I'll let you know tomorrow."

We talk for another minute and then hang up.

I go back into my room and think about it. If we work together, I'm sure we'll both get A's. We're the best students in the class. We do both care about the subject. Also, our library's not that big and if we're both taking books out, there may not be enough to go around. Decisions. I also think about what Bonnie said about Zack having a crush on me. That makes me nervous. But he's a nice kid and I do like being around him. It doesn't have to be romantic. We can just be friends. Maybe I should work with him. Who knows? Why can't life be less confusing?

I lie down on the bed and try to think things out. Maybe I should call Bonnie and ask her to lend me Moose. Sometimes I think it's easier to talk to stuffed animals. They never hurt your feelings or confuse you.

Chapter 6

I've made my decision. I'm going to work on the project with Zack. It's silly to worry so much. It's just a project.

Next period's law. I'll tell him then.

I sit at my desk and think about Melissa. I wish she were around to talk to about all these things. I guess she and Mike are doing O K, that she's not afraid of getting hurt. I wonder why I turned out this way.

I can't even just have fun. I always have to worry and wait for disaster to strike.

The bell rings.

I go up to class. Zack's waiting outside the door. When he sees me, he grins.

I feel so glad to see him that I almost decide we shouldn't work on the project. That's how dumb I am, how scared.

"Well?" he asks.

I nod.

"Great." He smiles.

I smile back. Why can't I say anything?

We go inside.

Mr. Matthews is standing there talking to Ms. Richmond, the home ec. teacher. Bonnie found out they go

316

together. I guess that's all right. She's really nice and he's too old for me.

After she leaves, Zack and I go up to him.

"Lauren and I are working together," Zack says. "We're going to do our project on child abuse."

Ed Harmon's standing nearby. "Yeah: And they're going to take some little kid, beat him up and bring him into class to talk about how it feels."

"That's not funny. You're an idiot," Zack says.

"Why don't you go back to California and wait for the earthquake? Or wouldn't your father keep you? And who do you think you are, trying to make it with a freshman? You're just a punk kid."

The next thing I see is Zack taking a swing at him.

Ed punches him in the stomach.

Mr. Matthews moves in to separate them, but Ed keeps swinging. He hits Matthews in the face.

Zack punches Ed in the stomach.

Somebody runs to the phone and calls the office.

Ed takes another swing at Zack.

It's all happening so fast. I don't know what to do.

Ian Tomlin's holding on to Ed.

Zack's being held by Mr. Matthews.

"I don't want to see anything like this ever happen in my class again. We have to try to work things out without being physical. Now I want the two of you to calm down." Mr. Matthews' nose is bleeding a little.

The Vice-Principal, Mr. O'Brien, barges in yelling. That's the way he always handles situations. "What's going on in here? I demand an explanation."

317

Ed yells, "He started it. He hit me," and points to Zack.

"Wrong," Mr. Matthews says. "He didn't start it. You did, with your comments."

Ed says, "It's a free country. I have the right to free speech. He doesn't have the right to assault me."

Mr. O'Brien's yelling again. "You two are going to be suspended."

Guilty without hearing the story. It doesn't seem fair.

Mr. Matthews says, "I think that once you hear the extenuating circumstances, you may want to review the punishment for both. Zack was provoked."

Mr. O'Brien says, "You teach your classes. I'll handle the discipline."

"But . . ."

"All right, you boys, march right down to the office."

After they leave, everyone just stands there for a minute.

I hand Mr. Matthews a tissue and say, "Your nose is bleeding."

He says, "Thanks. Look, everyone, take your seats. I'll be back in a minute. Just sit there quietly."

He goes out and we all sit down.

I hate when something like this happens. Some of the kids like it, but I don't. School should be more exciting, but not like this. And I'm upset about Ed's comment about Zack's trying to make it with a freshman.

When Mr. Matthews comes back, I raise my hand.

"Yes, Lauren?"

"I don't think it's fair that Zack's going to get in

trouble. Ed asked for it."

"Ed was just talking. It was Zack who started the slugging." That's from Ed's friend, John Miller.

"Ed's the one who hit you," Laurie Wilson tells Mr. Matthews.

"It's not fair," I call out. "Mr. O'Brien didn't listen to the facts. Isn't there any justice in this school?"

Mr. Matthews sits on his desk. "O K, now settle down, everyone. Let's discuss this calmly, rationally."

That's one of the things I like about him. Most teachers would've told us to just take out our books and work quietly, pretending that nothing had happened.

Instead we get into a discussion about rules, why they are necessary and how to be fair about the punishment. Also about whether students have any rights in school or whether the administration can make all the decisions.

I can tell that Mr. Matthews didn't like the way O'Brien handled the situation, but that he's trying not to be unprofessional and tell us that. I sort of wish he would.

We spend the entire period talking about the rules of the school and the problems kids have had: accused of cheating when they didn't, unfair detentions, no say in the food served in the cafeteria, the classes that are required. After we talk about all that, Mr. Matthews has us examine what it would be like to be an administrator or teacher, how we would act. Then we try to make some decisions based on the entire situation.

It's a good class.

I'm sorry that Zack's missing it.

Maybe they'll take into account that it's his first offence

and that Ed's a troublemaker. It's hard to know.

When the bell rings, I get up to leave.

"Lauren." It's Mr. Matthews.

"Yes?"

"When I talk to Zack after school, I'll tell him that you defended him. He's going through a difficult time. I think it's nice that you two are becoming friends."

I guess we are becoming friends, no matter what other people think.

There are a couple of kids standing around the desk, waiting for a chance to talk to him.

I say, "Thank you. See you around." Then I leave.

Bonnie meets me in the hall. "Is it true? Did you really have a fight in your class? Is Zack OK? What about Matthews? I hope they get Ed this time. Nothing like that ever happens in my class. The most excitement we've had was when Roberta Weinstein had trouble getting out of the lotus position and Ms. Sebold had to untangle her."

I nod. "I'd rather see that than what happened in my class. It was awful. I don't even want to talk about it now."

She changes the subject. "I saw David last night. He's got a friend he'd like you to meet.

I shake my head.

She pushes back her fringe. "Come on, Lauren. You can't spend the rest of your life staying at home on Saturday nights."

"Thanks, but no thanks. If I want to do something, I'll let you know. Anyway, there are still parties and things to go to. I don't have to have a date to do things."

320

"Well, OK," she says, "but I know this guy would like you."

"Maybe some day," I say, to keep her from bugging me.

I wonder what's happening with Zack.

By the time I get home, it's late and I have to set the table, as usual. There ought to be a law against one kid getting stuck with all the chores. With Melissa out so much, I have even more stuff to do now and I'm tired of it. I think that I should directly receive the money that the government takes off my parents' income tax as a deduction for me. After all, when I was born, they got a free servant. That's my function in the family, to be the good one. I once decided it was the only way that I was going to get any attention. Now I think it's all taken for granted, and I'm expected to do it all.

Linda's lying down on the kitchen floor, with Gopher on top of her.

"What's going on?" I ask.

"I think he's got a tick on him and I'm trying to get it off. Want to help?" she asks.

"Yaag. I'll go set the table." I debate helping and then bringing in the tick as an extra-credit project for Ms. Solomon but decide against it. It's not going to make any difference. Nothing's going to help in that class. She hates me, and when a teacher hates you, there's no hope.

Linda comes in just as all the dishes are on the table. "Hey, Lauren. Do you have a thumbtack?"

"Well, I have a toe, and now I have a tick." She holds up the wretched thing. "All I need is a tack to complete the game. Get it? Tick, tack, toe?" She falls down on the floor in a fit of hysterical laughter.

I wonder whether they will ever invent a medication that will cure her.

"Do you know what you get when you cross a dog with a hen?" she asks.

I step over her body and say, "Just this one, twerp. No. What do you get when you do that?"

"Pooched eggs." She's banging her fists on the floor and giggling.

"Don't you have any homework? Don't they make you do anything intelligent in fifth grade?"

She looks up at me. "Yeah, in health class today I learned where baby ears of corn come from."

"At last," I say, "schoolwork."

"Yeah, the stalk brings baby ears of corn."

"OUT!" I yell, just as my mother walks in carrying several boxes.

"What did you bring me?" Linda and I both yell at the same time.

She laughs and puts down her bundles. "Amazing as it may seem, nothing. I went to the shopping mall today and they were having a sale on clothes, and I finally decided to buy myself some things." She grins. "For me."

"What did you get?" I ask.

"A couple of pairs of slacks, a dress, and two sweaters. Lingerie. It's been so long since I bought something that I wasn't even sure what size I was. But I found out soon enough. It was great fun."

She starts taking stuff out of the cabinet. A quickie

dinner. Spaghetti. Yeah. I love the way she makes it.

"I think that's great. You haven't bought anything since Melissa graduated from high school."

"And guess what else I did," she says. "I don't even believe I did it. I'm not even sure that I like it. But I think I do."

"What?" The suspense is killing me.

She pulls back her hair. Her ears are pierced.

I don't believe it. "Mom, when? Why? What's Dad going to say?"

She looks at me as if she doesn't believe it either. "I was walking past the store, looked in, thought about yours, and just went into the store. Before I realized it, I'd done it."

I giggle.

"I don't know what your father's going to say, but I don't think he'll divorce me for it. Anyway I decided I really need things for subbing."

My father walks in.

The packages are lying out there.

"What is all of this?" he asks.

"Things I bought to start subbing."

He doesn't look too happy.

"I'm going upstairs to start on my homework. Call me when dinner's ready," I say. I don't want to be around while they discuss this, especially when he discovers that her ears are pierced.

Linda says, "Me too."

Linda and I walk up the steps together.

I remember that I haven't checked my ears for a couple

of days.

I feel them. Oh, no! Lumps!

We go up to our room.

I look in the mirror. The earlobes are infected. How gross.

Peroxide.

Q-tips.

I squeeze the earlobes.

Goop comes out.

It's almost as disgusting as dissecting a frog.

My body is diseased.

I can hear my parents fighting.

Maybe the infection's going to spread to the rest of my body.

I go into the bathroom and put on the stuff that Mom used when my toe was infected.

Maybe I've caught it in time. It might not have spread to my brain yet.

The phone rings. I run to get it.

Linda gets to it first. "And who shall I say is calling?"

She listens for a minute, bats her eyelashes at me, and hands over the phone. "For you. Someone named Zack." She stands there.

I say, "Would you please get the hell out of here? Oh, Zack, I don't mean you." The kid doesn't move. I hate having the phone out in the hall, just because our parents wouldn't choose one room to keep it in.

"Excuse me for a minute," I say to Zack. "LINDA, GET OUT OF HERE!"

Zack says, "Did I pick a bad time to call?"

I laugh. "Around here there's no way of knowing what's going to be a good time. It changes from one second to the next."

"So what's new?" he asks.

Should I tell him that I've turned into a walking pus bomb? That my parents are downstairs arguing? I decide to ask about him instead.

"Not much. What about you? Are you suspended?"

"Yeah. I got one day and three generals."

Generals. That's the big-tie detention where you have to put your hands on the desk in front of you and do nothing for forty minutes but stare ahead at the space in front of you. It's inhuman. Even teachers who you think are nice turn into animals when they have general. You've got to do something really bad or just annoy O'Brien to get it. I got it once and don't ever want it again. Mine was for throwing the piece of worm at Harry Warner, who put it in my purse. O'Brien wouldn't even give me the chance to complain. It was a victimless crime. You have to be human to be a victim, and Harry Warner isn't.

"What did Ed get?"

"A three-day suspension and five generals," he said. "Mr. Matthews came in and defended me, so O'Brien relented a little. Boy, do I hate this school. It's so full of cliques and unfair rules. I wish I had never come here."

I wonder why he's telling me this, and then I realize he probably just wants a friend. That's the other thing I do a lot, be everyone's friend, have them tell me all their problems. It's a little like the way that I do the work around the house. So that people notice me.

"Ed just got me so angry," Zack tells me. "That comment about beating up a little kid and bringing him into the class to talk about it. And then that comment about making it with you—that's none of his business. He's a . . ." There's a pause. "Anyway, I wish I'd really hurt him even though I don't like to fight. He deserved it. But now my mother's really upset because of the fight and she's grounded me. The only way I can get out of the house is for schoolwork, so I told her we were doing a project together and that I promised to go over to your house to work on it. I hope you don't mind, but I'll go nuts stuck in this house all the time."

I debate bringing him into my house and taking all the teasing that will go on. Oh, well, I can live through it. And I know how bad it is to get grounded. I do keep thinking about his saying it's none of Ed's business about making it with me.

"Sure," I say. "Why don't you come over after dinner? Or we can meet at the library."

"Let's do that," he says. "Meet you at the library at six thirty."

"Make it seven." I think of the dishes I'm going to have to do.

By the time I get downstairs, everyone else is already at the table and eating. My parents seem to have worked things out. At least things seem calm.

"Lauren, so who is this Zack?" Linda asks.

I sit down.

Everyone's staring at me.

"You're not planning to elope, are you?" That's from

my father.

I get all set to yell until I see the smile on his face. Sometimes he's got a weird sense of humour. I'm not always sure what he's going to do, yell or make some dumb joke out of it.

"No," I say. "I thought I'd meet him behind the bushes, though."

"Lauren Allen, what way is that for a young lady to talk?" He's losing his sense of humour fast.

"Just kidding, Dad," I say. "Look, he's just a kid from school. We're working on a law project together."

"On suing your parents for malpractice?" my father says.

"No, on child abuse," I answer.

He chokes on a strand of spaghetti.

My mother laughs. "Surely that's not an accusation against us, is it?"

I shake my head. "No, it's just something I've become interested in and so is he."

My father says, "I've never met him, have I?"

Twenty questions time. My father thinks he's got to know everything about every guy who comes to visit or calls. Sometimes it gets embarrassing. Once he asked Bobby how many other girls he had dated and whether he had respect for me. I could have died right then and there. It was awful. Melissa said that it was even worse when she started dating. Maybe that's why I'm so messed up.

"Look, Dad. He's just a kid, an eighth grader."

"One whole year," Linda says. "Big deal. I'm never going to get married."

"We weren't discussing marriage, just child abuse." I debate threatening her with the spaghetti spoon when I notice that she's eating hers with chopsticks. She's cornered the market on weirdness.

She says, "How can you stop a buffalo from charging?"

"Take away his credit cards," my mother answers.

My father turns to her. "You should know that one. Now that you're going back to work, I bet you're going to be spending like mad, living outside my salary."

"Why don't you just accept it and not feel so threatened?" My mother raises her voice. She hardly ever does that.

I can feel the knot in my stomach and I feel like I'm going to jump out of my skin.

"Who feels threatened?" he yells. "That's ridiculous. Just because you won't have to depend on me, need me any more, why should I worry?"

So that's why he's acting this way. He thinks it's the money that makes him important. Sometimes I just don't understand his brain.

"Why can't you ever celebrate anything?" she yells again.

I throw my spoon on the table. That's it. I'm leaving.

Linda follows me out. It's like a revolution. Nothing like this has ever happened before.

I can hear him yell, "See what that job is going to do? It's making me unimportant to them, too."

I grab my coat and say to Linda, "I'm going to the library. Tell *your* parents I'll be back whenever I get

328

done."

Linda nods.

I slam the door on the way out, hoping that the entire house will crumble and that I'll be left an orphan.

As I jog to the library, I wonder what kind of man acts that way. It's a good thing that I don't ever want to get involved. If that's what it's all about, I want no part of it.

Chapter 7

I debate hitching a ride to the library. That would serve them right. I'll probably get kidnapped and hurt and then they'll be sorry that they caused me so much grief. The kidnappers would ask for a lot, though, and my father would say, "Oh, well, we'll just have to let her go. We have two others left, so what's the hassle? I never much liked her with the pierced ears anyway."

I keep on jogging and pass Donny Collins. He waves and calls out, "Hey, Lauren." I wave back and keep on jogging. Donny's the fleabrain who discovered that when you throw a hot paper towel up to the fire detector in the toilets, the fire alarm goes off. One day we had eight alarms and had to go out for each one of them. I caught a cold and my hair frizzed up. The school finally caught him, called his parents, and gave him generals for a month. They also had the fire department prefer charges against him. Then they had to explain to everyone how dangerous and expensive it was. Donny's reformed a little, but now he's known as "Smokey the Bear". He'll never live it down. Once you get a nickname like that around our school, it sticks for life. Or at least until you graduate and go away someplace where no one knows you and hope that no one from your past ever shows up and tells.

In front of the library is a whole bunch of kids I don't know. It's sort of a hangout, because kids tell their parents that they have to go there to work and then they just meet friends. If there's one thing I hate, it's walking past an entire group of unfamiliar kids who hang out with each other. I'm always afraid that they'll make fun of me, call me Frizzhead or something. That's the way some kids get, in a gang. They do things they wouldn't do alone.

As I pass them, I look straight ahead and recite the Gettysburg Address silently to myself. That way I look as if I don't even notice them. Having no eye contact is important in cases like this.

I make it. Inside the library. Safe in a place filled with books. And I'm even in luck. My favourite librarian, Ms. Jensen, is on duty. She's been helping me pick books since I was five.

I check the place out. No Zack. But I am really early on account of having left the house before dinner was over. Maybe they'll make Linda do the dishes alone. Then they'll see how much I really do.

"Hi, Lauren Allen. How are you tonight? Read any good books lately?" Ms. Jensen always says that and she always smiles.

"No," I say, "I've decided to be a functional illiterate when I grow up."

"A noble ambition," she says. "But I doubt that. Not you. Not with your brains."

Ms. Jensen deserves an A in Librarianship. She not only

331

knows her books, she knows how to make people feel good.

"And how's your family? I mean to ask Linda but she's always got her head buried in a joke book."

"My mother's going to work as a substitute," I tell her.

"How exciting." She stamps someone else's book choices, smiles at her, and says, "Enjoy them. See you soon."

"Mom bought some new clothes and had her ears pierced. I got mine done too, first."

She grins.

"My father's acting flippy about the whole thing," I say, not wanting to get too personal but wanting to talk to someone about it. "I just don't understand why."

She nods. "People get that way sometimes when things change. He'll survive, though. My husband did when I went back to work, when the kids all were in school. Now Mr. Jensen likes having the extra money and I have a job that I really love. So you see, it worked out well for us."

"I hope it works out OK for them," I say, playing with a lock of hair.

"I hope so too," she says. "Now, what are you here for? Anything special? May I help?"

"A friend and I are doing a law paper on child abuse. Where can I find the information?"

"Family relations, psychology, sociology, and law. Surely you know where those are?" She never lets me get away with not finding things on my own. Once she told me that she thinks it's more fun to check out the catalogue and wander among the stacks so that you have a chance to discover things. I still try to take the lazy way out, but she never lets me. She's always willing to help with recommendations though. I think it's turned into a game over the years.

I go to the card catalogue. Might as well do some of the preliminary research so that when Zack gets here, we can get started.

"Lauren," Ms. Jensen calls out. "We just got a new joke book in. Why don't you take it home to Linda?"

I look at her and cross my eyes. "I won't contribute to the delinquency of a minor. Do I have to?"

She laughs. "I think she's funny. Come on, admit it. You do too. With your sense of humour, you must."

My sense of humour. I guess she's right. I do have some good points on my own. With all the strong personalities in my family, I sometimes feel like a nothing. But I guess I do have some things going for me. I'm glad Ms. Jensen's there to remind me.

"Oh, O K. I hope they're better than her last set of jokes. She could drive me up a tree."

She says, "I'll leave it here and you can check it out with your books."

While I'm going through the card catalogue, I feel someone tug on my hair.

It's Zack. "I thought you were going to be later."

"Family problems," I say. "Had to make my escape."

He nods. "I know that one well. In California, I used to have to escape all the time. Now it's only sometimes."

I say, "There's not too much in here. Where else should we look?"

333

He says, "I got some books out of the school library already, and we can look in some of the real law books for sections on child abuse. Don't worry. We'll find stuff—and Matthews saw me after school at my locker and says he'll give us an extension since we can't work on it while I'm sitting in the generals."

We go to the study section of the library and sit down at one of the tables.

I pore over some of the books. There are some interesting cases. It's sad though to realize that some kids are so damaged by their own parents. Physically. Not like the stuff that goes on in my house.

I look up and there are Bobby and Sandy, walking arm in arm. I want to die. Vanish. But I can't show it.

Instead I move closer to Zack and show him an article.

Bobby looks over and sees me. He doesn't look any more comfortable than I feel.

I'm not sure I'm going to survive this, but I'll never let Bobby know how I feel. Actually I'm not even sure how I feel.

I keep talking to Zack, but have trouble not looking at them.

They sit down at the empty table near us. Sandy takes out a compact and puts on lipstick. When she looks up, she notices me, gives me a dirty look, then puts her hand on Bobby's shoulder.

I turn to Zack and say, "Do me a favour. Act like we go out."

He says, "Here?"

"Don't do anything extreme. Just act like it's more than

working on a term project. I'll explain later."

He leans closer to me and bites my earlobe, right near my pierced ear. I hope he doesn't get infected. Then he whispers, "Do you think I should get down on my knees and propose?"

I laugh.

He continues to whisper. "Is there anything else you would like me to do? I'm beginning to enjoy this."

"You're only in the eighth grade. You're not supposed to," I whisper in his ear.

He puts his arm around my shoulder and says, "I'm from California. We start earlier there."

That's it. I can't stop laughing. All of a sudden, I don't even care if Bobby's watching or not. Zack's crazy and I love it.

"We'd better get out of here before we disturb everyone else. Come on, we'll check out these books and come back tomorrow for more."

I nod. Out of the corner of my eye, I can see that Bobby's still staring at me and Sandy's poking him in the arm.

Zack and I get up. He grabs some of the books with one hand and holds my hand with the other.

We get to the checkout desk.

Ms. Jensen says, "Oh, it was Zack you were waiting for. How nice."

I blush.

So does he. But he doesn't stop holding my hand.

I wonder if there's any spaghetti sauce dried out on my hand.

When we get outside, past the crowd of kids, I say, "It's all right. You don't have to do this any more."

He smiles. "Do I have a choice?"

I look at him. "Yeah, I guess you do. That means I do also."

He shrugs. "Women's liberation. That's fine with me. Especially if you don't let go."

I keep my hand in his.

I guess that answers his question.

"Look," I say, "I want you to know what that was all about. My old boyfriend was there with his new girlfriend and I . . ."

"Yeah, I know. Bobby and Sandy. A good lawyer always finds out all the facts beforehand." He grins.

I stop short.

"But you're in the eighth grade and I'm in the ninth."

He says, "That kind of junk doesn't matter any more. Don't you want to go out with me?"

I think about it. Maybe I do. But what will everyone say? Even Bonnie will think it's weird.

It doesn't have to be anything serious. And I kind of like Zack. Who knows? For a person who planned never to go out again, this is awfully confusing.

"Let me think about it," I say.

"OK. Is hand holding off limits until the verdict comes in?" Zack says.

"I guess not," I say, not sure what I feel. "Listen, do you normally go home this way? Do you live near me?"

He says, "Not too far. About five blocks. I told you. A good lawyer always does preliminary research."

336

"Who have you been talking to?"

"And never reveals his, or her, sources," he says. "I plead the Fifth Amendment."

We walk along. It feels kind of comfortable being with him, sort of relaxed and friendly.

"There's something I want you to know about me," he says.

"Yes?"

"I don't want you to think I get into fights a lot." He looks nervous. "It was just that comment about child abuse and beating up a little kid."

We stop.

He lets go of my hand and stands there biting his lip. "Well, it's just that . . ."

I wait for him to continue.

"It's just that my parents got a divorce because my father used to do that to my brother and me all the time. That's why we moved so far away. He's not allowed to see us any more. That's what the judge ruled." He looks like he's going to cry. "My mother thought we'd be better off here where she grew up."

I don't know what to say.

He continues. "So when Ed made that crack, I just belted him without thinking about it. I hate to hit people. I just wanted you to know about my family. But please don't tell anyone else."

I promise and grab his hand. I don't know what else to say so I just hold on.

And I think I have it tough. There are so many people with problems you never know about. It's depressing.

Especially to have it happen to someone you know and like.

We walk back to my house.

"Zack, there's something I've been wanting to ask you."

"What?" he says. "Ask me anything."

"Anything?" All of a sudden there's so much to choose from. I decide to stick to the original question. "Remember when you said you already knew about me?"

He nods.

"Well, how did you? Was it my charm, wit and stunning appearance?" I pretend to model.

He grins. "No, actually it was books."

"Books?"

"Yeah, books. I moved here during a vacation and didn't know people. So I spent most of my time reading books from the library. Almost every book I picked out had your name in it. Same with the school library. I figured we probably had the same interests. So I checked up on you a little. If I hadn't run into you and Bonnie that day, I would have met you some other way."

Books. I can't believe it. Books.

"You do have all the other things you mentioned," he says. "But I do wish you'd change one thing, though."

I wonder what it is. He must have discovered that I'm really a jerk or that I pick my toenails.

I wait for him to go on.

He says nothing, but smiles.

The suspense is killing me.

He's not going to say anything unless I ask.

"Well," I yell. "What is it?"

I stop, close my eyes, and wait to hear the worst.

"I wish you'd read a little faster. There are a couple of books I put on reserve that you have out."

I look at his grinning face.

The library. Ms. Jensen. That's how he found out so much about me. I bet she's got this secret hobby of matching people up by the type of books they read. Just wait 'til I see her.

We get to my house too soon. I wish we could have talked more.

"Look," I say. "Next time I'll invite you in but I don't think it's a good idea this time."

Zack says, "I'll talk to you tomorrow. Good luck with your parents."

He leans over and gives me a fast kiss.

He's going down the street almost before I realize what's happened.

I go into the kitchen, feeling confused.

Melissa's home. How unusual. She usually comes in way after my bedtime or says she's staying at the dorm. She and my parents are sitting at the table, having coffee and looking very serious.

I run up to her and hug her. I want to talk to her about so many things.

My father says, "Lauren, I want you to go up to your room immediately. We're in the middle of a discussion. I don't want to see you until I tell you you may come out. And then when you do, I plan to talk to you about your actions at the dinner table tonight."

I look at my mother. She's been crying.

Melissa hugs me and says, "I'll talk to you later, Lauren."

I leave. Once his majesty, my father, has spoken, that's it.

Linda'a sitting on her bed, playing with her Barbie and Ken dolls.

I don't believe the positions she's put them in.

"Lin, what are you doing?"

She looks startled and separates them.

Maybe she does think about something besides lousy jokes. But I don't remember ever doing that with my dolls.

She says, "They make you come upstairs too?"

I nod. "What's it all about?"

"I'm not supposed to know, but when Melissa came in tonight, I heard her talking to Mom first."

"About what? What's going on? Is there a problem?" I ask.

"She's going to move in with Mike. Why did Daddy get so angry? On television they do that all the time."

Melissa's moving in with Mike. What am I going to do? Who am I going to talk to about Zack? What are they going to do with her room? Who am I going to switch clothes with? Is Melissa doing the right thing? Sometimes I feel like I'm part of a soap opera, only it's the real thing.

Now I know why Mom likes quiz shows and not soap operas. With quiz shows, you know right away whether you're a winner or loser. Once it's over, it's over. It doesn't work that way with things about real everyday life.

I think I like quiz shows better too.

I lie down on my bed. Will Melissa really leave home and live with Mike? Will Lauren go out with Zack and have to put up with the remarks from other kids? What will their father do? Will the Ken doll get the Barbie doll in trouble? Will my father forget to yell at me for running out of the house? Tune in for the next episode.

I bet the answers won't be easy.

Chapter 8

It's official. Melissa's moved out. She left a week ago. She and Mike came by today, Sunday, to pick up her stuff.

We weren't even allowed to stay in the house when they came over. My parents took Linda and me to some dumb movie. When we got back, I went into Melissa's room. It looks like a ghost town.

There's a note on the bureau for me. From Melissa.

> Lauren:
>
> I just want you to know that I love you very much and am sorry it's got to be this way. I don't want to get married until I'm sure it's going to be a good thing. I don't want to end up in a marriage like Mom's got. Please come visit Mike and me as soon as we get settled. Just call and we'll make arrangements. Know that I'll always be around if you need me.
>
> Love,
> Melissa

* * *

I look at it for a few minutes and try to memorize the phone number she's written on the bottom.

342

There's also a note for Linda.

Linda comes into the room and I hand it to her and walk out. I figure she may want to be alone when she reads it. It's awful knowing that my father can get away with acting like this.

I don't even know what's going on in my mother's head. She looks like she's been crying but she hasn't said much, anything as a matter of fact. The whole time we were out she didn't say anything to anyone.

My father said enough for both of them though.

I hate him.

First I put Melissa's note in the shoe box under my bed and then I go downstairs to get a soda.

He's sitting at the table reading the paper as if nothing's happened. My mother's peeling carrots and slicing them as if she's chopping off their heads.

My father says, "Lauren, I don't want you to end up like your sister. In my day, a girl who moved in with someone would be called a tramp. I hope you realize that I have to do what I'm doing so that your sister doesn't set a bad example for you and Linda."

I want to kill him. I want to scream out that what about how Melissa's always making the honour roll, about all the volunteer work she's always done, about what a nice person she is. But I don't say a word. Neither does my mother, who's now tearing a head of lettuce to shreds.

It's a good thing he's never seen Linda play with her dolls.

He continues, "Perhaps if she and Mike decide to marry, things will be different."

My mother mumbles something to herself. I can't hear it.

I don't see what difference one dumb ceremony and a piece of paper are going to make. I think of all the people who do marry and end up divorced. Would he rather that happen to Melissa?

I go upstairs. I know if I stay there we'll get into a gigantic fight.

I'm afraid to even bring Zack into the house. With the names my father's calling Mike, I don't think he's ever going to want to see another male visitor in this house.

My parents should have had only boys. Better yet, they should never have got married; then I wouldn't have had to go through this.

My father said he's going to make Melissa's room into a study. The only good thing that could have come out of this is that I could have had my own room—the only good thing. And then he says that. My mother said we should leave the room the way it is, that Melissa should be able to come back if things don't work out.

Now my parents aren't speaking to each other.

This house is a terrible place to be. I go to sleep.

When I wake up, it's morning. Time to go to school. It'll be better than being home.

I think it will. But I'm not sure what's going to happen once people figure out that Zack and I are hanging around together. Maybe they'll think we're just friends. But I don't even know if that's all we are.

I haven't even got up enough nerve to talk to Bonnie about it, and she's my best friend.

344

I check out my earlobes. They're better but not good enough to put in the earrings that Ms. Alda gave me, the independence ones. I hope they get better fast. I'm going to need all the help I can get. In another week I should be able to put them in.

I sneak out of the house without even having breakfast and go over to Bonnie's.

We walk to school. On the way, Bonnie says, "Lauren, Dave said that Bobby saw you at the library with some guy last week. He asked Dave who he was. Dave didn't know, so he asked me. How come I don't know?"

This is it. Faster than I thought. I was so sure I'd have more time to think about it. "It's Zack. We're doing a law project together."

Bonnie frowns. "Dave told me that Bobby said you acted like you were going out with him."

I don't say anything. We're almost at school.

Bonnie says, "Lauren, you just can't go out with Zack. Everyone's going to think you're some kind of creep who can't do any better than an eighth grader. Come on, I can fix you up with someone else."

I turn to her. "Look, I don't need to be fixed up with anyone else. Sometimes you act like I could never get a boyfriend without your help. And I think Zack is nicer than anyone else I know. I don't even know if I am going out with him. I just know that I like being with him. Is that such a crime?"

"At this school it is," she says. "Nobody but a creep would go out with someone younger."

I turn to her. I've had it. Her attitude. My father's

345

attitude. It's all getting to me.

"So now I'm a creep. If that's what you think, we don't have to be friends any more. I know how you'd feel hanging around with someone who's a creep."

I storm off and go to my locker.

I want to cry.

My best friend. If she feels this way, what's it going to be like with everyone else?

Word spreads fast in our school.

Go to the library once with someone, walk down the halls, and people have you practically engaged.

Mindy Donner comes over. "Hi, Lauren. I hear you're robbing the cradle these days."

I turn around and look at her.

She's smirking.

I walk past her without saying a word and go into homeroom.

Bonnie's already in there, talking to someone else as if I don't exist.

If that's the way it's going to be, that's OK with me, I think.

But it's not really OK. She is, was, my best friend. What am I going to do? In a few days, my sister moves out and I lose my best friend. And to top it all off, people say I'm robbing the cradle. That makes me nervous. Mindy's got a whole group of friends who follow whatever she does. When she's nasty to someone, they all are. And here I am, with Melissa gone and my best friend not talking to me. All because of Zack and I'm not even sure of how I feel about him. What if he and I don't end up friends? I'm

346

not going to have anyone, not anyone who's real important to me.

The bell rings. Biology. Wonderful. Bonnie's my lab
partner, and we aren't even talking to each other.

We get to the class, put on our lab aprons and go to our
table. Silence. Then Bonnie whispers, "You don't have to
be so touchy."

"You called me a creep."

Ms. Solomon says "That does it. The two of you have
detention for whispering. Now, I'm splitting the two of
you up. Bonnie, you will work with Mitchell, Lauren,
you with Erik."

Erik comes over to my table.

Bonnie goes over to Mitchell's.

Great. Now Erik is going to find out that he's got a frog
mutilator for a partner and that I'll probably mess up his
work. Then he'll hate me too. I hate Biology. All these
weeks on one dumb frog—and all those charts she makes
us do in class—when will it ever end?

I want to take the dissecting instrument and plunge it
into my heart.

Instead, I just stand there and watch Erik Marks,
F.M.D., Future Medical Doctor, start working on
Ferdinand.

He looks at me and says, "What did the two of you do
to the frog? It looks like you could be arrested for
frogslaughter."

"It was dead when we got it. I plead the Fifth."

He grins at me.

Ms. Solomon comes over. "What seems to be the

problem?"

Erik says, "No problem. But do you think we could have another frog?"

She nods. "I knew you would disapprove of this work. I put you at this table to make sure that Lauren learns something."

She goes to get another frog.

Erik whispers, "I hope you don't mind. I don't want to get you in trouble. It's just that this frog would be impossible to work with and I really do want to do this right. If I'm going to be a brain surgeon, I've got to start somewhere."

I nod. "It's O K. With the way my life's been going, this is minor."

Ms. Solomon brings the frog and then goes to check on someone else. It's amazing. She doesn't say a word when Erik and I talk, just when Bonnie and I did.

"Do you mean all that talk about you going out with Zack?" Erik asks.

"How do you know already?" I can't believe it.

"It was the homeroom topic for the day. Look, most of the kids in this school act like morons. Zack's in the chess club. He's nice," Erik says.

I vow never to make fun of rubber bands popping out of Erik's mouth. We work on the frog. This time I can actually see the different parts of the frog before they're all sliced up.

When the bell rings, I walk out before Bonnie has a chance to call me a creep again.

Someone comes up to me in the hall and puts a hand on

my shoulder. I jump. It's Zack. He's grinning.

I do like him. I really am glad to see him. I look around to see who's watching. Some people are. They are also whispering.

Zack notices too, because he says, "Lauren, how about tucking me into my cradle?"

I look at him. He's grinning and acting as if he enjoys the whole thing. No wonder. I bet no one's calling him a creep. It makes me laugh though. There are still some people who are trying to listen.

I sigh. "OK, Zack. I'll do it, but I'm getting sick and tired of having to pick up your teddy bear every time you throw it out."

He says, "I promise I'll only throw out the rattle."

I say, "I guess you've been hearing stuff too."

He nods, "Mostly from the eighth-grade girls I didn't pay any attention to. The boys think I'm really something, though." He's grinning.

"Doesn't it bother you?"

"No. Last year, in California, a lot of my friends were older. And anyway, I like you. I don't care about what anyone says."

I think about that. I wish I could be that way. And then I remember how Zack reacted to what Ed said. Maybe it's not as easy as he makes it sound.

Finnegan comes up. "All right, you two. Get to class."

We both rush off.

It's a difficult day. In Spanish class Julia Simpson tells me I must really be hard up for a social life. I turn around and tell her that if she calls going out with Andy Bradford social life, she's in serious trouble.

Bonnie and I don't even sit together at lunch. She's already sitting with someone else, so I go off and sit at a table by myself. I feel like the whole world is staring at me and there's no place to hide. By the time I get to law class, I'm exhausted, just wiped out. Zack sits down and says, "How's it going?"

I shake my head.

Mr. Matthews starts the class. There's no time to talk. We spend the entire period making assignments for the fact sheet. I volunteer to write an editorial about the rights of students who get detention without a fair hearing.

When the bell rings, Zack and I walk out together.

He says, "Want me to walk you home?"

I nod yes, and then I remember. Solomon's detention. "I've got detention. Biology."

"I'll hang around and wait for you. After last week's generals, I'm used to staying late."

He walks me to my locker, then down to biology. I can't believe how many looks we get. Sometimes I wish I went to a really big school where everyone didn't know everyone else's business.

Bonnie and I have to sit there and listen to Ms. Solomon give us a lecture about how we're letting our friendship get in the way of our academic lives. She should only know that we aren't even speaking to each other. Then we have to write a hundred times each, "I will not use biology class time frivolously."

I get done before Bonnie, turn in my paper, and leave. Zack's waiting outside.

350

He says, "Why don't we go over to my house and work on the project? My mother's got a date right after work, so there'll be nobody there to bother us."

I think about what my mother will say about that and decide it doesn't matter. I don't even care what my father thinks, not the way he's treating Melissa.

I nod.

We walk over to his house. It looks smaller than most of the others on the block. I guess that's because there are only two people living there.

Once inside, he's a little nervous all of a sudden. "Listen, can I get you anything? A Coke? An English muffin with peanut butter and jelly on it? That's what I always have when I come home."

"I think I'll just have a Coke. Do you have a special place you want me to hang up my coat . . . or should I keep it on?"

He laughs. "Think you'll feel safe taking your coat off?"

I laugh too. "If that's all I have to take off."

We sit down in the living room after he brings in the Coke and hangs up our coats.

The living room's decorated beautifully. I wonder what his mother looks like, is like, how she'd feel if she knew I was here. So I ask, "How would your mother feel about your entertaining an older woman in the house all alone?"

"She's not going to care," he says. "Look, I don't understand what the big deal is. Some of those kids are so dumb. What's it matter to them what we do? And anyway, one of the guys my mother's dating is two years younger than she is, and no one makes a big deal about it."

"She's not in the ninth grade, with him in the seventh. It's different, maybe, when you get older."

"Look," Zack says. "I haven't had to wear nappies in years. This whole thing is silly. Do you know how to play backgammon?"

I nod. "I thought we were going to work on our project. Do you always lure women to an empty house to play backgammon?"

He grins. "Only the ones who look like they can play it well."

"I play to win."

"That's O K," he says. "So do I. Play to win. It'll be fun."

I jump up. "Where's your phone? I've got to call my mother and tell her I'm going to be late."

"Why don't you stay for dinner? Then we'll have time to work on our project too."

"I'll ask her."

I call. She says that it's O K. I neglect to mention that Zack's mother is out on a date.

We play backgammon for a while. He wins the first game. I win the second. And the third. He doesn't seem upset that I've won, just glad that we both play well. Bobby used to get angry when I did anything better than he did.

Zack makes the dinner: two chicken pot pies and chocolate ice cream for dessert.

During dinner, I tell him all sorts of things I didn't think I could talk about. Like how much I miss Melissa, how mean my father can be, how I hate sharing my room. He's real easy to talk to.

He tells me how much he misses his older brother, how hard it was to move, and how he still loves his father, even though he can't see him. He says it's hard when you love someone and hate him at the same time.

I can understand that.

We clean up the kitchen. There's not much to do when all you've had is chicken pot pies and chocolate ice cream.

Neither of us mentions the way some people act because we're together. I feel sort of funny bringing it up again.

"Lauren, all my books and my desk to work on, all that stuff's up in my room. Do you want to go upstairs and work on the project?"

"In your room?" I ask.

He nods. "Unless you want to help me carry the books and the desk downstairs."

I laugh. "How heavy is the desk?"

He pretends to look very serious. "Very heavy. It took the moving men, all four of them, two hours to carry it up. And one of them ended up with a hernia and we had to perform an emergency herniactomy on him, right here in this house, right on top of the desk."

"I'd hate to see that happen to you," I say. "Biology's not my strongest subject. We'd better study upstairs," I say. "By the way, is herniactomy a word?"

On the way up, he says, "I just made it up. Sounds

good, though, doesn't it?"

We go into his room. It's really nice. Rock posters all over the walls. A skateboard and surfboard in one corner. A large, but not that large, desk. A bureau and matching bed. A bed. What if Zack's like Bobby? Why am I up here? What if my father finds out that I've been alone with some guy in his bedroom. He'll throw me out, turn my half of the room into an extension for his study.

I must be staring at the bed a lot.

Zack says, "Lauren, come on, I promise it's OK." He pulls two chairs up to his desk and sits down on one of them. He opens one of the library books. "Now, stop worrying. What's the problem?"

I sit down and open one of the books.

We work quietly for about five minutes.

Then I say, "Listen, I used to go out with a sex maniac."

Zack smiles. "Me too."

"Somehow I think we have different reactions to the same situation," I say.

He says, "Look, do you you want me to sign a contract stating exactly what I will and won't do?"

"Let me learn more about law and contracts first. Then we'll do that. I don't want to be taken advantage of by an unscrupulous future lawyer."

He pretends to be smoking a cigar, doing an imitation of Groucho Marx. "How would you like to be taken advantage of by a scrupulous future lawyer?"

All of a sudden, I'm not so nervous. Zack's not Bobby, and I'm not even the same Lauren who went out with

354

Bobby. I'm different. This is something new. Not all guys have to be alike. I mean even when I really thought Bobby was wonderful and that it was real true love, I never felt this "nice" about the whole thing . . . I never thought that Bobby and I were friends, just that we went together. With Zack, I feel like I've got a friend.

"Better watch it," I say. "If we're ever going to be able to open law offices, we better do well in this course."

He shakes his head. "Somehow I doubt our careers are going to depend on a junior high project. But OK, I'm ready to get to work."

We start working on the project.

Each of us takes half the books, skims them, and decides which ones are going to be the most useful.

Zack's really working hard.

I'm the one who's sitting there, trying not to think about what it would be like to make out with him. I also begin to wonder what the problem is—doesn't he think I'm as attractive as the last sex maniac he knew?

It's all too confusing.

Maybe I should just solve this once and for all by taking him in my arms, throwing him on the bed, and doing all sorts of things that my father would never approve of.

Zack looks up at me. "What are you thinking about?"

I can feel myself blush.

He says, "Me too."

He leans over and kisses me.

I kiss him back.

It's very nice.

It's also very uncomfortable trying to make out, sitting

355

at desk chairs.

We move over to the bed and sit down.

"Are you sure this is a good idea?" I ask.

"Positive," he says, and grins.

"OK, but we can only make out for five minutes," I say.

He laughs. "Should we set the timer my mother uses for baking . . .? Or how about a stopwatch?"

I laugh. "The timer. That way we don't have to stop to check it out."

He tries to look very serious. "I thought maybe you'd want to be absolutely accurate, not go a second over five minutes."

I nod. "I'm willing to give up a slight bit of accuracy for the sake of the sound of the timer."

He rushes downstairs for the timer, rushes back, and sets it.

While he catches his breath, I check that he's got it timed right.

He does. "On your mark, get set, go," he yells, throwing himself down on the bed.

I just stand there.

"Come on, Lauren, you're wasting valuable time."

I sit down on the edge of the bed.

He sits up.

"You must think I'm crazy," I say.

"A little. But you play backgammon well and read good books."

"Is that why you like me?"

He nods. "Couldn't you have asked me this before we

set the clock radio?"

"Yeah, but then I couldn't have wasted the time. Are you getting mad at me?"

"Maybe later, after the timer goes off. Not now. I don't want to waste the time."

I look at him. He does have great cheekbones. But that's not enough reason to make out with someone. At least not for someone who's been as sheltered as I have been. No wonder Melissa left home.

I like him. I want to be held by him. I feel so lonely without Bonnie and Melissa to talk to. And I like being with Zack. He's nice and attractive and bright and funny.

I lean over and kiss him.

He's definitely much nicer than Bobby, makes me feel different. And he likes me even if I am messed up about making out.

When the alarm rings, we both sit up.

"What about the time we missed while you were talking?" he asks. "Can't we count that like a time out in basketball?"

I shake my head. "Look, I've got to get home before it's too late. I don't want to get my parents angry at me."

He nods. "OK, let's go. I'll walk you home."

We get our coats.

I look in the mirror. My frizzy hair is definitely not neat. I take a comb out and put lipstick on.

"Did you have to do that before I kiss you good night?" Zack says. "That looks like one of those flavoured lipsticks I hate."

It is flavoured, strawberry.

"For one so young, you certainly do know a lot."

He grins.

I take out a tissue and wipe the lipstick off.

He gives me a kiss.

"Is this the good night one? I thought you were going to walk me home," I say.

"This is the good night from my house kiss. After I walk you home, I'll give you a good night from your house kiss. Maybe along the way, I'll give you a halfway there kiss." He starts counting on his fingers. "Then I can have one for the road . . ."

"Enough!" I grin at him. "If you don't walk me home soon all you'll end up with is a fight with my father."

"Is your father very strong?" Zack asks as we walk out of his house.

"Very strong. And very mean. I'm thinking of suing him for malpractice."

Zack starts to laugh. "That's wonderful. Of course, I don't think you'd win. But could you imagine what it would be like if everyone were able to sue their parents for malpractice?"

I nod. "But my mother says my father would counter-sue if I took him to court."

He grins. "I'd be a character witness for you."

"You mean you'd come to my defence."

"Yes." He leans over and kisses me.

We stand in the middle of the street for a minute.

"I'm almost home. We better get there so that my parents don't get mad and say I can't see you any more."

"You really are afraid of them, aren't you? They've got

you trained."

He makes it sound like I'm a dog or something. But I think about it. They do have me trained, better than Gopher. I come in when I'm supposed to, try hard to be a good little girl. I practically do everything but roll over and play dead. I'd probably even eat the case of dog food my mother won, if they asked me.

We get to the door. This time we go inside, even though I'm nervous.

I introduce Zack to my parents and Linda.

Linda says, "What's red and dangerous?"

"A herd of stampeding apples," Zack answers.

Linda grins and sticks her tongue out and touches her nose with it. That's her very special trick, a sure sign that she's impressed with Zack.

Zack grins at her.

I can see her falling in love with him the way I used to fall in love with some of the guys Melissa used to bring home.

My father asks us, "Well, did you get work done? Let me see it."

My heart drops. "We left it at Zack's."

"I can run back and get it to show you," Zack says. "If you wish."

My father shakes his head.

My mother asks him some questions about where he used to live, how he likes it here, basic parent questions. It seems to go all right.

I walk Zack out to the porch. "If my father had said he wanted to see all the work, what would you have done?"

Zack whispers, "Thrown myself under a passing truck."

I grin. "Well, we're O K so far. He hasn't killed you or me."

We give each other the good night from my house kiss, and I go back inside.

My father says, "Just remember what I told you. I don't want to see you end up like Melissa."

I want to scream that I don't think Melisssa's done anything wrong, but I don't want to get into another fight with him. Sometimes I think the only way to handle him is by pretending he doesn't exist. That seems to be what my mother is doing. She hardly talks to him any more. Maybe that's not the best way to act, but it's the only one that seems to work with him.

I say, "Well, I guess I better go upstairs and wash my hair. Good night."

I go up to my room.

Linda's sitting there, not doing anything.

"What's wrong?" I ask.

"Nobody's ever around any more. Melissa's moved and now you don't come home until late."

"But this is the first time," I say.

"Yeah, the first. But not the last, I bet." There are tears forming in her eyes. "I'm going to be the only one left in this house, 'cause I'm the youngest. And things are getting worse."

I hug her. There's not much else I can do. She's right. Things are getting worse. And she will probably be the last one out.

I want to tell her things will end up fine. I want her to tell me that also. I end up hugging her and saying nothing.

Chapter 9

Announcement over the loudspeaker. "Will all teachers please check to see if their phones are on the hook. Someone's is off and the buzzing is driving everyone in the office crazy."

That's it. The school's office staff has finally flipped. It was bound to happen, having to deal with the whole student body, administration, faculty, and parents. I knew all it would take some day would be some kid sneaking the phone off the hook and letting it buzz. Since the front office can't tell where it's coming from, they have to track it down over the loudspeaker.

I look up. Ms. Lawrence is holding the cut wire from her phone. The receiver is missing. Someone from our homeroom has done it.

She sends one of the kids to the front office to report it. Then Mr. O'Brien arrives, screaming that unless someone confesses, we'll all have detention forever.

It's not fair.

I raise my hand and tell him so, and that we have some rights.

He says, "You're students. While you're in this school, you must do what you are told."

Bonnie speaks up. "It's not right to punish the entire class for the work of one criminally minded fiend."

"Criminally minded fiend" makes me laugh.

Bonnie laughs too.

I really miss her.

O'Brien extends our homeroom time.

He searches all the boys, and the nurse searches all the girls. Finally, it's found. Ed Harmon's got it hidden inside his gym sneaker.

The bell rings and everyone but Ed is allowed to leave. No one apologizes to the rest of the class for the accusations and search.

I walk out the door. The fire alarm rings.

How gross. It's damp outside. My hair's going to get all frizzy. I'm probably going to catch pneumonia. It's cold, and we're not allowed to go to our lockers for our coats.

I walk outside. Behind me someone says, "Stay away from our eighth-grade boys. Stick to someone in your own class."

I ignore the comment, but from behind, I hear someone call, "Lauren."

I turn around and there's Mindy Donner smiling. "I just want you to know that I think it's fine that you're going out with an eighth grader. I mean, if that's the best you can do . . ."

Before I have a chance to say anything, I hear Bonnie say, "You are the lowest of low. I think you're just jealous that Lauren's going out with someone nice and bright and cute. The only reason you get to go out so much is the free movie passes your father is always giving you."

Mindy turns and walks away. I can tell that Bonnie's comment got to her.

Bonnie confronts me. "Now can we talk? You've been avoiding me."

"Avoiding you? It's you, not me," I tell her. "You haven't talked to me at all."

"Wrong." She shakes her head. "You're the one who walked away just because I was sitting with someone else. You could have joined us. It's never bothered you before. You haven't said anything or sat with me at lunch or called at night. What am I supposed to do? Not say what I think? But that didn't mean we had to stop being friends."

I think about it. She's right. I did do a lot of the pulling away. "But you think I'm a creep now, right?"

She shakes her head. "No, I don't. But I do think you are making things hard on yourself by going out with Zack. Look what's happening. People are being awful. You must like him very much."

I nod.

She puts her hand on my arm. "Well, that's good enough for me. And I think he's nice. If you'd given me the chance I would've told you that before. Come on. I don't want to fight."

"Me neither. I'm sorry."

She smiles. "Apology accepted."

We get to biology a few minutes late. Detention. Back to the old days. It's even worth the detention. I'm glad Bonnie had enough sense to make up. I don't know why I didn't. I feel overwhelmed, I guess.

After class, Bonnie says, "Let's throw a party, the two of us. We'll invite kids from all different classes. That way everyone will get a chance to know each other. The only thing is that when I tell Dave, he's going to want to invite Bobby and Sandy."

Bobby and Sandy.

I'd almost forgotten they existed.

"That's O K. It doesn't matter," I say. "At least, I don't think it does."

She says, "It's a deal then. We'll have it at my house. My mother won't mind buying the stuff for it. We'll get together tonight and make up the guest list."

"I think that's a great idea," I say. "And listen, thanks."

She grins. "I'm doing it because you didn't snitch on the time I almost fainted after getting our ears pierced. And anyway, Moose misses you."

Things are better for the rest of the day. It's good being friends with Bonnie again. And she helped me to realize that I haven't been giving people the chance to let me know that they don't all feel the same way about me going out with Zack.

Law class. The kids from my homeroom who are in the class discuss what happened in homeroom, how we all got accused and searched. We decide to include the incident in the newsletter that's supposed to come out next week.

After class, I tell Zack about the party Bonnie and I are planning.

He frowns. "I hate parties. I don't want to go."

"Why not? It'll be fun. You'll meet a lot of new

people."

"I don't want to meet a lot of new people, at least not at a party. I hate parties. Come on, Lauren, we can just go to a movie or something."

I don't say anything, not all the way home.

He keeps trying to get me to smile. I don't want to. In fact, it takes everything I have not to cry. Life's not fair. Just when I think everything's straightened out.

"Look, Zack, I'll talk to you later," I say as soon as we're at my house. I go into my house without really saying anything else to him.

I wish I had someone to talk to who wasn't directly involved. I go up to my room and lie down on the bed. Melissa. If Melissa were here, I could talk to her. I go under my bed and pull out the shoe box to find Melissa's phone number. I lie back down on my bed and try to think everything out for myself.

No matter what I do, nothing seems good. Bonnie and I make up and she wants us to throw a party and Zack doesn't want to come. Either way, one of them is going to be mad at me. And no matter what happens at school, I never have any rights. And all of those kids are being mean to me.

I start to cry. I've just got to call Melissa. She's known me all my life. And she said she'd be there if I wanted to talk.

I go out into the hall, making sure no one is there— although I have this feeling that my mother wouldn't mind.

As I dial her number, I try to calm down. I hope she

answers, not Mike.

She does. "Hello?"

I start crying immediately.

"Who is this? What's going on?"

I try to catch my breath, so she doesn't think it's some kind of "phoney", a kid calling to fool around. "It's me, Lauren."

"What's happened? Is anything wrong at home?"

"Nothing's wrong. It's just me." I try to get calm. "I feel bad about everything. I want to talk to you."

"Is it any one thing?" she asks.

"My life's a shambles," I wail. "I miss you. I need to talk to you."

"Do you want me to come over and get you?"

That's more than I hoped for. "Oh, yes, please. How soon can you get here? But how can we do it? You know what Dad said about you never darkening his doorstep again."

Melissa says, "Look, I'll meet you outside. That way I don't have to come near his doorstep. Anyway, I've been to the house during the day to see Mom. He just doesn't know that."

I didn't know that. And Mom's never said a word.

Melissa continues. "Mike's studying for an exam. I can use his car. I'll be there as soon as possible."

"OK." I feel relieved somehow.

"I'll meet you down the block. That way you won't have to put up with a scene. Just get Mom aside and tell her where you're going, so she won't worry."

We hang up. I go downstairs. My mother says,

"Honey, what's wrong? Have you been crying?"

I say, "I'm OK," but I go over to the sink where she's washing dishes. No one else is in the kitchen, but I don't want to take any chances. My father might have the place bugged.

I whisper, "I'm going over to Melissa's for a while. Don't worry."

"How are you getting there? Are you sure everything's all right? Don't you want to tell me? Maybe I can help you."

"It's OK," I whisper. "I just want to talk to her. She's picking me up on the corner soon."

My mother nods. "Tell her I'm still trying to get your father to relent, to realize he's not being fair."

I can't say anything to her about that. If I were her, I wouldn't let him get away with murder, the way she does. I wouldn't let him treat his daughters so badly.

On the way out the door, I run into Linda. She's carrying library books.

Oh no, a new set of jokes.

"Did you hear the joke about the roof?" she asks.

I decide to go along with it. Melissa can't be at the corner yet. "No, I haven't heard the joke about the roof."

"That's just as well. It's probably over your head."

I leave before she has a chance to say any more. I stand on the corner, hoping Melissa gets there before my father gets home. I just hope he has to stay late writing up some insurance policy. Maybe they'll invent a new policy to be given at birth to kids. If things turn out badly, they can collect on insurance and have a chance to start over.

Melissa arrives.

I get into the car, hug her, and start to cry again.

She says, "Put on your seat belt. We'll go back to the apartment and talk."

"But Mike's studying for an exam. I don't want to bother him."

"It's O K. He said we should come back there. He studies in the living room. We can talk in the bedroom. It's my place too."

"Oh, O K."

She turns a corner. "Want to stop for some ice cream on the way home?"

I'm confused until I realize she means on the way to her home, not mine. I nod again. If I open my mouth, I just know I'll start crying again.

"Applegate's has a brand new flavour." She smiles at me. "Watermelon fudge ripple with cashews."

My stomach lurches. "You're kidding, aren't you?"

She nods. "Yes. I'm kidding."

I smile at her. "You almost got me that time."

"It wouldn't hurt." She's still smiling.

We ride along in silence for a few minutes.

Applegate's. I get a cone, one scoop of banana, one of cherry vanilla coconut. Melissa gets a single dip of raspberry with sprinkles. We drive on. The ice cream starts to drip a little. I'm probably the slobbiest ice-cream eater in the world.

We pull up into a parking lot right next to a railroad station. "That's my apartment building over there." She points to it. We cross the street and enter this sort of courtyard, with some trees, which is not very well kept.

"Hi, Melissa." A couple of really cute guys are walking down the steps.

She nods and says, "Hi. This is my sister Lauren."

I want to die. I look awful from crying and now I'm probably covered with ice-cream drippings. They both smile and say hello. Melissa and I continue to walk up the path.

She says, "They live right above us. They're on the hockey team. Sometimes they practise at home. Once Mike went up and threatened to ram a hockey puck if they didn't stop. Another one is a weight lifter. Sometimes he drops the weights. There are times I could kill them, but they're usually pretty nice. Wild parties though."

I wonder how she can take it. We go in one of the doors. "We're one flight up," she says.

I can hear people yelling in one of the downstairs apartments. We get up to her apartment. She takes out a key and opens the door. Mike looks up from his books, smiles, and says, "Hi."

Melissa walks over and kisses him on the forehead. I look away.

"Lauren and I are going into the bedroom to talk. First I'm going to give her the grand tour."

Grand tour. We can walk through the entire place in a minute and a half.

"This is the living room." There's not much of it. A single bed with large pillows on it, a desk, and the stereo.

"The kitchen." Lots of plants, a folding table and a

couple of chairs, and a midget refrigerator. The stove and sink. Also two cats.

"Lauren, meet Batman and Robin." Cats. I didn't even know she liked cats.

"The bathroom." Small. But it's got everything you need.

"The bedroom." Two bureaus. One giant bed. Giant! A rocking chair. And that's it. Except for the bamboo shades.

"Sit down on the bed. I'll hang our coats up." She goes over to the closet. I plop down on the bed and roll over on my side.

She giggles. "I forgot to tell you. It's a water bed."

I kind of roll back and forth on it. Then I giggle. "Can you actually sleep on this?"

She nods. "At first I thought I was going to have to take motion sickness pills to survive, but now I like it a lot." She comes over and sits next to me. The bed sort of rolls around and then settles down.

"Now what's the matter, Lauren? Let me try to help. Is it Dad?" She's biting her lip.

"Oh, it's O K. I feel better now."

She says, "Oh no, you don't. You're not going to avoid it. If you were so upset, you really should talk it out."

I decide to level with her. After all, she's my only choice. I tell her how hard it's been with her gone. How things are developing between Zack and me. About not talking to Bonnie. How we made up and how she wants to have a party. And how Zack says he doesn't want to go. The tears have started. I can't stop crying.

Melissa holds me.

"I wish I were dead," I cry. "Nothing ever works out for me. Or I wish I could run away like you did and get my own apartment."

She holds me until I calm down. "First of all"—she shakes her head—"I didn't run away. I walked. I'm nineteen, and Mike and I had been talking about the move for a while. We were together for a while. And you're right, I did want to leave home. I've wanted to for a long time, but I didn't until I thought it was right. Do you really think it would be right for you now? And do you think you're doing what's best about Zack?"

"You mean I shouldn't go out with him. Is that what you think?"

She shakes her head. "No, I don't think that at all. I remember when Tracy Mitchell went out with someone who was younger. They had a rough time. But they both thought it was worth it. So they just kept going out. It took a couple of years, but eventually everyone accepted it. If you want to go out with Zack, I think you should. In fact, if you want we'll have both of you over to dinner."

I sigh. "He probably won't come here either."

"Did he say that he positively wouldn't go to the party or that he didn't want to go?"

I think. "Didn't want to go."

"Did you talk to him about it or just get mad and act the way you did with Bonnie?" Melissa asks.

She knows me well. "I didn't talk to him, just got mad."

She shrugs. "Maybe you should try to find out why he

doesn't want to go. It's probably been difficult for him too."

I think about it. She's probably right. A party with lots of new people and when all those people may not approve of you—well, it's just not easy. But it's not going to be easy for me either.

She says, "I think you should talk it out with him. I know it's hard, but you've got to. Lauren, it's difficult for people like us, coming from a family where nothing is ever discussed, where nobody can talk about what's really going on. And nothing's ever direct. I always thought all the fights were because of money. But that's not it. Mom and Dad use that as a weapon against each other instead of talking about the real problems. I didn't realize that 'til I moved out. Now, with Mike, I have to be real careful not to do some of the same things our parents do in fights. It sounds like you've picked up some of their bad habits."

"Like what?"

"Not finding out what's really bothering a person, not really trusting others, not showing real feelings. It's hard to change our behaviour. But we've got to. It doesn't work for our parents. It won't work for us."

I think about it. It's so hard to understand myself, let alone what's happening in other people's heads.

Melissa says, "You don't have to be perfect. You couldn't be if you tried."

I smile. "Not even if I try real hard?"

She shakes her head. "And no one expects it. Zack cares about you. So does Bonnie. I do. And you're just going to have to accept the fact that some people need to make themselves feel bigger by putting others down. They think you're an easy target because you're going out with someone younger. Don't let them get to you."

"Doesn't it bother you that Daddy's so awful to you?" I ask her.

She nods. "I used to cry about it a lot. But I'm doing what's right for me now. I've had to learn that there's no easy way. But I've also learned that a person can survive if she does what's right for herself in spite of what others think."

"Are you happy?"

"With Mike?" Melissa smiles. "Very. But we work hard at the relationship. It doesn't come easy."

"Did you ever go out with anyone younger?"

She giggles. "Yeah, Mike. He was born two weeks after I was."

I laugh. "Maybe it runs in our family."

"Somewhere, right now, there's an eight-year-old just right for Linda."

"Do you think so?"

She shrugs. "Maybe Linda's going to end up with someone who's ten years older and people will complain about that. Who knows? But I bet it won't be easy for her either, no matter what. It's just a myth, a fairy tale, that relationships are easy. Look, would you like to stay for dinner? Call Mom and tell her." She strokes my hair.

"My hair's frizzy," I say.

"And mine's too straight. I've always been jealous of yours. Want to trade?" She tickles me.

"No. I guess I'll keep it."

374

I call home. My mother answers.

"Mom, I want to stay here for dinner. Think we can manage it?"

She says, "Sure, Lauren, if you want to eat at Cindy's and then study, that's fine with me. Just be sure to be home by nine thirty."

For a second I think she's gone off the deep end. I don't even know a Cindy. Then I realize. He must be standing nearby, and since I don't know someone by that name it's a safe alibi. If she said "Bonnie," we'd be in trouble if Bonnie called.

It's really lousy that we've got to lie about all of this. Just because he's so strict.

"Well, thanks, Mom, see you later." I hang up.

Mike, Melissa, and I sit around and talk.

They're really nice to each other. They listen to each other. It sounds like they do try to work things out. Maybe I can learn to do that. Bonnie and I managed to get our problems straightened out. I bet Zack and I can try. I hope it works.

Why do people have to act so dumb and always pick on other people? Maybe kids outgrow it, but I don't think so. I know a lot of adults who act the same way. But Mike and Melissa try not to. And Bonnie. And Zack. And me. And some others. Maybe there's hope. Not for everyone. There's no hope for my father. There's no hope for Mindy. There's no hope for those rotten eighth-grade girls who make fun of me. When I become a lawyer, I'm going to try to get an amendment to the Constitution passed, outlawing meanness.

Chapter 10

When I get home, Linda tells me that Bonnie called, and Zack's called twice. "Boy, he certainly sounded like he wanted to talk to you. I hope some day some one wants to talk to me that much."

I call him back.

"Lauren, I hate large parties. They drive me nuts," he says immediately. "Couldn't you ask me to do something easier, like spend the night in a cage with boa constrictors?"

"How about doubling with Bonnie and Dave? Would that be easier?" I think of that as we talk.

"Anything," he says. "But do you think they'll want to be with me? I mean, isn't Dave in the eleventh grade? A junior isn't going to want to double with an eighth grader."

"I don't know," I say. "I'll find out. I just wanted to check with you to see if it would be O K, since I did the other thing without discussing it with you, and it caused a real mess. I'm sorry."

He says, "I'm sorry too. If it's really important to you, I'll go. But I hate parties where I don't know anyone, and with everything else that's going on, I just don't think I can stand it."

"What else is going on?"

He says, "Do you have any idea how many kids are betting on us? That we're going to break up. That we're going to stay together. Charlie Kaletsky has started a pool, like football, only we're the game."

"Are you kidding? What did you say when you found out?" I gasp.

There's silence on the other end for a few minutes.

Oh, no. I bet he slugged Charlie and is going to get into trouble.

"Well," I yell into the phone. "Well, what happened?"

"Promise not to get mad?" he says.

Oh, I knew it. He's got into another fight.

"Please tell me. I want to know."

"We have to go together for twenty-two years. That's the number I took in the pool." He laughs. "Twenty-two years. I'll split the winnings with you."

I have to laugh, too. "Zack, how could you? Bet in a pool about us."

"I figured I had the best inside information. And we could just fix it. What's twenty-two years?"

Incredible. We've practically just met, and he's betting on twenty-two years!

We talk for a few more minutes and then we hang up so that I can call up Bonnie. She answers immediately. "Guess what. I just about have the guest list made up. It's going to be so much fun."

I'm afraid she's going to kill me, but I've got to tell her. "Bonnie, I spoke to Zack about it, and he just can't stand big parties. Would you be really angry if we doubled instead?"

There's silence on the other end. Oh, no. Our friend-ship is over again. I can't stand it. Finally she speaks. "I'm not sure about the doubling. It's O K with me. I'll have to check with Dave. And I can throw the party myself. But even if Zack won't come, will you?"

It's the least I can do, and anyway, it's been a long time since I went to a party.

She says, "Listen, do you have any idea how long the two of you will be going out?"

What a strange question. And then I remember. The pool. Not my best friend too.

I say, "Zack bet twenty-two years. He promised to split the winnings with me. What kind of deal can you offer?"

She giggles. "Sixty-forty? And I'll go with you when you get your ears double pierced."

Double pierced. My ears still haven't stopped dripping from the first time. Fat chance I'll be doing that.

"Look, I'll think about it," I tell her. "But seriously, you're not upset about the party?"

"No," she says. "When I talked to my mother about it, she said we hadn't planned well. I told her the whole story about what's been happening, how you and Zack have been getting picked on by some of the kids. Then she asked me if we'd consulted Zack. When I said we hadn't, she told me this might happen. I guess she and his mother have been talking about it."

It's nice to know that some people understand.

"Then it's OK?" I ask.

"Sure. I'm just glad we're still friends."

"Thanks," I say.

My mother comes upstairs. "Lauren," she says. "It's late. Bedtime."

I hang up after saying good night to Bonnie.

My mother says, "Your father figured out that I was covering for you. I'm not a very good liar. He also figured out that I've been using some of the food money to give to Melissa. I guess he's known for a while, kind of, but just now decided to let me know—especially when he realized that we're both going against his wishes. He's in a terrible mood. Also angry because I start subbing next week. Just stay clear of him, though. He promised me he won't yell at you for going over there."

"Why does he have to be so awful?" I ask.

She shrugs. "He really thinks he's doing this for everyone's best, that he's got to make everyone's decisions for them. For years I've been able to get him to do things by letting him think they were his ideas, but this time he's been impossible."

I say, "How can you stand it?"

She shrugs and walks away without answering.

Twenty-two years. Zack bet twenty-two years. That's longer than my parents have been married. I can't see how some people manage.

I wonder what I'll be doing in twenty-two years, whether I'll end up like my mother or any of the other mothers I know.

Twenty-two years. I won't be living at home again. I

379

won't be going to school again. I'll really be on my own.

I wonder if I'm ever going to marry. Have kids. Really be a lawyer like I want to. It's hard enough to know what it's going to be like tomorrow, let alone that far in the future. It's even a little scary thinking about it. Like what I'll be doing. Where I'll be living. Whether I'll live long. Will my parents be around when I get older? Or what if they die? Who will care about me then? Even though my father's sort of a lousy parent, I know he does care about me. What if he has a heart attack and dies? I'd be upset. And who'd take care of my mother? I'm not sure she can take care of herself. What if I do have kids and they hate me and won't listen? I wish there were a mail-order catalogue you could use to get the kind of life you want, so that there would be no questions, no wondering, no worrying. And if you weren't happy with your purchase, you could get a trade-in on the old life-style and buy a new one.

At night, that's what I dream about. Some guy, like a car salesman or an insurance agent, trying to pressure me into buying a life-style I really don't want.

I'm really glad when the alarm goes off and it's time for school. I dress up a little. Now that Zack's at school, I take a little more time, put on a little mascara and lipstick. I mean, what if he decides that he's made a mistake or something? By the time I get over to Bonnie's house, I'm running a few minutes late.

She rushes out. We walk quickly. She says, "Did you hear the news? Bobby and Sandy broke up."

I smile. I can't help it.

380

"Don't you have anything to say about that?" she asks, rearranging the fringe on her forehead.

I just keep smiling.

"Come on. Lauren. Say something."

I smile. "Couldn't happen to two more deserving people. What happened? Did he develop an allergy to her pom-poms and megaphone?"

She says, "He decided they just didn't have enough in common."

Ha! I could have told him so.

"What if he wants to ask you out again? Would you go?" she asks, trying to sound very nonchalant.

I think about it. Going out with Bobby again. Being able to go out on dates in a car. Seeing R-rated movies more easily. It would mean not going out with Zack. Not having to deal with everyone's abuse.

"Well?" She asks.

I have to know. "Did Bobby ask Dave to have you find out the answer?"

She stops short. "Come on. What makes you think that?"

"Is it true? He did ask, didn't he?" I'm smiling.

She says, "My lips are sealed. Dave would kill me if I said that it was true. So I'm not saying anything."

That's good enough for me. I grin. She doesn't have to say it out loud. I know it's true.

We walk silently to school.

I think about it the whole time. Going out with Bobby again. Why should I even want to when Zack is so nice? Why should I still care about Bobby? Why do I want to go out with him?

School. Homeroom. Bio. The frog's almost finished. Solomon tells us there's going to be a test next week.

I hate tests that I have to really study for and will probably do lousy on no matter how much time I spend. I wish my brain were all-around useful, instead of just in some things.

On to law class. Zack's waiting at the door for me. It's the first time I've seen him all day.

"Where have you been?" I ask. "I kept looking for you in the halls."

"Would you believe a secret spy mission for the Intergalactic Council?"

I shake my head. "Try again."

"Searching the world for the perfect wave."

"And you found it already? Where's your surf-board?"

He grins. "In my locker. No, really I had a doctor's appointment. My yearly checkup."

"Anything wrong?" I'm always terrified that something's going to happen to someone I care about.

"Nope," he says. "Perfectly healthy. Guaranteed to last at least twenty-two years. Just think of how much interest we'll have in the pool in that time. We'll be able to go to Europe on our winnings."

Twenty-two years again. What if I do decide to go back with Bobby? How's Zack going to feel? How will I feel? Why did Bonnie ever tell me?

I decide not to think about it. "Europe? On the interest? Don't you think we should put the money away for a rainy day?" I listen to myself. It sounds like something my father would say. Yeech!

Zack shakes his head. "Oh, no. By that time, we'll have made it through lots of rain. At the most, we'll use a little of it to buy an umbrella to take with us to Europe."

Mr. Matthews comes out. He puts his hand on Zack's shoulder. "Want to help fold the law newsletters? They just got here. Both of you worked so hard on this, I think you'll be pleased."

We rush in. The newsletters look great. We did work hard to get them done. The kids who typed them did a fantastic job, hardly any errors. We all read the articles for a few minutes. We've already read them in class, but it looks different all done on mimeograph and everything. Professional. Like the real thing.

Then we fold them. Two sheets. Information on both sides. Editorials. Articles. Cartoons. All about laws that affect young people. Some things about what happens at the school.

As we're folding, Mr. Matthews tells us we've done a great job, most of us. We all know he's thinking of the creeps like Ed who didn't do much, trying to con their way into getting a passing grade. But I don't think it's going to work in this class. "I will evaluate each of you on your understanding of the material, the way you wrote it up, and your participation in class. I'm extremely proud of most of you."

We applaud ourselves.

"We'll get these all folded, counted out and placed in homeroom mailboxes. The homeroom teachers will pass them out in the morning," he says. "I just want you to remember we're publishing some things that are going to cause comments and maybe even anger."

"Will you get fired?" someone asks.

I think of the articles—about the administration, and the teachers who give unfair detentions, stuff like that. Even though the articles are unsigned, I bet some of the people are going to try to find out who's responsible for which writing. And then they'll blame the student and Mr. Matthews. He'll get into a lot of trouble, I bet.

He shrugs. "I've got tenure. They won't be able to fire me easily. I can use the law to help me. don't worry. I've made the choice, and I hope there won't be a problem. If there is, we'll just use the experience to learn how to best deal with the situation."

I look at Matthews. He's brave. I also know that he's almost done with his law studies, and will soon take the bar exam to become a lawyer. It must be easier to do something like this when you know you're not going to be around much longer anyway. It's a shame the way a lot of the good ones leave and go on to other things. The good ones who stay almost always have outside jobs. I don't know who made the rules that teachers get paid for what they do. It's not fair that Solomon and Matthews get the same money and everything. Maybe that's why Matthews went into law—to try to make things fair in education for everyone.

I also look at Zack. He's so nice, so much fun, so cute. I must be crazy to even consider going out with Bobby again.

384

I am crazy. I'm still thinking about it. I don't know what to do. Maybe I should call Melissa tonight.

But she hasn't even met Zack yet. And anyway, I know what she's going to say, that I have to do what's best for me. How can people always know what's best for themselves? Damn.

We fold all the papers. The bell rings. Some of us sit around and plan strategies in case there is trouble. Something tells me the administration isn't going to be too happy about the newsletter. Finally, everyone gets up to leave.

Zack says, "Let's go over to my house."

I grin. "To visit your timer?"

He laughs. "With any luck. Could we set it for seven minutes?"

"Six and a half."

"It's a deal," he says.

We go over to his house. His mother's home already. She's gorgeous. Long curly brown hair. Curly, not frizzy. Cheekbones like Zack's. Green eyes. No wonder he looks so good. And she acts as if she doesn't even know how beautiful she is. If I had a body like that, I'd be so grateful.

She says, "Hi. Welcome home."

Zack says, "I thought you were working late tonight. And then going out."

She shakes her head. "A change in plans."

"Oh."

She gives him a look. "Does this ruin your plans? I should hope not. Aren't you and Lauren here to study?"

I could just die of embarrassment. But not Zack. "Mostly," he says.

She smiles. "Mostly? Well, why don't you two have a soda with me, then you can study, and Lauren, you're invited to dinner. Zack's told me about you. So has Bonnie's mother. I've really wanted to meet you."

We all sit down and talk. Ms. Davids is very nice. And funny. A sense of humour a lot like Zack's. I guess he takes after her.

It's fun except I keep thinking about the six and a half minutes. It's awful to think about how much you want to make out with someone when you should just be thinking about things to say to his mother for the first time.

I can tell Zack's mind is not totally on the conversation either. He keeps looking at his watch.

"I can tell that the two of you are anxious to study. I can remember what it was like to be young and want to study." She's grinning. "You two may go upstairs, but don't study too hard. I'm serious about that."

Zack laughs. "Got you. OK, Mom, we'll see you later."

Zack and I go upstairs and sit down on his bed.

"Somehow I don't think she expects us to study the whole time."

He grins. "We're not supposed to study too hard. That's her way of telling us not to do too much."

"I can't believe she's a mother."

"I can. I live with her. Since she's got to be the only parent, we talk a lot. She knows I like you a lot, but she also told me we're too young to do too much. I told her I

386

know that.''

"Can you really talk to her about all of that stuff?" I think of my mother.

He nods. "Yeah. But I still don't tell her everything. It's not good to tell parents everything. You've got to do some things on your own and learn to be your own person."

"That sounds really good," I say. "For one so young, you really know how to handle yourself."

He says, "Don't tease. You'll be sorry."

"What are you going to do?"

He leans over and tickles me. I tickle him back. He kisses me. I kiss him back. The timer! I've forgotten all about it.

"Zack. Stop. We've got to the set the timer."

He says, "Don't worry. I've got an automatic one that goes off in my head."

"So do I. That's why we've got to set the timer. Somehow I don't trust the one in our head."

He grins. "Five minutes the other day. Six and a half today. By next week, we'll be up to an hour."

"Fat chance. Look, we have to be good."

He just grins.

"I didn't mean that kind of good."

He just keeps on grinning. I just sit there for a few minutes until he gets up and sets the timer. I wonder if his mother has noticed that it's vanished.

I look at him and think of Bobby. It's so confusing. Why should I think of Bobby when it's Zack I really like.

He comes back and sits down again. "What's wrong?"

"Nothing," I say. "Come on. The clock's ticking away."

He looks at me. "What's bothering you? I never know what's going on. Sometimes you act happy with me. Sometimes you don't." He looks at me. "Come on. You can tell me." Then he grins. "Is it my mouthwash? My deodorant? Do you hate rugby shirts?"

I smile. "No. I've just got other things on my mind."

"Like Bobby and Sandy breaking up?"

"How do you know about that?" I can't believe it.

He says, "One of the girls at school made sure it was the first thing I heard when I got back from my doctor's appointment. Before I even got into the office for my pass, she came running up to me in the hall to tell me."

I don't say anything.

"That's it, huh?" he asks.

I just sit there, confused.

"Do you want to go out with him again?"

I start to cry. "I don't know. I don't think so. But then I keep thinking about all the trouble we have because we go out, and I don't know what I want, what's best for both of us. I just don't know."

He says, "I think it's worth it. You're the best friend I have."

I think about that. Zack's one of the best people in the world. Nicer than anyone else I've ever gone out with. More fun. More considerate. But I hate the way everyone is making a fuss about us going together.

I'm the kind of person who just likes to fade into the woodwork, not stand out in a crowd or anything. And

388

going out with Zack makes me stand out. People are taking bets on what I'm doing. Girls are making nasty comments to me in the hall. I'm just so confused.

He says, "Look, do you want to be alone for a while to think things out? I'll go downstairs and help my mother get dinner ready. You can think about everything."

I nod. He gives me a kiss and leaves.

I lie down on the bed and cry. He's so good. Why did he have to be born a year too late? Why did I have to be born a year too early?

I just lie there and try to sort things out. The alarm goes off. I'd forgotten about it. Six and a half minutes and we didn't use any of it. I don't have an answer yet.

Why couldn't my parents have raised me to be sure of myself and to know what to do? I really do wish there were a way to sue them for malpractice. Then I could hire advisers who could tell me what to do, what would be the best for me. But I can't.

And I'm not sure that even advisers can answer this one for me. I wish Bobby and Sandy had never broken up. I wish I weren't so confused. I wish that most of the world would vanish and let me live life the way I choose. I wish I really knew how I want to live.

I hope that when I come back reincarnated, I come back as a piece of pickled herring. Somehow I don't think pickled herring has as much to deal with.

Chapter 11

All hell's broken out in the school. The newsletter came out.

The Principal and the Vice-Principal practically had heart attacks when they saw it. Ms. Solomon vowed to track down the writer of the editorial on unfair detentions. Some of the parents are pretty upset. Some aren't. My father wants me to drop out of the class, but I won't.

Some of the teachers are furious. Some aren't. Mr. Matthews is pleased. He says that we did a good job, and now everyone is more aware of the issue of children's rights.

Some people want him fired.

I'll be glad to graduate and get out of this school. I hope the high school's better. Except that Zack's got another year here. It's like I get paroled a year before he does.

I still don't know what to do. Bobby called last night. I'm going to see him tonight. I've told Zack. He said O K, but I know he's upset. I would be too. I am upset, in fact.

Bobby sounded so nice over the phone, telling me how much he's missed me, what a mistake it was to break up with me for Sandy. He told me how great it would be if we got back together. How things would be different.

How the good things would be even better now.

I told him I wasn't sure. I told him that I was willing to talk to him, but that there would be no guarantees.

He said he was sure that once we saw each other again, everything would be fine.

I just don't know. I've got no idea what's going to happen. So far tonight I've tried on eight different outfits. None of them looks right for the occasion.

I finally decide on blue jeans and my grey sweat shirt. That looks very casual, not like I'm trying to impress him or be sexy or anything. Sort of like I'm making time to see him between jogging engagements. I also wear the independence earrings Bonnie's mother gave me.

Linda's sitting on her bed staring at me. "Don't you have anything better to do?" I ask her. "You're making me nervous."

She shakes her head. "Do you think there'll ever be a time when I have to make the choice of two guys? Sometimes I don't think there'll ever be one."

"Don't worry," I say. "It'll happen. Sixth-grade boys just mature later than the girls. Boys always do, well almost. There are exceptions." I think of Zack and wonder what he's doing tonight.

She says, "Do you think I'll ever be as nice-looking as you and Melissa?"

It's so funny. I don't think I'm that nice-looking.

I say, "You look wonderful now. Don't worry."

She lies down on her bed and stares at the ceiling. "John Pollack asked Judy out. He's in the sixth grade."

Judy again.

"Linda, do you really care about going out because you want to or because other people in the class are starting to go out?"

She sighs.

'Well?"

"I don't know. A little of both, I think."

"Don't you think you should just relax a little and then do what you really want to do?"

She looks at me. "What about you? Is that what you do?"

Wham. She's got me. That's not what I do. At least I don't think I do. I mean I can't even decide what I want with Zack and Bobby. And I am letting other people make the decision for me. I think that's what I'm doing. I really don't even know any more. I go downstairs to wait for Bobby.

My parents are sitting at the kitchen table, working on their chequebook. That's always a good time to stay clear of them. I go into the living room to wait.

My stomach's in knots. I wonder what Zack's doing. I even wonder what Sandy's doing. I wonder why it's taking Bobby so long to get here. He's a half hour late. He used to do that all the time. I'd forgotten about that.

Finally I hear the horn honk. He's not even coming up to the door. He did that after we'd been going out for a while. I would have thought he'd come up to the door this time to show that things would be different. I guess he's pretty sure of himself.

I go out. He's sitting behind the wheel. I get in on the other side. He smiles at me. He's wearing a football varsity jacket.

"Hi," I say.

He keeps smiling and says, "Let's go for a soda and hamburger. We can talk there."

I nod.

Neither of us says much for most of the ride.

As we pull up into Stewart's, Bobby says, "I've missed you. I'm glad we're getting back together."

I shake my head. "I didn't say that we were. I just said we'd talk about it."

He says, "But I know we will. Remember all the fun we used to have? You know you like hanging around with the high-school crowd. Being driven places. And you know I'm just crazy about you."

He pulls into a parking space, turns off the engine, and leans back, looking very sure of himself.

I take a good look at him. He's very attractive, tall, kind of strong-looking, the kind of guy that most of the kids who have been teasing me would love to go out with.

I say, "If you are so crazy about me, why'd you break up with me?"

He frowns. "I just got tired of your being such a scared kid about sex, and I knew Sandy wasn't."

I say, "Well, what makes you think I'm any different, that things will be different?"

He says, "Well, you're getting older, and I'm sure that you've got to be getting bored with that little kid you've been hanging around with."

He looks so sure of himself. I debate telling him that Zack turns me on more than he ever did, and that I really don't think he should be so sure of himself, that maybe he should go back to Sandy.

I don't say anything yet.

We order from the guy who comes out.

It is nice being able to go out with someone who has a driver's licence. Zack won't have one for almost four years.

Bobby says, "There's a party at Marty's on Friday. I'll pick you up at eight."

For a second I'm tempted to say yes; then I realize there was no question.

"How can you assume I'm going with you?" I ask him. "You don't even ask, you just tell."

He says, "I know you want to go out with me again. Remember how upset you were when you found out about me and Sandy, when I told you it was over? And now I'm telling you I was wrong. Doesn't that make you happy?"

I wait until the guy bringing the order puts it on the window and leaves.

"Bobby, you're unbelievable. You walk out and then expect to come back as if nothing had ever happened."

He looks at me. "But I told you I'm sorry."

I look at him. He seems so sure of himself in his varsity jacket, with his driver's licence, being seventeen. I think of Zack. He's smarter, nicer, more fun. I think of what I told Linda about doing what she wants to, not what others think she should do. Next I think of how the kids act to me in the hall. I don't even like them. Why do I have to worry about what they think of me? I wouldn't want them as friends anyway.

Bobby says, "Look, I'm giving you the chance to go out with me again. If you don't want to, just tell me. There are a lot of girls who would love the chance."

I almost laugh. When they handed out egos and conceit, Bobby must have got a double dose.

First I bite into my hamburger. Then I say, "I think maybe you should give one of them the pleasure of your company. I don't think I want to go out with you. In fact I know I don't."

He looks stunned. "But I thought . . . I mean, you were so upset when . . ."

"I was. But I'm not now. Look, Bobby, I don't think you know me any more. You didn't even ask me what's new or anything. I don't want to be with someone who doesn't look at me and really see me."

"But I do."

"No." I realize it's true. "You don't, and you never did. Everything's always the way you want it."

He says, "Well, if that's the way you feel, there's no reason for us even to stay together any longer tonight." He turns on the engine.

"Don't you think you should honk so the guy gets the tray before you drive off?" I ask him.

He frowns. Bobby never likes to be told that he's goofed, considers it a sin. He honks. We drive back in silence.

When I get out of the car, I say, "It would have been nice if we could have ended up friends even without going out. But that's not possible because I don't think we've ever been friends."

He just frowns.

I go back into my house.

My parents are fighting over something in the cheque-book. It sounds as if Mom wrote out a cheque to Melissa. I sneak past them. There's no way I'm getting involved in that.

Linda is still lying on her bed when I enter the room. "Everything O K?" she asks.

I nod and smile.

"No Bobby?"

"No Bobby."

"Good." She grins back. "Zack's a better audience for my jokes. And I like him better."

"Me too." I say.

I lie down on my bed to think about it. There are still going to be nasty remarks at school from some of the kids. My life's not going to drastically change. It hardly ever does when you're a kid. My parents certainly aren't going to change that much. It doesn't look like Melissa's going to be allowed to visit soon. I don't think I'm going to turn into a bio brain, like Erik Marks. I'm not even sure whether Zack and I will end up winning the pool, staying together for twenty-two years.

What I am sure of is that I finally did something for myself, that I'm learning to do what I think is best for me.

Maybe suing my parents for malpractice isn't as important as making sure that I don't do malpractice on myself. For the next newsletter, I'm going to write an article about that. I'll even sign it.

In the meantime, I'm calling Zack. We owe each other six and a half minutes.